W9-CES-370

CLAWS
of the
CAT

CLAWS
of the
CAT

A SHINOBI MYSTERY

Susan Spann

Minotaur Books

A THOMAS DUNNE BOOK

New York

A THOMAS DUNNE BOOK FOR MINOTAUR BOOKS.
An imprint of St. Martin's Publishing Group.

www.thomasdunnebooks.com
www.minotaurbooks.com

LIBRARY OF CONGRESS CATALOGING-IN-PUBLICATION DATA

Spann, Susan.
    Claws of the Cat : a Shinobi mystery / Susan Spann.—First Edition.
        pages cm
    ISBN 978-1-250-02702-3 (hardcover)
    ISBN 978-1-250-02703-0 (e-book)
    1. Ninja—Fiction.   2. Samurai—Fiction.   3. Murder—Investigation—Fiction.   4. Kyoto (Japan)—Fiction.
5. Mystery fiction.   I. Title.
    PS3619.P3436C58 2013
    813'.6—dc23

                                        2013011675

Minotaur books may be purchased for educational, business, or promotional use. For information on bulk purchases, please contact Macmillan Corporate and Premium Sales Department at 1-800-221-7945 extension 5442 or write specialmarkets@macmillan.com.

First Edition: July 2013

10 9 8 7 6 5 4 3 2 1

For my mother, Paula,
who always believed I could do this.
And for my son, Christopher,
who made sure I did it well.

Acknowledgments

E very author acknowledges how many people help to produce a novel, but nobody ever told me how impossible it
would be to thank everyone properly. I cannot begin to ex-
press my appreciation for those who have supported me across
the years and helped bring this dream to reality—the list
would run as many pages as this book.

But there are a few who require special mention:

To my husband, Michael, and my son, Christopher—thank
you for the constant love, support, and reinforcement that
kept my dreams focused and my butt in the chair.

To my incomparable agent, Sandra Bond, and my fantastic
editor, Toni Plummer—thank you both for believing in Hiro
and in me. Working with each of you is an honor and a pleasure for which I am grateful every day.

To my peer editors, David and Amanda—thank you for
your time, skills, friendship, and patience as I learned to accept the critique my work so desperately needed. You make
me better than I am alone.

To the amazing ladies of my critique group, the infamous

SFWG—Heather Webb, Janet Taylor, Marci Jefferson, Candie Campbell, L. J. Cohen, Julianne Douglas, Evangeline Holland, Amanda Orr, DeAnn Smith, and Arabella Stokes—you bless me daily with your help, comments, suggestions, support, and friendship.

To my family, Paula, Spencer, Robert, Lola, Spencer (III), Anna, Matteo, Gene, Marcie, and Bob—thank you for loving this crazy scribbler and encouraging her to follow her dreams.

Thank you to Joe, Master of the Interwebz, for more help and favors than I can count.

Domo Arigato Gozaimasu to Tomoko Yoshihara for her help with translations and maps of Tofuku-ji.

And last, but certainly not least, thank you to Erika Mailman; to Laura, Wing, Peter, and Steve (the Saturday Dim Sum Gang); to the men and women of <Invictus> and <Blood Vigil> of Feathermoon server; and to all the other friends—online and off—who encouraged me along the road. The name on the cover is mine, but I could not have done this without your friendship and support.

CLAWS
of the
CAT

Chapter 1

Father Mateo strolled through the narrow yard, hands folded and face cast down in meditation. His shoulders bent against the predawn chill. The first two weeks of May had been warm in Kyoto, but this morning the switch to his summer kimono seemed just a bit premature.

At the other end of the garden a shadow snaked over the wall and into a cherry tree with no more sound than a spring wind rustling leaves.

The priest walked on, unaware.

He passed the koi pond without a glance. It was still too dark to watch the fish. At the back wall of the garden the Jesuit crossed himself and knelt before a statue of a man nailed to a cross. The priest's knees sank into the dampened ground as he bowed his head in earnest prayer.

The shadow moved farther up the tree. Rain-slicked leaves and slippery bark made climbing treacherous, but the *shinobi* did not falter. His hands and feet found purchase where none existed for other men.

A branch grew over the path between the koi pond and the house. The assassin stretched his body along the limb. He moved out over the path without dislodging a single leaf.

And there he waited.

Minutes passed. The eastern sky purpled with dawn's approach. A fish jumped in the pond, and a delicate splash resonated through the yard.

The priest's lips moved without a sound.

The shinobi's black eyes glittered in the depths of his hood.

As the sky turned pale Father Mateo concluded his morning prayers. He stood up and brushed stray leaves from his brown kimono, then frowned at the damp patches over his knees. When the moisture did not rub away he shrugged to himself, nodded to the statue, and turned back toward the wooden house that served as his home and church.

The shinobi's breathing slowed until even his dark blue tunic ceased to move.

Father Mateo passed the pond without stopping. As he stepped beneath the tree, the assassin dropped to the path with no more sound than a breaking twig and laid a slender hand on the Jesuit's shoulder.

Father Mateo spun with a startled cry. The shinobi's hands flew up in defense as the priest's face tensed and then relaxed in recognition.

"Hiro!" Father Mateo exclaimed. "How many times must I tell you not to do that?"

Dark eyes sparkled within the shinobi's cowl. "I will stop on the day that I fail to surprise you."

The Jesuit frowned. "Have you been out all night again?"

Hiro pulled down the cloth that covered his mouth and

pushed his hood back onto his shoulders. "I don't answer that sort of question, remember?"

He reached into the pouch that hung at his side. "I brought you something."

"Other than heart failure?" Father Mateo asked.

Hiro raised an eyebrow in amusement and pulled out a small, dark object. It squirmed.

"An presenta," he said in Portuguese.

"Um presente," Father Mateo corrected. Hiro's Portuguese was startlingly good, considering that the shinobi had studied the language for barely eighteen months. The priest's Japanese had far more flaws, despite two years of study before his arrival and eighteen months of living in Kyoto.

"Presente," Hiro repeated.

The present struggled and mewed.

Father Mateo stepped back. "That's a cat!"

"A small one," Hiro agreed. He switched to Japanese. "Since you talk to the fish, I thought you would like it."

The priest switched languages, following Hiro's lead. "Where did you find a cat?"

"Abandoned by the canal. It's not a lucky color, but you claim you don't believe in luck."

"God controls my fortune," Father Mateo confirmed, "but lucky or no, I can't keep a kitten. Cats make me sneeze."

Hiro considered the squirming ball of fur. "What should I do? I don't want it to die."

"Have you become a Buddhist overnight?" Father Mateo grinned at his own joke.

"You know better than that." Hiro frowned at the kitten. "It needs a home."

"I can't touch it, but it can stay. It's your cat now, if you want it."

The kitten spun in Hiro's grip and clawed at his arm. He clutched it to his chest to stop its struggling.

The kitten gave a muffled mew.

"You're squeezing it," Father Mateo said.

"It's stabbing me," Hiro retorted. "I'd say we're even."

The kitten began to purr. It retracted its claws and relaxed in Hiro's hands. He looked down at the tiny bundle of marbled black and orange fur. A white patch gleamed at the kitten's throat, and the tiny cat squinted at him through greenish yellow eyes.

Loud banging echoed through the air. It came from the front of the house.

"Open up!" a male voice yelled. "I need the foreign priest!"

"Who did you insult this time?" Hiro arched an eyebrow at the priest.

Father Mateo started for the house. "No one I remember, not intentionally anyway."

Only a handful of foreigners had the shogun's permission to live and work in the Japanese capital. Many samurai found even that limited presence offensive.

"At least they're not Shogun Ashikaga's men, or the emperor's." Hiro followed the priest to the wooden veranda that circled the perimeter of the house.

The men slipped out of their sandals and stepped up onto the smooth, unpainted wood.

"How do you know that?" Father Mateo asked.

Hiro followed the priest inside. "The emperor and the shogun do not knock."

The room that served as Father Mateo's bedroom and study

had a built-in writing alcove instead of a desk and no Western furniture at all. Only the crucifix mounted in the tokonoma, the decorative alcove that normally showcased pieces of Japanese art, hinted at the room's foreign occupant. Although the Jesuit mission had purchased the house from a Japanese family two years before, in the spring of 1563, Father Mateo lived as a Japanese and had permitted little change.

Father Mateo crossed the floor, slid open the door, and stepped into the central room beyond. The open room at the center of the house had a sunken hearth and tatami mats on the floor, and it served every purpose from parlor to family room and even church. Father Mateo turned right, toward the small entry chamber at the front of the house, and ran a hand through his dark brown hair.

He turned to look for Hiro.

The shinobi had disappeared into his own room, which shared a wall with the priest's. Hiro couldn't let anyone see him in assassin's clothing. Moreover, a messenger would think it strange to find the household alert and about so early.

Father Mateo started to run his hand through his hair again, but caught himself and stopped. He faced the swinging door at the front of the house and called, "Who's there?"

His Portuguese accent often made people pause, but this time a male voice answered at once. "Mateo Ávila de Santos? You are wanted at the Sakura Teahouse."

Father Mateo opened the door. "So early?"

The visitor wore a simple kimono belted at the waist with a wide obi. A dagger hung at his hip but he carried no sword. His close-cropped hair was thinning on top, a situation made even more obvious by the fact that his head barely reached the Jesuit's chest.

The messenger startled at the sight of the foreign priest but recovered more quickly than most. "There has been a murder. A man is dead."

"Was the victim one of my students?" Father Mateo avoided the term "converts" in the company of strangers.

"No. The murderer asked for you."

"The murderer?"

The messenger nodded. "Sayuri, an entertainer."

Father Mateo stepped backward and shook his head. "That's impossible. Sayuri would never kill anyone."

"She did, and a samurai at that. You'd better come quickly if you want to see her."

"Is she going to commit suicide?" Father Mateo asked.

"You'd better come quickly," the messenger repeated. "She hasn't got much time."

Hiro emerged from his room wearing a smoke-colored silk kimono and a pair of swords. The short *wakizashi* hung down from his obi, while the longer *katana* stuck upward through the sash with its black-lacquered bamboo scabbard jutting several feet behind his back. Somehow, the shinobi had also found time to retie his long hair in a samurai's oiled topknot. Not a strand was out of place.

The messenger's eyes went wide at the sight of a samurai. He dropped to the ground and laid his forehead in the dirt.

"Get up," Hiro said as he reached the doorway. "Where is the Sakura Teahouse?"

The messenger stood and bowed from the waist. "Honorable sir, it lies on this side of the Kamo River, on Shijō Road, east of Pontocho. It's the third house east of the bridge. You will know it by the stone dogs in the yard."

Hiro scowled. "I will bring the priest. You may go."

The messenger bowed twice more and hurried away.

"We could have gone with him," Father Mateo protested as Hiro shut the swinging door.

"Samurai do not follow commoners." Hiro looked the priest up and down. "More importantly, that's your old kimono and you need to put on your swords."

"You know I don't like to wear them, and we need to hurry."

"Why did I train you to use them if you won't wear them?" Hiro shook his head at the priest's stubbornness. "Nevermind. As you say, we should hurry. Change and get your swords."

"Why are the swords so important?"

"Two years in Japan, and you still have to ask?"

The priest crossed his arms over his chest.

Hiro pointed at the swinging door. "You saw the way he reacted when I appeared. Only samurai have the right to wear two swords and to order men to obey. The shogun's edict granted you the rank of a samurai, and today you must use it. If this woman is in trouble, you will need your swords to save her."

"We have yours," the priest pointed out.

"Mine are paid to protect you," Hiro said. "My clan and I owe nothing to a girl we do not know."

And have every reason to let her die if doing so saves your life, he thought.

But he didn't say that part aloud.

Chapter 2

Hiro and Father Mateo left the house and walked west along the narrow earthen road that led to the Kamo River. The priest stood three inches taller than his Japanese protector, but the status he gained by his six-foot height was destroyed by his katana. The longsword wagged behind him like the tail of an overexcited dog.

Hiro shook his head and fought a smile. "That would stop if you practiced wearing the swords, you know."

"Yes. Just like the last ten times you told me." Father Mateo smiled to remove the comment's sting.

After half a mile they passed the white torii gate at the public entrance to Okazaki Shrine, which marked and guarded Kyoto's eastern border. A white-robed Shinto priestess sold amulets by the gate. She nodded respectfully to Father Mateo. Shinto acknowledged a multitude of divinities. The priestess considered the Christian god no threat.

Father Mateo returned the silent greeting. He saw the woman often on the road, and, though he disagreed with her theology, he bore her no ill will.

At the river Hiro and Father Mateo turned south along the unpaved road that followed the eastern bank. Cherry trees lined the way. A month before, their blossoms fell like snow, but Hiro preferred May's leaves to April's flowers. They made better camouflage.

A bridge spanned the river at Sanjō Road. Had they crossed, the street would have led them to Pontocho, a twisting alley connecting Sanjō Road with Shijō Road to the south. Teahouses and brothels crowded the narrow thoroughfare, barely leaving space for three people to walk abreast.

Hiro glanced at the bridge and the city beyond. He hated Pontocho. Tight spaces didn't bother him, but large concentrations of dishonest women did.

East of the river, Sanjō Road was residential. Well-groomed gardens and trees surrounded the dwellings. As the messenger promised, stone dogs stood guard at the third house on the left, a two-story structure with a raised foundation and a steeply peaked roof. Long eaves overhung the wide veranda that circled the house, and a gravel path led to gates at both sides of the building. Wooden fences shielded the yards beyond from public view.

Crowded Pontocho had no room for private gardens. Then again, the average teahouse patron wasn't paying to see a landscape.

Father Mateo walked to the door and knocked with a familiar confidence that made Hiro wonder how much time his pious friend spent in teahouses.

The door swung open to reveal a woman in a formal kimono embroidered with dark purple blossoms. Her hair and makeup looked flawless despite the early hour, and though her thinning face suggested age, no lines or wrinkles marred her powdered features.

She inclined her head to the priest.

Father Mateo bowed. "Good morning, Madame Mayuri. Sayuri sent for me?"

The similarity in the names suggested mother and daughter or master and apprentice. Hiro guessed the latter. He could hardly imagine a less maternal figure than the tall woman standing in the doorway.

Mayuri's gaze shifted to Hiro as if drawn by his thoughts.

He bowed just enough to show manners but not quite enough for respect. "I am Matsui Hiro, Father Mateo's translator and scribe."

The assumed surname fell naturally from his lips. He had used it so long that it almost felt like his own.

"I have not seen you here before," Mayuri said.

It was neither a question nor an accusation, and also both.

"His previous visits concerned only his religion," Hiro replied, "but this time he may encounter words he does not understand."

Mayuri nodded but did not bow. Hiro decided to overlook the slight. Teahouse women stood outside the social structure, and though they usually indulged male guests to the point of obsequiousness, this was not a normal morning and, strictly speaking, Hiro was not a guest.

"Mayuri owns the Sakura Teahouse," Father Mateo said.

Hiro didn't need the explanation. Successful entertainers often bought or inherited houses when they retired, and although she was now too old to sing and dance for men's amusement, Mayuri would have won hearts and emptied pockets in younger days.

She stepped back from the door. "Come in."

The cedar floor of the entry gleamed like honey beneath her sock-clad feet. Hiro pitied the servant tasked with keeping it clean. He stepped out of his geta and onto the raised floor, but paused to let Father Mateo enter first. Hiro always reinforced the impression that Father Mateo deserved great deference and respect, while Hiro himself was merely a low-ranked scribe.

A shinobi's first and greatest defense was misdirection.

Six tatami covered the entry floor. Most entries measured no more than four mats, and the extra space conveyed a sense of luxury and light. A decorative screen by the eastern wall showed merchants and samurai cavorting with courtly ladies.

Hiro inhaled the scent of expensive cedar mixed with something faint and sweet that reminded him of distant flowers in bloom.

Ahead and to the right, an open doorway led to the central foyer, but before Mayuri could lead them through Father Mateo asked, "Has there really been a murder?"

Mayuri raised her painted eyebrows at his directness.

Hiro pretended not to notice. The Jesuit tried to behave like a Japanese, but his Western nature showed through under stress. At least he hadn't run his hand through his hair yet.

Mayuri kept silent long enough to indicate her disapproval. "A samurai is dead."

"Surely Sayuri didn't kill him," Father Mateo said.

Mayuri's lack of reply said more than enough.

"I don't believe it," the priest insisted. "May I see her?"

Mayuri inclined her head in consent. "Follow me."

She led them into the square, twelve-mat foyer. Sliding doors on the eastern and western walls led to private rooms, three on either side, where the teahouse women entertained their guests. Unlike prostitutes, who needed only space for a futon, true entertainers required room to sing and dance as well as a hearth for serving meals and tea.

Another door, in the northern wall, stood open to the informal room beyond, where the women gathered for meals and conversation or to wait for guests to arrive. Hiro averted his eyes. Polite people did not stare into private spaces and he had already seen enough to know the room held no imminent threat.

Mayuri knelt on the floor before the second sliding door on the western side.

As she arranged her kimono around her knees Father Mateo whispered, "Why is she kneeling?"

"No proper entertainer opens an interior door while standing," Hiro murmured. "Didn't Sayuri do the same?"

"I told her Christians kneel only to God."

Before Hiro could reply Mayuri looked up. "Sayuri will explain what you see, but be warned. You may find the scene . . . disturbing."

"You haven't cleaned it up?" An edge of frustration clipped Father Mateo's words.

Hiro made a mental note to refresh the priest's memory of etiquette. Dead samurai didn't mind insults and accusations, but the living often felt differently.

Mayuri sat up straighter and raised her chin. "Akechi-sama's family has the right to see what happened."

Her powdered face betrayed no emotion, but the words told Hiro more than she realized. Teahouse owners protected their performers like samurai guarded their honor. Mayuri's refusal to clear the scene meant she thought the girl was guilty.

Mayuri fixed her eyes on the men. She clasped her hands, but not before Hiro saw them shaking.

"Why are you waiting?" Hiro asked.

"We have seen death before," the Jesuit added.

"Not like this," she said, and drew back the door.

Chapter 3

T he scent of copper wafted from the room.

Father Mateo froze in the doorway. Hiro stopped short behind him, barely avoiding a collision. As he looked over the priest's shoulder, he was grateful for the samurai tradition that forbade emotional responses to tragedy.

Because Hiro had seen death like this before.

The north wall of the room was spotted and streaked with blood. Circular droplets spattered the tokonoma and streaked the wall on both sides of the decorative alcove.

A crescent-shaped pool of drying blood soaked the tatami in front of the tokonoma, and a wavering bloody trail connected the pool to a dead samurai lying faceup on a thin mattress beside the central hearth. He was naked except for a blood-drenched loincloth clinging to his hips.

The Jesuit stepped through the door and Hiro followed. The coppery scent grew stronger, with undertones of salt. Hiro inhaled carefully but detected no smell of sweat. The dead man had not put up a very long fight.

Rusty droplets spattered the dead man's legs from thigh to

knee. Multiple jagged slash marks gouged his ruined throat. They seemed to start on the right-hand side, about where neck met shoulder, and ended just short of the samurai's left ear.

Three vertical stab wounds marked the dead man's chest, like punctures from short, thin daggers. A metallic glimmer in the center wound suggested a broken blade, but Hiro couldn't see it well enough to judge the type. He fought the urge to step closer. Most Japanese considered death defiling, and though Hiro didn't hold with superstition he wouldn't risk his cover to satisfy his curiosity.

He looked for the samurai's clothes. A neatly folded blue kimono and obi lay on the floor before the alcove, just below the blood-spattered vase of hydrangeas that sat on the toko-noma shelf. The bloody drops that marked the clothing suggested it was folded before the attack.

Hiro's eyes were drawn to the vase. Hydrangeas symbolized love and heartfelt feelings. He wondered if the samurai lived long enough to see his feelings spattered on the wall. The amount of blood and the vicious wounds suggested his death came quickly and by surprise.

A tiny girl, perhaps sixteen years old, knelt to the right of the tokonoma. Her long-fingered hands rested in the lap of her bloodstained kimono and her face tilted downward toward the floor. Her posture suggested patience but her shallow breathing betrayed her hidden fear.

Father Mateo knelt before the girl. She looked up, and her smooth lips trembled as she raised her hands to hide her mouth. Tradition allowed her more emotion than a man, but not by much.

Skin-colored tear trails lined her powdered cheeks and dark shadows hollowed her midnight eyes, but Hiro had rarely seen a more beautiful girl. In fact, he knew only one, and he usually tried not to think of her at all.

"Father Mateo." Sayuri regained control and lowered her hands. "I'm so glad you came. I worried you might refuse. I didn't do it. It wasn't me."

"Of course not," Father Mateo said. "What happened?"

Mayuri remained kneeling in the open door, so Hiro stood by the entrance. He never turned his back on potential threats, and at that moment everyone was a threat.

"Akechi-san came to the teahouse as usual." Sayuri nodded at the corpse, but kept her eyes on Father Mateo. "I entertained him several nights a week—just singing and dinner and talk, nothing you said was forbidden."

"This is a high-class house." Mayuri sniffed. "The brothels are in Pontocho."

Hiro gave the woman a sideways look. The priest would interpret her words as defense of Sayuri, but Hiro heard only concern for the reputation of the house.

"I haven't come to condemn you," Father Mateo said, and Hiro knew he meant it. The Jesuit's capacity for trust and forgiveness never ceased to impress his shinobi guardian. On occasion, Hiro also found it irritating.

"Akechi-san stayed very late," Sayuri continued. "Most of the guests had gone home. I was tired and wanted to go to bed, but he wouldn't leave. I said I needed to visit the latrine but he didn't take the hint, so I went to Mayuri and asked her to intervene."

She looked to the doorway. Mayuri nodded.

"Then I went to the latrine," Sayuri said. "When I returned, Akechi-san said he wanted to spend the night. He was too drunk to ride home. I sang to him and he fell asleep.

I must have been a little drunk myself, because I fell asleep shortly afterward.

"When I woke up he was dead."

Sayuri's lips quivered. A single tear rolled down her cheek. Her right hand rose to wipe it away and then returned to her lap.

Hiro thought it a perfect performance—too perfect for the truth.

"It's not your fault," Father Mateo said.

"It must have been a shinobi," Mayuri offered. "I was in my room all night, and I heard nothing."

"Shinobi," Father Mateo repeated. "That's the same as *ninja*, isn't it?"

Mayuri looked down her nose at the priest. After a very long moment she said, "Yes, though only a Chinese would pronounce the word that way."

Hiro's gaze returned to the corpse. The samurai's oiled pigtail had come loose from its leather band. Strands of graying hair hung around his face and trailed on the floor.

Hiro shook his head. Not even a dead samurai deserved the shame of ruined hair. Then he noticed something worse. The killer had gouged out the corpse's eyes. The empty sockets were crusted with drying blood.

Hiro had seen many corpses, but that was a first.

He looked over the corpse very carefully. Once again he noticed the glimmer of polished metal in the dead man's chest. This time he decided to look more closely.

He faked a cough and raised a hand to his stomach. "I am sorry. May I get some air?"

Mayuri frowned as Hiro started across the room toward the sliding veranda door.

"Don't touch anything," she snapped. "I don't want the scene disturbed."

Hiro wondered if she was lying or just didn't realize that the body had been moved.

As he passed the corpse he eyed the cuts in the samurai's chest. Drying blood obscured the wounds, but the parallel slits seemed identical in diameter and almost but not quite equidistant, like slashes from a tiger's claws. A fragment of metal glinted in the center wound. As Hiro suspected, the killer's blade had broken.

He saw no more before he reached the door, pushed it open, and stepped outside. Long thatched eaves extended over the porch, supported by round pillars at ten-foot intervals along the veranda's edge. Beyond the porch lay a narrow yard punctuated with cherry trees. Beneath them, flowers bloomed in ornamental gardens. Granite lanterns and a black stone Buddha stood between the flower beds. Bright green moss covered the Buddha's rounded belly.

Aside from a scattering of leaves on the grass, most likely dislodged by the previous night's brief but violent storm, Hiro saw no sign of disturbance in the garden. No footprints marked the grass and the only broken flowers were bent down by the force of rain. No bloody footprints stained the veranda, either. Hiro hadn't expected any. The prints in the room stopped at the door, with the last ones positioned roughly side by side. Whoever made them had stopped to put on shoes, or at least remove bloody socks. The trail ended there.

To the right, a small rectangular building protruded beyond the end of the teahouse. Hiro stepped to the edge of the porch and peered around the eaves. The outlying building had a thatched roof and an open door on the narrow end.

Lanterns hanging outside the entrance and slatted windows near the roof suggested a latrine.

A pair of ancient cherry trees stood between the latrine and the garden wall that separated the Sakura from the house next door. The larger tree stood almost thirty feet high, with the smaller one only three or four feet shorter. They reached over the wall toward the neighboring house like giant thieves determined to pick the neighbors' pockets.

Hiro returned to the open doorway and looked back into the room. Mayuri had disappeared and the interior door was closed. Father Mateo knelt beside Sayuri. Their heads were bowed in prayer.

As Hiro stepped across the threshold, shouting echoed through the walls. It came from the front of the teahouse—angry, demanding, and male.

Hiro hurried to place himself between the priest and the inner door. Unless he missed his guess, the dead man's relative had arrived.

Chapter 4

The door slid open. A young samurai stormed into the room with his hand on the hilt of his katana. He took two steps toward the hearth and froze in shock.

The stranger stood half a head shorter than Hiro, with a shaved forehead and long black hair pulled back in a samurai knot. He looked very young, no more than nineteen, and slender, with a narrow face and a thin mustache that looked more like a shadow on his lip. He wore baggy *hakama* trousers and a wide-shouldered surcoat of bright patterned silk, and he swaggered more than appropriate for his age.

His clothes and attitude suggested a *dōshin,* or local policeman, come to investigate a disturbance.

Hiro wondered who had called him. Although all policemen were samurai, only commoners needed the help of magistrates and police. Samurai families enforced the law themselves.

The stranger's nose reddened. The flush spread all the way to his half-shaved scalp. His pigtail quivered and his hand trembled on his sword. His eyes remained locked on the corpse.

"What happened here?" he gasped.

Mayuri had not stood up after opening the door. She bowed her head to the floor at once, and when she pushed herself to a kneeling position she looked very small and vulnerable. Fear thawed her icy exterior like boiling tea on snow.

"I apologize a thousand times, Akechi-sama," she said, using the highest honorific to show respect. "We did not . . . we hoped you would see . . . an assassin is to blame."

The samurai whirled and pointed at Mayuri. "He was murdered in your teahouse. You are to blame." He turned to the dead man and dropped to his knees. "Find something to cover my father."

Hiro's mind buzzed a warning. Membership in the Kyoto police was generally inherited, with positions passed from retiring father to son. A dead samurai meant trouble for Sayuri. Dead policemen were trouble for everyone, especially with an arrogant *dōshin* son.

He wished he and Father Mateo had arrived later, or not at all.

Mayuri bowed to the floor again, but not before Hiro saw the terror in her eyes.

Sayuri stood and lifted the dead man's kimono.

The *dōshin* whipped his head around and snapped, "What do you think you're doing?"

Sayuri froze, eyes wide. The silk kimono unfolded in her hands and slipped toward the floor. She clutched it to her chest to keep it from falling.

The young man's eyes brimmed with unshed tears but his fists were clenched at his sides. "How dare you defile his kimono with bloody hands!"

The kimono was already ruined, but Hiro suspected the dead man's son wasn't thinking very clearly. With good reason.

Hiro held out his hand for the garment. "I'll do it."

The young samurai blinked and his eyebrows rose in surprise. They lurched downward again as he noticed the foreign priest. He jumped to his feet. He stood barely as tall as Sayuri but his rage made him seem much taller.

"Who are you?" he demanded. "What are you doing here?"

Hiro bowed. "I am Matsui Hiro, interpreter and scribe. This is Father Mateo Ávila de Santos, a priest of the foreign religion, from Portugal."

The young man's face turned purple. He rounded on Mayuri. "How dare you allow a foreign ghost in this room!" He shifted his glare to Hiro and his hand returned to the hilt of his katana. "Remove him at once, before I remove his head."

Hiro admired the way the youth channeled his grief into anger, but recognized the threat of a violent outburst. Keeping himself between the samurai and the priest, Hiro retrieved the kimono from Sayuri and spread it over the body. He took care not to touch the corpse.

When he finished, he said, "The priest is under shogunate protection. Ashikaga Yoshiteru personally invited him to live and work in Kyoto."

"That gives him no right to defile my father's body."

"The presence of a priest does not defile the dead," Hiro said. "He has not touched your father. He came to comfort this woman, who shares his faith."

Hiro switched to Portuguese. "We should leave."

"What did you say?" the samurai demanded. "Speak Japanese!"

"Father Mateo does not speak our language well." Hiro hoped the priest would play along. "I told him that you wanted him to leave."

The young man narrowed his eyes at Hiro. His hand remained on the hilt of his sword, and he trembled like a wild boar preparing to attack.

Adrenaline rushed through Hiro's limbs, though he kept his hands at his sides. He didn't want to kill a policeman if he could avoid it.

Father Mateo seemed unaware of the danger. "I'm not leaving," he said in Portuguese. He nodded at Sayuri. "She needs our help."

Hiro turned his head just enough to catch the Jesuit's eye. "We need to go now, immediately."

"I'm taking Sayuri with me." Father Mateo beckoned to the girl and started for the door.

The gesture needed no translation.

"Stay where you are!" the young man barked.

Sayuri froze, mouth open and eyes wide.

Father Mateo drew a breath. At the last moment he seemed to remember that he didn't know Japanese well. He closed his mouth and said nothing.

"She claims she didn't kill your father," Hiro said. "There is no reason for her to stay."

"Please, Nobuhide." Fresh tears appeared in Sayuri's eyes and her knuckles whitened as she gripped her hands together. "Don't kill me."

Nobuhide ignored her. "This is the woman my father spent his evenings with. Her kimono is stained with his blood, and I see only a woman's footprints on the floor."

He pointed at the trail of tiny prints that led from the silk-draped body to the door. Hiro agreed that they looked feminine, but wasn't as quick to make damning assumptions based on circumstance.

Then again, it wasn't his father lying by the hearth.

Sayuri knelt and bowed her head to the floor.

"It wasn't me," she whispered. "When I woke up he was just as he is now."

The samurai looked at the wall and the bloody floor as if trying to reconstruct the crime. "I see footprints in here but none on the porch. How did a killer enter without notice and vanish without a trace?" He drew his katana.

Hiro's muscles tensed as the blade hissed against its scabbard. Only years of training kept his hands and body still.

"I have the right to avenge my father's death," Nobuhide declared, "first as his son and second as the *yoriki* in charge of Pontocho."

Hiro drew a sharp breath. *Yoriki* were police commanders and assistant magistrates, with as many as thirty *dōshin* at their command.

"Please, no," Sayuri begged.

Mayuri watched from the doorway, as mute as the stone dogs that guarded her teahouse.

"Wait," Father Mateo said.

Nobuhide turned. "You said he didn't speak Japanese."

Hiro's hand moved toward his katana, but he resisted the urge to draw it. Thus far Nobuhide had only threatened Sayuri, and Hiro still preferred not to kill a grieving man. Not with witnesses, anyway.

He took a step toward Nobuhide. "I said he did not speak our language well. I never said he could not understand it."

The young samurai held his katana at waist level with his left hand almost touching the guard and his right at the base of the hilt. Hiro recognized the fighting stance. He also knew that resheathing swords without shedding blood caused samurai shame and loss of face, and that policemen didn't take embarrassment well.

He had to diffuse the situation at once or someone would die.

"We have to do something," Father Mateo said in Portuguese.

"It is the law," Hiro replied. "He has the right to avenge his father."

"She didn't kill his father," the priest protested. "Her death accomplishes no justice."

"Speak Japanese," Nobuhide growled, raising his sword to emphasize the threat.

Father Mateo stepped between Sayuri and the samurai with a confidence that suggested either ignorance or foolishness. Nobuhide's eyes widened and he lowered his sword a fraction.

The priest told Hiro, "Translate," then bowed to Nobuhide and continued in Portuguese. "Honorable sir, I respect your customs and your law, but this woman is under the protection of the church, which is itself protected by the shogunate.

"Shogun Ashikaga granted my predecessor, Francis Xavier, permission to reside in Kyoto and teach our religion to all who wish to accept it. This woman has recognized Jesus Christ as her Lord and savior. She is governed by God's justice as well as by Japanese law."

The Jesuit's right hand twitched. For a moment Hiro thought he would raise it, but the priest resisted the nervous gesture. Hiro noted the restraint with satisfaction. He had often warned Father Mateo about the importance of control to samurai.

Hiro translated the words as politely as possible and watched Nobuhide's reaction. The shinobi wouldn't kill without provocation, but he would act without hesitation to save the priest.

Nobuhide sneered. "She is a murderer. She has no rights under any law."

"A Christian must have the right to prove her innocence," the priest persisted, still in Portuguese. "The law of the church requires it."

Hiro suspected the Jesuit was bluffing but translated anyway.

"I've never heard of such a thing," Nobuhide said, "and samurai are not bound by your Christian laws."

"But Sayuri is," Father Mateo countered, "as you are bound by the Bushido code, which requires a samurai to temper justice with benevolence."

When Nobuhide heard the translation, he stepped back in surprise and lowered the tip of his sword by several inches. He scowled at Hiro. "He didn't really say that. You made it up to help him."

"Father Mateo is a student of Bushido as well as of Christ," Hiro said, glad that the priest's quick mind had appealed to samurai honor and not just religious law.

"How can she prove her innocence?" Nobuhide demanded. "She is clearly guilty."

"She must have two days to prove otherwise," Father Mateo insisted, "the amount of time our Lord spent in the tomb before He proved His divinity by rising from the grave. This is a central tenet of our faith. Surely you would not deny Sayuri a final religious expression?"

As Hiro finished the translation he added, "You can kill her just as easily two days from now."

"She will run away." Nobuhide glared at Sayuri.

The girl remained kneeling with her forehead on the floor.

"She won't run," Hiro said. "If you're concerned, post *dōshin* outside the teahouse."

He didn't care what happened to Sayuri, but convincing Nobuhide would enable the Jesuit to leave with his head on his shoulders.

"How will I run my business with policemen at the doors?" Mayuri sounded horrified.

"It's a trick," Nobuhide said. "The priest will smuggle her out in the night."

"I give you my word he will not." Hiro had no intention of ever returning to the Sakura. "Give the girl two days, under guard. If she cannot prove herself innocent, execute her. Men will remember your dedication to justice."

As Nobuhide considered the suggestion, Hiro could see Bushido honor struggling with vengeance in the young man's thoughts.

"Very well." Nobuhide took a hand off his sword and pointed at Father Mateo. "But I hold him equally responsible."

The priest bowed. "I give you my word that Sayuri will not escape."

"Not for that," Nobuhide said. "My men will secure the teahouse. I hold you responsible for my father's death. If you prove Sayuri's innocence by noon two days from now, I will execute the killer and set her free.

"But if you fail, I will kill you both."

Chapter 5

"Have you lost your mind?" Hiro barely restrained himself until he and Father Mateo reached the street. "What were you thinking?"

"He won't kill me," the priest replied. "I'm under the shogun's protection."

"You forfeited special status when you offered to help the girl. How do you know her anyway? I've never seen her before."

"I met her a month ago, in Pontocho."

Hiro stopped short. "What were you doing in Pontocho? I thought you didn't like women."

"There are other reasons for taking a vow of chastity," Father Mateo said.

Hiro raised an eyebrow. "Not in Japan."

"If you must know, I went to Pontocho for the cherry blossom dances. I missed them last year and heard they were something to see. Sayuri danced her formal debut this year. She is a talented entertainer."

"And she talked to you?" Hiro could hardly believe it. Most entertainers only had time for paying clients.

"You don't have to look so surprised. But as it happens, I didn't talk with Sayuri at the dances. I ran into her on the street a few days later. She was going to have her hair styled, and I walked her there and back. Since then, we've met for tea several times. She became a Christian only a week ago."

"How convenient," Hiro said, "just in time for you to defend her."

"She didn't do this," the Jesuit said. "She wouldn't lie."

"All women lie," Hiro retorted, "and she's not even good at it. That samurai was awake when someone killed him, and she couldn't have slept through it."

"How do you know that?"

"The blood on the walls all sprayed in the same direction, the one he was facing when someone cut his throat."

They had reached the Kamo River, but instead of turning homeward Hiro started across the bridge.

"Where are you going?" Father Mateo asked.

"*Yoriki* answer to the magistrate." Hiro paused and waited for the Jesuit to follow. "As Nobuhide's superior, the magistrate can absolve you of liability. I'm going to see him and explain you have no part in this."

"But I do have a part in it." Father Mateo caught up and fell into step. "I'm going to help Sayuri prove her innocence."

"What? You hardly know her!"

"She is a member of my flock and my sister in Christ. Would you let your sister be wrongfully executed?"

Hiro looked away at the mention of sisters. That topic ranked high on the list of things the shinobi did not discuss, even with friends.

When Hiro did not answer Father Mateo added, "I cannot sit by and watch someone put an innocent woman to death."

"You can and you will, even if she is innocent, which I doubt. I swore an oath to keep you safe, and I don't intend to fail."

"I'm trying to save a woman's life and you're worried about your salary?"

"Salary?" Hiro made a sound, more bark than laugh. "If you die, it means my head."

"Shogun Ashikaga would understand that I acted on my conscience. I'll write a letter saying you were not to blame."

"You overestimate samurai understanding," Hiro said. "The Iga *ryu* sent me here, not the shogun, and Iga does not forgive failure."

"The shogun will make them."

"The shogun controls Kyoto," Hiro said, "but his reach does not extend to Iga Province. Even if it did, shinobi clans do not answer to warlords, including the shogun."

"Then you'll have to convince the magistrate some other way," Father Mateo said. "I'm helping Sayuri no matter what the cost."

Two samurai boys were sparring at the far end of the bridge. The crack of their wooden swords echoed off the buildings that lined the bank. The older boy stood half a head taller, but the younger one showed more skill. He ducked beneath his opponent's blade and brought his wooden *bokken* down on the tall boy's skull with a thump that rang across the water.

"*AI!*" The younger boy yelled in victory. He raised his sword and stepped back, ending the fight.

The older boy bent double and rubbed his head. Hiro winced in sympathy. He remembered the ache of *bokken* strikes, despite the many years since he felt a blow.

The priest shook his head. "That's got to hurt."

"Better hurt than dead," Hiro replied.

"Why has the older one got a forelock?" Father Mateo asked. "I thought samurai shaved their heads at sixteen. He looks older than that."

"It varies," Hiro said. "A boy shaves his forehead after *genpuku*, when he receives his sword and also his adult name. Every father decides when his son is ready."

The boys gaped at the foreigner, mouths wide like gasping fish. Father Mateo ignored their familiar surprise, but Hiro scowled and laid his hand on the hilt of his katana.

The boys bowed low and returned to their sparring. Hiro smiled to himself. A man didn't have to draw his sword to use it.

The men continued up Sanjō Road. Hiro glanced down Pontocho as they passed. The alley looked dark and silent in the morning light. Teahouses and brothels woke at sunset and slept at dawn.

A couple of blocks farther on they turned north and passed the walled police compound at the entrance to the administrative ward. The guards at the gate nudged one another and whispered at the sight of the Jesuit priest.

Hiro also heard the word *"ronin,"* followed by snickering laughter. He was used to men mistaking him for a masterless samurai, or ronin, who served the foreign ghost because he had no other option. Most men would have found the disdain offensive, but Hiro considered it useful and slightly amusing.

The magistrate's compound lay a short distance past the police. Two samurai in leather armor guarded the gates, and a small crowd of merchants and laborers had already gathered at the entrance to the compound. Their expressions ranged from concern to nervousness. Most were men, but here and there a woman waited in her husband's shadow.

No one spoke.

A sweaty smell rose from the crowd. Normally people bathed enough to avoid offensive odors, but a visit to the magistrate inspired fear, even when men thought their causes just.

The crowd stared as the foreigner approached. A child pointed but his mother hushed him before he made a sound. The guards decided the order in which people pled their cases, and no one wanted to make a scene that might drop them back in the line.

Hiro put on a swagger as he approached the guards. The man on the right would not meet his eye, so he spoke to the one on the left. "We wish to see the magistrate."

"The magistrate is sleeping," the guard said. "Come back later and wait your turn."

"The matter cannot wait," Hiro said. "It concerns a *yoriki*'s murder."

The guard blinked and stood straighter. "Murder? What happened?"

Hiro glanced at the crowd of merchants. "It is a delicate matter. Perhaps the magistrate would prefer to discuss it in private."

Comprehension dawned on the guard's round face. He nodded slowly. "Yes, he may want to speak with you before the official hearing."

The guard disappeared into the compound. His companion glanced at Hiro and looked away, trying not to stare at the foreigner. Instead he glared at the commoners, who shuffled a little farther away from the gate. Discomfort flowed through the social strata like water running down a hill.

A few minutes later the guard returned. "Magistrate Ishimaki will see you at once. Follow me."

Hiro and Father Mateo followed the guard across the graveled court toward the wooden building that dominated the yard. Wide-spreading eaves overhung the weathered veranda. Slatted covers barred the windows, allowing the passage of air but forbidding light, and a pair of dark stone lanterns flanked the doorway like tusks beside a gaping mouth.

The guard led them through the entrance and into a wood-paneled room with a pit of white sand at the center. Behind the pit sat a wooden desk on an elevated platform. Even seated, the magistrate would look down on everyone in the room. Charcoal braziers and oil lamps provided a flickering light that dispelled the darkness but filled the room with a gentle haze of smoke.

"What's the sand for?" Father Mateo whispered.

The guard had left, but the dark, low-ceilinged room inspired respect.

"It represents justice and purity," Hiro said. "The accused kneels there while awaiting the magistrate's judgment. Don't .and in it."

"Won't we have to?"

"We're here as informants, not supplicants."

A door to their left slid back with a soft rustle as the magistrate entered the room. His black kimono blended with the shadows, but his hair and forehead glowed pale in the dim light. For a moment he looked like a ghostly head floating through the room.

His shape took on definition as he climbed the stairs to his desk. Once seated, he looked at the visitors. His snowy eyebrows raised at the foreign priest, though not enough for real surprise. The guard must have warned him about the Portuguese.

Hiro bowed. Father Mateo followed.

"I am Matsui Hiro," Hiro said, "translator and scribe for Father Mateo Ávila de Santos of Portugal. Thank you for meeting with us in private."

The magistrate nodded slowly. "A *yoriki* has been murdered? May I ask his name?"

"Akechi." Hiro paused, suddenly aware that he didn't know the dead man's given name.

"Nobuhide?" The magistrate's expression did not change. "A pity, though murder is not unheard of in Pontocho. May I ask the circumstances of his death and why a foreigner is involved?"

"Not Nobuhide," Hiro said. "His father. Akechi-san was killed last night in a teahouse across the river from Pontocho."

The magistrate leaned forward and placed his hands on the desk. "Akechi Hideyoshi was not a *yoriki*. He was a general, retired from the shogun's army." His forehead wrinkled with concern. "You say he was murdered? In a teahouse?"

Hiro suddenly wished they had not come. This wasn't turning out as he expected.

"How is the foreigner involved?" the magistrate asked.

"He is not involved," Hiro said. "He is merely the spiritual counselor of the accused, an entertainer named Sayuri."

"Of the Sakura Teahouse?"

Hiro struggled to hide his surprise. "You know her?"

The magistrate nodded. His white pigtail bobbed gently atop his head. "I am familiar with the house, though not personally acquainted with the girl. The priest is her counselor, you say?"

"Yes, she has accepted the foreign god." There was no harm in speaking. The damage was done. "She sent for him this morning after the crime. Nobuhide arrived a few minutes after we did. He wanted to execute the girl at once, but Father Mateo intervened."

The magistrate raised his eyebrows in surprise and looked intently at the priest. "Why would he do that?"

"His religion grants the accused an opportunity to exonerate herself. As an adherent, Sayuri has this right. In addition, the followers of the foreign god treat one another as siblings. Father Mateo considers Sayuri his sister, and on that basis he asked Nobuhide to give her a chance to prove her innocence."

"Really?" The magistrate leaned forward. "Fascinating. I would like to hear more. Does he speak Japanese?"

"A little," Hiro said. "Not well."

The magistrate leaned back again. "A pity. I would have liked to discuss this law with him in depth." He folded his hands on his desk. "I take it Nobuhide did not appreciate the finer points of foreign religious laws."

"Not exactly," Hiro agreed. The magistrate's joke suggested a possible ally. "He granted the request, but intends to hold Father Mateo responsible if Sayuri cannot prove her innocence. He threatened to execute them both in two days' time."

The magistrate raised a hand and rubbed his chin. "Most unfortunate indeed. I assume you came to ask me to intervene."

Hiro nodded.

"I'm afraid there is nothing I can do. Had the murder occurred within Pontocho, I could order Nobuhide not to touch the foreign priest, but the Sakura Teahouse lies outside his jurisdiction. His authority there stems from his status as Hideyoshi's son. I cannot control his actions in that capacity, and, as you know, the law permits a samurai to avenge his father's death."

"I also know that the death of a foreign priest could complicate the shogun's relations with the Portuguese," Hiro said.

The magistrate nodded. "I will speak with Nobuhide and see what I can do."

"You can do nothing."

Hiro spun around with his hand on his sword, chastising himself for letting down his guard. Nobuhide stood by the supplicants' entrance, face and forehead red with ill-contained rage. He bowed perfunctorily to the magistrate.

"I have the legal right to avenge my father." Nobuhide pointed at Father Mateo. "This man inserted himself into a private matter. He chose to assist the woman. For all I know, he helped her commit the crime."

"Ridiculous," Hiro snorted. "He was at home all night. I was there."

"He could have helped her plan, or given her the weapon," Nobuhide said. "Doesn't the other Portuguese sell firearms?"

"Enough!" The magistrate thumped his hands on his desk.

He looked at each man in turn. His hand crept back to his chin, and he rubbed it as he thought his way through the problem. The gesture suggested uncertainty, but when the magistrate spoke his voice conveyed both confidence and regret. "If you cannot prove the girl innocent within the allotted time, I cannot stop Nobuhide from taking vengeance."

He shifted his gaze to the young samurai. "But I can require you to cooperate with their investigation. You may not interfere with their efforts in any way.

"Have I made myself clear?"

Nobuhide scowled but bowed in assent. As he turned to leave, he pointed at Hiro and said, "Sakura Teahouse, noon, two days from now. Make sure the priest is there."

He stalked from the room, feet thumping the wooden floor.

"I wish I could do more," the magistrate told Hiro. "Justice is in your hands now."

Chapter 6

As they left the magistrate's compound, Hiro asked Father Mateo, "Have you got a plan?"

"A plan?"

"Yes, to find the killer."

The Jesuit ran his hand through his hair. "I hadn't really thought that far ahead."

"I didn't think so," Hiro said. "You should leave Kyoto. Nobuhide cannot kill what he cannot find."

"Run away? I have to help Sayuri prove her innocence."

"Assuming she is innocent," Hiro said, "which is far from certain. The bloody footprints in the room were a perfect match to her tiny feet."

"She might have walked in blood by mistake."

Hiro gave the priest a disbelieving look. No one should take trust and forgiveness that far.

"How many Japanese willfully touch defiling blood?" Hiro asked. "If Sayuri didn't commit the murder she is certainly an accomplice."

They turned left past the police compound and followed

Shijō Road back toward the river. A gentle breeze fluttered the indigo *noren* in the doorways, indicating the shops had opened for business. Meaty scents wafted across the road, and Hiro's mouth watered at the thought of fresh stuffed buns. He looked for the bun shop but didn't see it.

"Sayuri couldn't kill a man," Father Mateo said. "She's just a girl."

The words brought Hiro back from his hungry reverie. "Japanese women are stronger than they seem, and entertainers are trained to feign innocence."

"But Sayuri is a Christian."

"She's also a liar."

"I don't like you saying that, even if you think it's true."

"Almost everything she told us was a lie," Hiro persisted, "and the way she looked at Mayuri suggests they both know what really happened. They're covering something up."

"Impossible," Father Mateo said. "You have no proof of that."

"But I do. Someone moved the body shortly after the crime. Given the bloodstained kimono, I'm guessing it was Sayuri."

"Why would she do that?" the priest asked. "And even so, moving him doesn't mean she killed him. She could have moved him this morning when she woke up and discovered him dead."

"The evidence says otherwise." Hiro made a sweeping gesture. "Neck wounds spray blood everywhere. You saw the droplets on the wall and on the floor.

"Hideyoshi was facing the tokonoma when someone attacked him from behind. The drops all sprayed in the same direction, which means he didn't fight. He probably didn't have time. Blood spattered the wall and pooled on the floor in front of the alcove, but there were only minor bloodstains on the futon, the kind that happen when blood has ceased to flow actively through the veins.

"Had Sayuri moved him hours after death, as her story implies, there would have been no blood on the futon at all."

"Maybe the killer moved him after the attack."

"Why would a killer do that?" Hiro waited, but the priest didn't answer. "A killer who rips out throats and gouges eyes doesn't stop to arrange the victim on a futon."

"Unless he wanted to throw suspicion on Sayuri," Father Mateo said.

"Did he smear blood on her kimono while she slept?" Hiro shook his head. "If you want to discover who killed the samurai, you have to stop accepting lies as truth."

"But how will we find the truth? If we can't trust Sayuri, who can we trust?"

"Trust the evidence," Hiro said. "Facts don't lie, and when people do, their stories still lead to the truth eventually. Follow a lie far enough and you will reach a fact.

"We know where and when the killer struck, but why that time and place? Why did someone want Hideyoshi dead? If we can answer those questions I think we can find the killer, but you must understand, if Sayuri is guilty I will turn her over to Nobuhide and you must not interfere."

"Agreed," Father Mateo said, "but Sayuri is innocent. You will see."

Four samurai stood guard outside the Sakura Teahouse, one at each of the garden gates and two more leaning against the stone dogs near the path. They wore baggy trousers and wide-shouldered surcoats, like Nobuhide's but more cheaply made. All four wore swords and carried hooked *jitte*, which identified them as *dōshin*, low-ranking policemen undoubtedly under Nobuhide's command.

The dead man's son had wasted no time putting his underlings on guard.

Hiro leaned toward Father Mateo as they approached. "Speak Portuguese if you have to speak at all."

Three of the *dōshin* had graying hair and the confident calm of experienced policemen. The fourth was no more than twenty, with the rounded face and slightly overweight build of a pampered son. His scraggly mustache, grown to show his manhood, had the opposite result.

The older *dōshin* nodded as Hiro reached the walk. The younger man leaned back against his statue, withholding respect to reinforce his authority.

"What is your business here?" the young *dōshin* demanded. "No one enters this house today."

Father Mateo began to bow but Hiro stopped him with a look.

"Is the house under quarantine?" Hiro asked.

The older *dōshin* glanced at his young companion, but the silent warning went unnoticed. The young man raised his *jitte* to block the path. The weapon shone like new, in sharp contrast to the *dōshin*'s fraying sleeves and faded trousers.

"We are guarding this establishment. There has been a crime."

Nobuhide must have told him not to mention murder.

"Precisely the reason for our visit," Hiro said. "Father Mateo Ávila de Santos, of the Portuguese foreign mission, is investigating the death of Akechi Hideyoshi."

The older *dōshin* stepped back to clear the path, but the younger man stood up and blocked the way.

"Foreigners have no jurisdiction here. This is a police matter." His knuckles whitened as he clutched the *jitte*.

"A police matter?" Hiro asked. "Under your jurisdiction?"

The older man's eyes shifted downward. The younger one drew his shoulders back and said nothing.

"Who is your supervisor?" Hiro asked. He knew the answer. The question served a different purpose.

"I don't have to tell you that."

Hiro looked at the older *dōshin,* raised an eyebrow, and waited.

"Akechi Nobuhide," he said, "*Yoriki* of Pontocho."

"Pontocho." Hiro glanced over his shoulder toward the bridge. "This teahouse lies outside Pontocho."

"That's none of your business," the younger *dōshin* snapped. "Go away before I call the magistrate."

The words rolled off his tongue with the facility of frequent use.

"A fine idea," Hiro said politely.

The *dōshin*'s eyes went wide as Hiro continued. "Magistrate Ishimaki ordered full police cooperation with the priest's investigation, but I'm sure he won't mind you interrupting his morning audience to ask for repetition of those instructions."

The young *dōshin* narrowed his eyes and seethed. His older companion shifted from foot to foot. Policemen did not disagree with their partners in public, but the more experienced man seemed on the verge of speaking.

At the garden gates, the other two men watched the scene with interest. They were too far away to hear the conversation, but would close the distance instantly if anyone drew a sword.

The young *dōshin* pointed his *jitte* at Hiro's chest. "No funny business. When you leave, you leave alone. No companions and no parcels. Is that clear?"

Hiro wanted to take the bully down a notch or two, but pragmatism required otherwise, for the moment at least. He bowed slightly and allowed the tension to defuse.

"Thank you for your cooperation. You are indeed an example for your companions."

What kind of example, Hiro didn't say.

Instead, he nodded to the older *dōshin* and followed the Jesuit up the path to the teahouse.

Chapter 7

Mayuri opened the door just as Father Mateo reached out to knock. He withdrew his hand awkwardly and lowered it to his side. Mayuri lowered her own hands even faster, but not before Hiro saw the dark smudges on her fingers and an angry burn on her left hand that hadn't been there earlier in the day.

Father Mateo noticed too. "Are you injured?"

Mayuri pulled her hand into her sleeve. "It is nothing. I burned myself lighting a fire. The servant ran away when she heard about the murder—superstitious little fool. Why do you think I've answered the door myself all morning?"

She cast a harried glance toward the road as though hoping the servant would return. As her eyes shifted back to Hiro, she forced a smile. "Did you forget something earlier?"

Father Mateo bowed. "We hoped to speak with Sayuri."

"And also the other women who work in the house," Hiro added.

Mayuri's smile wavered. "No one saw or heard anything. I spoke with each of them myself."

"Then it will be a short conversation," Hiro said. "Thank you for accommodating us."

"It will take some time," Mayuri said. "We are not prepared for company so early."

"We can talk with Sayuri while we wait." Hiro smiled pleasantly, knowing the teahouse owner could not refuse without bringing more suspicion on herself.

When she realized Hiro had no intention of leaving, Mayuri tilted her head in consent and turned to lead the men into the house. Her kimono rustled slightly, like a mouse in a sack of grain.

As Mayuri turned, Hiro noticed a scrap of paper caught on the back of her kimono. The trailing end of her obi had trapped it just above the hem. Hiro bent and plucked the paper from her dress, slipping it into his sleeve as he straightened. He said nothing. Teahouse culture valued neatness and beauty above all else. Mayuri would have been mortified to learn she was trailing scraps, and, although Hiro didn't care about her feelings, he also saw no reason to cause her unnecessary embarrassment.

Mayuri led the men to the first door on the western side of the large common room. As she knelt she said, "You may speak with Sayuri here, but please do not take too long. I have priests coming to purify the house."

Father Mateo entered the room as soon as Mayuri opened the door, but Hiro paused just long enough to ask, "You will tell me when the other girls are ready?"

Mayuri's mouth pressed shut in a very thin smile. "Of course."

Hiro stepped over the threshold and joined the Jesuit inside.

The room was identical to the adjacent one except for a welcome lack of blood and the absence of a corpse. An unspoiled vase of hydrangeas adorned the tokonoma. The flower arrangement showed more skill than the one in the room where the murder occurred. Hiro recognized it as a master's work. The spoiled arrangement was likely the work of a student.

Sayuri knelt in front of the alcove, facing the door, with her back to the vase of flowers. She had bathed and changed into a simple kimono of patterned silk. Without her makeup, she looked younger than before, and also more beautiful.

A shamisen lay on the floor to her right. The lack of ornate decoration suggested a practice instrument, something to pass the time.

"Make a useful comment," Hiro said in Portuguese.

Father Mateo recognized the coded cue at once. "What something would you have me say? Do you need more than this or have I said enough already?" He kept his voice even so the questions would sound like statements.

"That will do." Hiro turned. Mayuri knelt in the doorway as though she intended to stay.

"I apologize for the foreign exchange," Hiro said. "Father Mateo does not know the proper words for his request.

"His religion has a rite called 'confession,' in which an accused person speaks confidentially with a priest. Father Mateo requests permission to have confession with Sayuri now."

Mayuri frowned. "Is privacy required?"

Hiro nodded. "A translator may assist if necessary, but no one else is permitted to remain."

Mayuri looked at Sayuri. To Hiro's surprise, the girl nodded in agreement.

"Very well." Mayuri sighed. "I have business to attend to anyway."

Hiro remained by the door to ensure that her shadow disappeared.

Sayuri burst into tears the moment the door closed. "I'm sorry. This is my fault. I would not have asked you to come if I thought Nobuhide would kill you too."

"Don't worry," Father Mateo said. "Hiro and I will find the real killer."

Sayuri stopped crying and looked up through her tears. "Do you really think you can?"

Hiro fought the urge to laugh at her attempt to manipulate the priest until he realized, with dismay, that it had worked.

"Of course we will," Father Mateo said, "but we need you to tell us what really happened last night."

"I already did. I woke up and Akechi-san was dead."

"I don't think that's true." Father Mateo's unexpected firmness made Hiro wonder if the Jesuit saw through Sayuri's performance after all. "Are you scared to tell the truth? Has someone threatened you?"

"Of course not," she said, a bit too quickly for the truth. "A shinobi must have killed him."

"Who would want to assassinate Akechi Hideyoshi?" Hiro asked.

Sayuri looked at him, wide-eyed. "I don't know. Akechi-san was a good man. Mayuri says he always paid his bills."

"He was wealthy?" Hiro asked.

Sayuri thought it over. "He didn't buy me presents like the other girls get sometimes, but then, he wasn't my patron, just a regular visitor."

"Did he ever bring guests to the teahouse?"

Sayuri smiled. Her eyes sparkled. "He brought his brother, Hidetaro."

Hiro found it curious that Sayuri's first genuine smile came at the mention of Hideyoshi's brother. Nothing in teahouse culture prohibited a girl from entertaining both a man and his relatives, though a girl who accepted a man as her patron would generally refuse separate visits from his brothers or male relations.

"Anyone else?" Hiro asked.

Sayuri squinted at the ceiling. Her forehead wrinkled in thought. "A couple of months ago he entertained a cousin from out of town. Masuhide? No, but something like that."

"You don't remember?" Hiro asked. Entertainers were trained to remember names, to make a client's friends feel special on subsequent visits.

"No." Sayuri pushed a stray hair behind her ear as her cheeks turned pink with embarrassment. "I got the impression they had only met a couple of times. They didn't seem close, and Hideyoshi said the cousin was just passing through on business. I didn't think I would need to remember his name."

"What about Hideyoshi's brother . . . Hidetaro? Did he visit you often?"

"A few times, with Hideyoshi." Sayuri's radiant smile returned, but faded quickly. "Hidetaro can't afford teahouses. But he's very nice."

"When was the last time you saw him?" Hiro asked.

Sayuri looked at the floor. "Several weeks ago."

"What about Nobuhide?" Father Mateo asked.

"He's not allowed here anymore." Sayuri's eyes widened. She lowered her voice. "He got drunk and forced himself on one of the girls. We're not that kind of house. It made Mayuri furious. She told Hideyoshi his son was not welcome anymore."

"Do you know the girl's name?" Hiro asked.

"Umeha?" Sayuri shook her head. "I think it was Umeha, but I'm not sure. She hasn't worked here in over a year. I think—"

The door rustled open and Sayuri cut herself off midsentence.

Mayuri knelt in the doorway.

"I apologize for the inconvenience," she said, in a tone that said the opposite. "My women cannot speak with you this morning. It appears you have waited for nothing."

Chapter 8

Father Mateo started to protest but Hiro bowed and said, "Thank you. We will come back later."

Mayuri stood up to lead them out. Father Mateo gave Hiro a confused look. The shinobi shook his head slightly and followed Mayuri without argument.

When they reached the front of the teahouse Hiro said, "Since the other girls cannot speak with us, perhaps you can tell us where to find Umeha."

Mayuri's smile disappeared. Her lips parted in surprise, but she recovered almost immediately. "I'm afraid I don't know that name."

"You are afraid because you do," Hiro corrected, "and either you tell me where to find her, or I let it slip to our friends in the yard that she has information about Hideyoshi's death that you have tried to hide. We'll see how long it takes them to find her for me."

"They already know where to find her." Mayuri's smile faded and her expression hardened as she looked past Hiro at the *dōshin* standing in the yard. "You can find her at the House of the Floating Plums in Pontocho."

Father Mateo said nothing until they reached the bridge. As they crossed the river he said, "Why did we leave? We need to talk with the other women. Someone must have heard something."

"Do you think they would tell us the truth?" Hiro didn't wait for a response. "Mayuri is hiding something and her women will back her up, at least until we know enough to persuade them otherwise."

"Well, at least Mayuri helped us find Umeha," the priest said, "though I'm not sure why you want to know."

"When a dead man's heir has violent tendencies, it's helpful to find out how deeply they run."

The House of the Floating Plums lay deep within the shadows of Pontocho, a tiny two-story teahouse squeezed between seedy-looking brothels. The overhanging upper floors of the buildings kept the earthen road in near-perpetual twilight, making it difficult to read the signs that identified businesses. Sunset would transform the dingy alley into a glittering paradise of paper lanterns, silk kimonos, and painted faces, but daytime Pontocho reminded Hiro of an aging prostitute without her makeup on.

"This is it?" Father Mateo asked as they paused before the door.

Hiro tried to see the teahouse as it looked through the Jesuit's eyes. The pine façade had weathered to brownish-gray, with darker patches of rot beneath the eaves. The second story hung over the alley, almost touching the upper floor of the brothel across the street. No stone dogs or cherry trees adorned the entry. Instead, a hand-painted board read FLOATING PLUMS.

"This is a brothel," Father Mateo said.

"Probably." Hiro didn't share the priest's dismay.

He knocked. Footsteps approached on the inside and a woman opened the door. Her plain blue kimono and narrow sash identified her as a servant. She bowed deeply at the sight of Hiro's swords. As she straightened, she noticed the priest. Her mouth fell open in shock and her eyes grew wide. She covered her surprise with a second bow, though it didn't give her quite enough time to recover her composure.

"Is this the House of the Floating Plums?" Hiro asked.

"Yes, sir, but I am sorry to say we do not open until evening. A thousand apologies. The girls are resting now."

"We are not customers," Hiro said.

The woman clasped her hands and bit her lower lip. Hiro understood her inner turmoil. She could not invite them in without incurring her mistress's wrath, but leaving a samurai and a foreigner on the doorstep showed an appalling lack of hospitality.

"We are here on official business," Hiro added. "Please fetch your mistress."

The woman bowed and scurried away.

"That was a lie," Father Mateo said.

Hiro raised an eyebrow at the priest. "Not as big as the one you told Nobuhide. Besides, I am on official business. Nobuhide is an official and I want to know his business."

The priest did not return his smile.

Hiro grew frustrated. "I went along with your lie back at the teahouse."

"That was different. I told it to save Sayuri's life."

"Which makes it all right with your god?"

Father Mateo didn't answer.

Hiro laughed and the tension fell away. "I thought as much." Then he grew serious. "I didn't ask to get involved in this, and I still disagree with your decision, but we are involved now, and I will do whatever it takes to ensure that your head stays on your shoulders. A lie is only the beginning."

Hiro and Father Mateo stepped inside and seated themselves on the built-in wooden bench that ran along the left wall of the entry. Yellowish paper lined the wooden lattices. A smell of greasy smoke hung in the air, reminiscent of cheap food cooked too quickly and left out overnight.

Ten minutes elapsed. Hiro passed the time by finding patterns in the stains on the walls.

"I don't think anyone is coming," Father Mateo said at last.

"The mistress would need time to dress and fix her makeup," Hiro said. "She was probably still asleep."

A faint sound made Hiro look to the inner door. Moments later, a woman appeared in the doorway. She wore a silk kimono adorned with hand-painted butterflies. A purple silk obi glowed at her waist, and butterfly ornaments glittered in her graying hair. Her makeup did not quite hide the wrinkles around her eyes, though her cheeks and neck were smooth.

Hiro bowed. "Good morning."

The woman frowned at the visitors. "You are not from the shogun or the magistrate. This establishment does not open until evening."

She gestured toward the door as though expecting them to leave.

"I apologize for the inconvenience," Hiro said. "We would like to see Umeha."

"Did Nobuhide send you?" she asked.

"Are you expecting him?" Hiro countered.

Her face revealed nothing. "I didn't say that."

"We are investigating a murder," Father Mateo said. "We need to speak with Umeha."

Hiro fought the urge to cover his face with his hand. The foreigner had a good grasp of Japanese culture, but had not yet mastered the art of indirection. At times he reminded Hiro of an impulsive toddler or an elderly woman devoid of self-control.

"Murder?" The woman's left hand crept to her throat. "There's been no murder. Nobuhide was fine when he left this morning."

"Then Nobuhide was here," Hiro said. The priest's words may have been bullheaded, but they provided an opening the shinobi would not waste.

She nodded. "He spent the night with Umeha. A messenger came for him a few hours ago. He was alive and well when he left. Whatever happened, it didn't happen here."

"May we speak with Umeha," Hiro asked, "to confirm your story?"

"Wait here, I will get her for you."

Chapter 9

As they waited to see Umeha, Hiro examined a parchment on the wall. Many teahouses placed decorative scrolls in the entry. In a high-class house the hanging might contain a poem or a landscape. At the House of the Floating Plums, it displayed a list of names. They appeared in no obvious order, though Hiro knew the most expensive girls usually appeared near the top.

Umeha's name appeared about halfway down the list, not close enough to the top for a pure entertainer though not necessarily low enough to indicate a prostitute.

The establishment called itself a teahouse, but its location near the brothels at the center of Pontocho, as well as the scroll of names, suggested that its clientele could purchase more than merely drinks and singing. Umeha's transfer provided a further clue. High-end houses preferred pure entertainers, women who might accept a single patron but who did not sleep with men for money as a normal enterprise. A woman defiled against her will lost value and desirability. Only a house of lesser status could accept her without losing face.

Hiro decided to treat Umeha as a high-class entertainer and pretend that he knew nothing of her past. He needed information, and flattery loosened feminine lips.

The girl appeared in the doorway. She wore a pink kimono with a red-and-white-striped obi that highlighted her pale skin and delicate features. Although not as strikingly beautiful as Sayuri, she had an honest face and large, childlike eyes. She looked at most fifteen, though she had to be at least three or four years older. That, too, came as no surprise. Women in the pleasure districts treasured their youth and held it well. Their income depended on it.

Umeha startled in surprise at the sight of Father Mateo, but quickly turned the movement into a bow.

"Good morning, Honorable Gentlemen," she said. She struggled with silence, then blurted out, "Has something happened to Nobuhide?"

"No, he is well," Hiro said.

Umeha's forehead wrinkled with concern. "Madame said . . ."

"I'm afraid that was a ruse." Hiro gave an embarrassed bow. "I wanted to speak with you, so I might have allowed her to think Nobuhide was killed."

Umeha looked from Hiro to the priest. She clasped her hands at her waist, the universal gesture of teahouse women trying to keep still. "I don't understand."

"Nobuhide's father is dead." Hiro didn't care about spreading the news. Word traveled fast in the floating world of the teahouses, and the Sakura's location outside Pontocho made little difference where gossip was concerned. Every entertainer in Kyoto would know about the murder by evening, whether Hiro mentioned it or not.

Umeha flushed, then paled.

"He spent the night with me while his father was dying?" She covered her mouth with her hands and then tilted her head down so her fingers covered her face. Her shoulders heaved with sorrow, and possibly fear.

"It is very sad," Hiro said. "I am sorry to bear bad news."

He found the girl's reaction curious, mostly because it seemed genuine. A courtesan or a prostitute would normally show more restraint. It suggested Nobuhide meant more to her than just a purse—which, in turn, suggested that Umeha had not been Nobuhide's victim three years before. At least, not an unwilling victim.

The girl removed her hands from her face. Her eyes were red but free of tears.

"No, I'm glad you came." A lopsided smile played at the corner of her lips despite her attempts to control it. "Akechi-san left so quickly when the messenger came. He barely spoke. I thought I made him angry by drinking too much last night. I did drink too much. I even fell asleep before . . ." She caught herself. "I fell asleep too early."

She raised a hand to her chest. "I shouldn't feel better knowing his father is dead, but I hated thinking Nobuhide was mad at me."

"Is he often angry?" Hiro asked. He didn't expect an honest answer, so it surprised him when Umeha shook her head vehemently and without hesitation.

The lopsided smile returned, too, and this time she made no attempt to hide it. "Not at all. Nobu isn't like that. He's a wonderful patron. I don't see anyone else. Last night he even undressed me and put me into bed." She laughed. "My dress was so muddy! We must have gone to every bar in Pontocho."

"Do you remember which ones you went to?" Hiro asked.

"I don't remember anything after dinner." She giggled. "But then, I never remember anything when I drink like that."

Her forehead furrowed. "I hope he isn't angry, though."

Hiro gave her a reassuring smile. "I don't think anyone could stay angry with you for long."

She smiled. "He did say he would come back tonight if he could."

"Does he visit you often?"

"Every—" A red flush darkened her cheeks and crept across the bridge of her nose, like a little girl caught stealing candied plums. She shook her head. "I'm not supposed to talk about my patron. You know that."

"True enough," Hiro said with a smile. "You caught me."

"I'm so sorry his father is dead," Umeha said. "Nobuhide slept so well last night. I was sad to wake him when the messenger came, and now I'm even sadder."

"You did the right thing," Hiro said, less to comfort Umeha than to extract himself from a conversation that had already served its purpose.

Nobuhide's alleged rape now sounded more like an affair discovered, after which Umeha claimed attack to avoid admitting that she had provided unpaid services on the sly. After her transfer to a less expensive house, they had formalized their arrangement, apparently to their mutual satisfaction.

Umeha looked at Father Mateo and murmured, "I've never seen a foreigner. He's not as pale as I thought a ghost would be, and he dresses almost like a real person."

"He speaks like one too," Father Mateo said.

Umeha's jaw dropped open. Her hands flew up to hide her astonishment and she bowed repeatedly from the waist.

"I'm so sorry," she said. "I apologize."

Father Mateo laughed. "Please, think nothing of it."

Hiro didn't find it funny at all. If Umeha mentioned the priest to Nobuhide, the *yoriki* would know they had misled him about the Jesuit's language skills.

"Thank you for your time," Hiro said. "Again, I apologize for the unnecessary fright."

Umeha's smile returned. Open joy seemed to be her usual expression. "I don't care," she said, "as long as Nobu is all right."

"And as long as he's not angry," Hiro said.

Umeha nodded.

"I'm glad you don't mind me bringing Father Mateo along," Hiro added, "most people consider foreigners as unlucky as foxes and ghosts."

"Unlucky?" Umeha's forehead furrowed. "Why?"

"I don't know," Hiro said. "It's not true, of course, but some samurai are superstitious. Nobuhide, for example. He thought the priest would defile his father's body just by entering the room."

Umeha's breathing grew shallow and her right hand crept to the base of her neck. "Really?" She looked terrified.

Hiro bit his lower lip as though realizing the implication of his words. "I'm afraid he did."

Umeha looked as if she might start crying.

Hiro raised a finger as though he had an idea. "I tell you what. I won't mention our visit to Nobuhide. I don't want to get you in trouble."

Umeha sighed with relief. "Thank you so much."

As Hiro and Father Mateo walked up the twisting alley away from the teahouse, the priest said, "I can't believe you frightened that girl on purpose."

"I don't want her to talk," Hiro replied. "Nobuhide will be angry enough when he learns we were checking up on him. I'd rather not have him learn we lied as well."

"We did not lie," Father Mateo said. "At least, I didn't. I never claimed I didn't speak Japanese."

"You went along with it," Hiro replied, "and to samurai, that's a lie."

They reached Shijō Road and turned right, toward the river.

"At least we learned a little more about Nobuhide," Hiro said. "I think his vicious streak was an act, concocted to save his purse from Mayuri's wrath."

Father Mateo looked confused.

"Men pay a higher rate for special services at a high-end house—much higher when the owner doesn't want the girls to provide them, and astronomically high when the service and fee are not negotiated in advance."

Father Mateo nodded. "So Umeha claimed rape, and accepted dishonor, rather than confessing the affair." He shook his head. "No woman should have to make such a choice."

Hiro didn't answer. Despite the Jesuit's interest in assimilation, the priest had several obstinate blind spots. Hiro had learned to ignore them when he could.

A few paces farther down the road Father Mateo asked, "Wouldn't Nobuhide have to pay for Umeha's services anyway?"

"Yes, but if Umeha claimed assault, Mayuri could only charge him for one night."

Chapter 10

The sun stood almost overhead by the time Hiro and Father Mateo returned to the church. As the priest stepped into the entry, an elderly female voice called, "Oi, Father Mateo, you're back. I have your meal waiting."

Hiro followed the Jesuit inside as the woman rose from her bow. She had steel-gray hair and a dried-plum face that showed every one of her sixty-two years, along with a few that she hadn't even lived yet. Her wrinkled cheeks creased in a smile that set her black eyes twinkling. Anyone could tell she adored the priest.

"Have you had a nice morning?" she asked.

"Very nice, thank you, Ana," Father Mateo replied as he bowed.

The elderly housekeeper had served as the previous owners' nanny and maid and had stayed on when Father Mateo acquired the property. Her name was Ane, but she changed the pronunciation the moment she learned that Ana was a name in Portuguese.

Her smile faded when she saw the shinobi.

"Hiro," she said. "I suppose you want rice?"

She spoke like a parent addressing a child who spilled his food and asked for more, only to spill that too.

"Thank you, Ana." Hiro nodded respectfully. Samurai did not bend to servants, but the housekeeper inspired respect that transcended her station.

"Hm." She pointed to the hearth as she shuffled toward the kitchen. "Sit down."

Hiro and Father Mateo crossed to the hearth that dominated the *oe*, the large central room that functioned as a combination parlor and dining room. The sunken hearth sat six inches below the surrounding floor. It held a bed of dark sand upon which a small fire burned. A kettle hung over the fire, suspended on a chain that hung from a ceiling beam. Steam rose from the kettle and mingled with the tendrils of woodsmoke that curled toward the ceiling.

The hearth fire could have cooked a meal, and did in smaller homes, but the priest's house had a separate kitchen beyond the *oe*, where Ana did the cooking. Father Mateo initially tried to help, but the elderly woman resented any intrusion or assistance, particularly from a man whose efforts she viewed as a fire hazard.

The priest knelt before the hearth, in the position facing the door. He knelt directly on the tatami, like a Japanese would, without any cushion or chair. Hiro took the place to Father Mateo's left, on the side of the hearth normally used by the other members of a family.

The seat of honor to Father Mateo's right was already occupied by the final member of the Jesuit's household.

Luis Álvares was a portly man with skin the color of wilted primroses and an unusually large, red nose that looked to

Hiro like a cross between a berry and a gourd. He had long dark hair pulled back in a greasy ponytail and piggish brown eyes that missed only what their owner chose not to see. He wore a short-waisted, high-necked doublet and fitted hose that did no courtesies to his ample figure. Slashes in the doublet sleeves revealed a cream-colored blouse beneath.

"Good morning, Mateo," Luis said in Portuguese. He wiped his sweaty forehead with the hand that held his chopsticks.

"And to you, Luis," Father Mateo said. "I'm surprised you're still here at this hour."

"Been to the warehouse and back already," Luis said between mouthfuls. "One of the rice merchants made a major purchase."

"Curious," Hiro said. "I wouldn't think rice dealers had much use for firearms."

Luis looked down his nose at Hiro. "I sell more than weapons, you know."

"How are those textiles selling for you?" Hiro asked. "Wool, I believe you called them?"

Luis made an exasperated noise. A grain of rice flew from his mouth and sizzled in the fire. "The Japanese refuse to buy it. Yesterday a woman had the nerve to tell me it smelled bad!"

Hiro couldn't agree more. Wool smelled like a three-day-old corpse. He couldn't believe anyone wore it willingly, though the bolts in Luis's warehouse suggested that someone considered it worth the trouble to produce and sell.

"Silk kimonos are comfortable in this climate." Father Mateo sounded almost apologetic.

"I still can't believe you wear that ridiculous native costume," Luis said. "You look like a woman."

"You should try it," Father Mateo replied. "It's cooler than doublets and hose."

"And more difficult to rip," Hiro added, with a pointed look at the merchant's tunic.

"My sleeves are made this way," Luis said indignantly. "The style is very fashionable, though I suppose I shouldn't expect a Japanese to understand."

"I'm afraid not." Hiro smiled. "We ignorant natives prefer to buy new clothes instead of calling damaged ones 'fashionable.'"

Father Mateo changed the subject. "What did the merchant buy this morning?"

Before Luis could reply Ana scurried in and set a tray on the floor in front of Father Mateo. It held a bowl of miso soup with tofu, a teapot, and a pair of chopsticks balanced on an ivory rest.

She frowned at the men around the hearth. "Who brought that cat in?"

The tortoiseshell kitten had followed her into the room. As she pointed in its direction, it turned around and streaked into Hiro's room.

Hiro and Father Mateo exchanged a look.

"I did," Hiro admitted, "as a present for Father Mateo."

He hoped Ana's love for the Jesuit would prevent a scolding, but didn't count on it.

"Hm," she said. "Is it staying?"

"Yes?" Father Mateo asked.

She nodded. "Good. When it grows up it will keep the mice away. It's already started on the spiders."

"It eats spiders?" Hiro asked.

"Plucks them right off the wall." Ana gave Hiro a rare nod of approval as she turned back toward the kitchen.

"Three dozen arquebuses." Luis continued the conversation as though Ana had not spoken. The merchant acknowledged servants only when he had no other choice. "The man has been having trouble with thieves and wanted to arm his guards."

"They want muskets instead of swords?" Father Mateo asked.

Hiro thought the idea made good sense. A firearm beat a sword for stopping thieves.

"You don't have to sound so disappointed," Luis said. He set down his bowl and chopsticks and poured himself a cup of tea. "Francis Xavier approved this trade to finance mission work in Japan, and if the former head of the Jesuit order didn't mind you have no reason to object."

"Even you must see the irony in taking lives with one hand while the other tries to save them," the priest replied.

"The Japanese are quite capable of taking lives without my assistance," Luis snorted. "They were hacking each other apart with swords long before we landed."

Father Mateo did not respond. It was an old argument, and not one he would win.

The maid returned with a tray for Hiro. She set it down and disappeared without a word. As Father Mateo blessed the food, Hiro noted his own soup contained seven cubes of tofu—three more than usual—doubtless a reward for bringing the cat.

"Where have you been this morning?" Luis asked.

Father Mateo set down his bowl. "One of my converts was accused of killing a samurai."

Luis sipped his tea. "Did he?"

"She," Father Mateo corrected, "and no, she didn't."

"Pity," Luis said without feeling. "I take it you went to perform last rites? The murderous bastards doubtless killed her anyway."

"Actually, no. She has been granted two days to prove her innocence, and I'm going to help her do it."

"Why would you want to do that?"

"Because if he doesn't," Hiro said, "the dead man's son will kill him too."

Luis sputtered in surprise and lost his grip on the egg-shaped teacup. Hot liquid spilled down his doublet and onto his hose.

"Pestilence!" Luis swore as he brushed at the stain. "I'll have to change! Hiro, that isn't funny."

Luis realized no one was laughing.

"Mateo, please tell me he's joking."

"It's no joke," Father Mateo said, "but we'll find the killer in time."

"Blind faith won't save you from swords." Luis turned a sweaty glare on Hiro. "How could you let this happen? Why did you translate things that would get him killed!"

"It's not his fault," Father Mateo said.

"Get the magistrate to intervene," Luis continued. "They're always bragging about their powerful judges."

"The law allows a nobleman's son to avenge his father's death," Father Mateo said. "If I don't help, the girl is as good as dead."

"Then let her die," Luis said. "What is she, anyway, some kind of prostitute?"

"Entertainer," Father Mateo corrected.

"Prostitute," Luis repeated as he hoisted himself to his feet. "Let her die. Leave town if you must. She's not worth jeopardizing your work, or my profits."

Hiro watched in silence as Luis disappeared into his room. For the first time ever, he found himself agreeing with the merchant.

He swallowed the last of his soup. As he set the empty bowl on the tray the scrap of paper from the teahouse scratched his arm inside his sleeve. He pulled it out to toss it in the fire, but at the last moment he snatched it back from the flames.

The palm-sized fragment of parchment contained columns of names and figures written in a feminine hand. The lower edge was dark and smudged with dirt or ash but not actually burned.

Teahouses kept careful records and never destroyed their ledgers. Hiro wondered why this one had been torn, and whether its destruction was intentional or merely coincidence.

Given the ash, and Mayuri's burned hand, he decided against coincidence.

"What's that?" Father Mateo asked.

"A scrap I retrieved from Mayuri's kimono. It seems to be part of a ledger."

"From her kimono?" The priest leaned forward for a better look. "That's strange."

"More than you know," Hiro said. "We need to go back to the teahouse. Immediately."

"Why?"

Hiro offered the paper. "To find out why Mayuri destroyed her ledger this morning."

"Destroyed it? Are you sure?" Father Mateo examined the paper. "Maybe it was an old one?"

"The date at the side indicates this year," Hiro said, "and the smudge on the corner looks like ash. Curious, since Mayuri burned her hand in a fire this morning."

"Why would she burn a ledger?"

"More importantly," Hiro said, "why would she burn it today?"

Chapter 11

The *dōshin* in the teahouse yard barely acknowledged Hiro and Father Mateo upon their return. Hiro had no objection. He preferred disregard to harassment.

When Mayuri answered the door, she didn't even bother with a greeting. "How will I prepare for guests with you coming and going all day?"

Hiro hadn't expected a warm welcome, but the woman's lack of manners still surprised him. The teahouse culture frowned on rudeness, and Mayuri should have welcomed help to prove Sayuri's innocence—and her own.

"Are you entertaining tonight?" Hiro asked.

"Unless Nobuhide's *dōshin* chase our visitors away." She paused. "Akechi-san's death is unfortunate, but I have a business to run."

"We have no objection to your business," Hiro said. "Father Mateo has come to pray with Sayuri."

"And you?"

"I would like to speak with the other women."

Mayuri smiled without humor or warmth. "As I told you, I

spoke with them earlier. Everyone but Sayuri was asleep when Akechi-san was killed."

"Then I will not need to ask them many questions."

Hiro preferred not to draw attention to himself, by rudeness or otherwise, but subtlety would not find Hideyoshi's killer.

Mayuri threw up her hands in exasperation. A white silk bandage covered the left one all the way to the wrist. She flinched and lowered the injured hand to her side.

"Very well," she said, "follow me."

She took Father Mateo to see Sayuri and then led Hiro to the opposite side of the central common room. She knelt and slid open a door, using only her right hand.

"Wait here."

Hiro entered the room and knelt before the tokonoma in the northern wall. The alcove held an empty vase, narrow at the bottom but bulging near the top and with a mouth just large enough to hold a few flower stems. White glaze coated the porcelain and blue, hand-painted leaves flowed around the sides.

The door rustled open. Hiro heard feet on the tatami and a soft rattle as the paneled door slid closed again. Kimonos swished as the women settled on the floor a few feet away. No one spoke. Entertainers would not interrupt a visitor's meditation.

Hiro let them wait.

After a couple of minutes he turned around. Three women knelt in a line before him. Their plain but expensive kimonos were made of silk. The woman in the center wore dark purple, while the ones to her sides were clad in pale pink and blue. The women's faces looked strangely pale without their elaborate makeup, but their features remained as emotionless as masks. Even their eyes revealed nothing.

All three women were older than Sayuri, Hiro guessed in their twenties or early thirties.

"Thank you for meeting with me," he said.

The women on either side looked at the one in the center. She seemed more confident than the others, and she alone met Hiro's gaze without faltering. Even before she opened her mouth, Hiro knew she would speak for the group.

"I am Okiya," she said. "You have questions about last night?"

"Did you hear the killer, or anything else unusual?" These women were trained professionals. Hiro saw no reason to treat them as delicate flowers.

Okiya didn't look at her companions. "No. We all had guests in the early evening, but the rest of our visitors left before midnight. I was the last one upstairs except for Sayuri. The others had already taken off their makeup and changed their kimono. We had tea and went to sleep."

"You heard nothing?"

"Not until Sayuri screamed this morning."

"She screamed?"

Before Okiya could answer the woman to her right said, "It was more like a yell."

The speaker was younger than Okiya, and clearly more impulsive. As soon as the words left her lips, she covered her mouth with her hand and looked down at the floor. Her blue kimono emphasized the embarrassed flush that spread across her cheeks.

"Is there a difference?" Hiro asked.

The woman in blue uncovered her mouth. "A real scream doesn't have any words in it. Sayuri called for help."

"Riko is correct," Okiya said. "It was more of a yell."

"Who went to help her?"

"We all did," Riko said, "but Mayuri blocked the door. She said it wasn't something we should see."

"I'm glad I didn't look," said the woman on Okiya's other side. "I don't want angry ghosts haunting me." Her hands shook and her pink kimono trembled.

"Don't be stupid, Yoko," Riko said. "Ghosts don't haunt you unless you do the killing."

"Do you want to chance it?" Yoko hugged herself, then recovered her composure and returned her hands to her lap.

Riko shook her head and rolled her eyes.

"Did any of you speak with Sayuri afterward?" Hiro asked.

"Mayuri wouldn't let us," Riko said. When Okiya gave her a warning look, Riko added, "Well, she won't, and she didn't tell me not to say so."

"I wouldn't go in that ghost room for anything," Yoko said.

"It's not a ghost room," Riko retorted. "Mayuri had it cleaned and the priests are coming to bless it this afternoon."

"Buddhist priests?" Yoko clutched her hands and looked nervously at the others.

"Shinto too," Okiya reassured her, "from Kamigamo Shrine."

Yoko still looked worried but managed a little smile.

"Is there anything more we can tell you?" Okiya asked.

"Who were your guests last night? Did they know Akechi Hideyoshi?"

"I don't think so," Riko said. "Guests who know one another often combine their parties. It's more fun that way. We play games and sing songs. Men like that."

"Our guests were not acquainted," Okiya confirmed. "I entertained a silk merchant and his clients. They left about an hour before midnight."

"And you?" Hiro asked Riko.

"I had a very early night. Magistrate Ishimaki fell asleep in his tea before the sun went down. His servants had to help him onto his horse."

"Magistrate Ishimaki was here last night?" Hiro asked.

"Yes. He visits once a week, for dinner." Riko's eyebrows raised and her mouth formed a circle of surprise. She raised her hand to cover it and giggled. "But it's not what you think. He's much too old for a girl my age."

Hiro doubted most men would consider her age an issue but said nothing. Riko gave Okiya a questioning look. The older woman nodded.

"Magistrate Ishimaki is my grandfather," Riko said. "His son was my mother's patron."

"Is Mayuri your mother?" Hiro asked.

Entertainers often bore children out of wedlock. Most men would not flaunt tradition to marry a mistress, so the female children normally followed their mothers into the trade.

"No," Okiya said. "I am, though I thank you in advance for your discretion."

Hiro hid his surprise. Okiya did look older than her companions, but not old enough to have a daughter Riko's age.

"Of course." After a pause he asked, "Did you see the magistrate too?"

She shook her head. "He doesn't dislike me, but I am not his blood. Truthfully, even his interest in Riko came as a surprise."

"Does he acknowledge her publicly?"

"Oh, no." Riko sounded shocked. "He couldn't possibly. I'm glad to know him, though. He's nice."

Hiro turned to Yoko. "Who were your visitors?"

"Only one," Yoko said, "a merchant. I had never seen him before."

"Do you remember his name?"

"I didn't need to," Yoko said. "He was visiting Kyoto on business from out of town and only staying for one day."

"What kind of business?"

"Rice." Yoko made a face. "It was all he talked about. He was boring and he stayed too late. By the time I got upstairs Riko was asleep."

"Did he mention where he came from?"

Yoko thought hard. It was clearly an effort. "Nagoya? I think Nagoya. He didn't like that we didn't have red miso for his soup."

"Did he pay in advance?"

Yoko nodded. "He gave me a gold koban and told me I could buy myself a present."

A night's entertainment cost only a small fraction of that, even in an upscale teahouse.

"He paid in gold?" Hiro asked.

Kyoto merchants used silver.

"Yes." Yoko's eyes grew round as she realized the implication. "You don't think . . . did I entertain the murderer? The ghost is going to haunt me after all!"

She clutched herself and looked about to cry.

"Don't worry," Hiro said. "Ghosts don't like teahouses much."

"They don't?"

He shook his head. He didn't care about the girl's emotional state, but it embarrassed him when women cried and he hated interruptions.

"Do any of you know her visitor's name?"

"Shutaro," Okiya said. "He arrived before my visitors, and I heard the introductions."

He stood up. "Thank you for speaking with me. I appreciate your time."

Okiya hung back as the others left the room. When they had gone she said, "Shutaro was actually the last guest to leave—aside from Hideyoshi, of course."

"He claimed to come from Nagoya?" Hiro asked.

When Okiya nodded Hiro continued. "Lord Oda Nobunaga controls Owari Province, including Nagoya, and Lord Oda wants the shogunate for himself. He wouldn't let his merchants sell rice to Kyoto."

The woman nodded. "It sounded strange to me, too. That's why I remembered."

"Thank you," Hiro said. "I know you breached etiquette by telling me."

"Justice excuses a breach of etiquette." Okiya lowered her voice. "Thank me by finding the killer. I don't know what happened here last night, but Sayuri did not murder anyone. She does not deserve to be executed for someone else's crime."

Chapter 12

After Okiya left, Hiro crossed the teahouse and entered Sayuri's room. Father Mateo knelt near the tokonoma with his back to the door. Sayuri faced him. Their heads were bowed in prayer.

A shamisen sat on the floor at Sayuri's side. The instrument had a stringed neck about the length of a man's arm, attached to a rounded body covered with animal skin. The skin was stretched taut like the cover of a drum, and three silk strings ran from pegs at the head of the instrument to a single anchor peg attached to the base of the body.

The shamisen took years to play badly and much longer to play well. Only women with genuine talent trained in the difficult instrument.

Hiro knelt beside Father Mateo. When the priest said, "Amen," Sayuri looked up.

Hiro nodded toward the shamisen. "Do you play?"

"A little." The confidence in her voice negated her socially mandated humility.

"Would you play something now?"

Sayuri picked up the shamisen. She cradled its neck in her left hand and settled its body against her right knee. When the position suited her, she picked up the ivory plectrum and strummed the strings.

She played right-handed, in the standard style, and exceptionally well. Hiro recognized the haunting lullaby. His mother had played it often, and equally well, though he doubted Sayuri's shamisen pick had a blade concealed in its sheath.

When the final note died away Sayuri set the instrument on the floor as if lowering a sleeping child. Hiro felt a pang of regret. For a moment, the music had taken him back to Iga.

"Thank you," he said.

"Did Okiya and the others hear anything?" she asked. "Mayuri said no, but I hoped . . ."

"They heard no intruders," Hiro said.

The door whispered open. Mayuri knelt at the threshold.

"Have you finished?" she asked.

Father Mateo stood up. Hiro suppressed a desire to bait the woman by asking to remain. He didn't dislike her exactly, but he never liked acceding to rude requests.

"Have faith," Father Mateo told Sayuri. "God will protect you and we will find the killer."

She nodded. "I will pray."

As they left the room, Hiro leaned toward Father Mateo and whispered, "You need to use the latrine."

"I do not." Father Mateo blushed.

As usual, Hiro found the reaction amusing. He had never understood the Jesuit's shyness about discussing bodily functions.

He raised his voice. "Mayuri, Father Mateo needs to visit the latrine."

The priest turned a brilliant shade of red. His mouth opened and closed like one of his beloved koi.

Mayuri inclined her head and looked from one man to the other. "Did you say he needs to use the latrine?"

"Urgently," Hiro said.

The woman and the priest exchanged a stare. Hiro didn't mind embarrassing Father Mateo, and he knew Mayuri could not refuse the request.

After a very long moment Mayuri nodded. "Follow me."

She led the men through the family room and into the narrow four-mat storeroom beyond. A hallway led off the east side of the storeroom, and at the far end of the hall a wooden staircase led to the second floor.

Mayuri gestured to the sliding doors in the north wall of the storeroom. "The latrine is outside—the building on the left." She paused. "You will forgive me if I do not escort you there."

"Of course," Hiro said. "Thank you."

As he stepped across the room and opened the door, he wondered what lay beyond the sliding door in the storeroom's western wall. Another storage room, or perhaps a private office.

Hiro waited for Father Mateo to step onto the veranda, then followed him out and closed the door.

Three wide steps led down to the narrow yard, where a forked gravel path connected the teahouse to a pair of outbuildings. The latrine stood about forty feet from the house on the left-hand side of the yard. Hiro had seen it from the veranda earlier.

A second, larger building stood ahead and to the right. It had a thatched roof, wooden sides, and two entrances, one at the end of the gravel path and a slightly smaller one on the opposite end. A worn track in the grass led to the smaller door. Slatted screens covered the three narrow windows below the eaves, allowing light to enter but obscuring the interior from view. The design suggested a bathhouse, and the woodpile outside the smaller door confirmed it.

Hiro felt a twinge of jealousy. Like most residents of Kyoto he bathed several times a week, and like most people he used the public baths. Only the very wealthy could afford a private bathhouse, and the Sakura's looked particularly fine.

At his side, Father Mateo hissed, "I do not have to use the latrine!"

"Fake it." Hiro pointed at the left-hand building. "I need at least five minutes."

"What are you doing?"

"No time." Hiro hurried down the stairs and across the yard to the bathhouse. When he reached the smaller door he glanced over his shoulder. He noted with satisfaction that Father Mateo had started toward the latrine.

Hiro grasped the wooden handle and pulled open the swinging door. As he suspected, it led to the fire room adjacent to the larger bathing chamber. A large wood-burning stove dominated the tiny room. It was square and made from whitewashed bricks of clay, though dust and ash had darkened its sides to gray. A large iron cauldron sat atop the stove, and iron pipes ran from the cauldron to the wall, funneling steam and hot water directly into the bathing room beyond.

Hiro was impressed. The setup was far more efficient than some of the older bathhouses he frequented, where servants carried hot water from the stoves to the baths.

The iron door on the front of the stove was warm but not hot to the touch, and its slatted grate was closed. Hiro grasped the handle and opened the oven door.

Coals glowed in the belly of the stove, though the flames had died away. They flared red for a moment when fresh air swirled in through the door, but faded almost at once. A pile of ash at the center of the stove supported some half-burned objects that looked like ledger books—exactly as Hiro expected. Sheets of delicate ash fanned out from the half-burned spines.

Someone had thrown the books into the fire but hadn't stayed to ensure that they burned completely. The bottom books were destroyed but the top one had escaped the worst of the flames. The heavy covers and dense pages kept the fire from breathing and the closed oven grating had not allowed enough air for proper combustion.

A practiced tender would have left the grate open, but Hiro suspected Mayuri had little experience with fires and even less with destroying evidence.

He picked up the tongs and removed the half-burned book from the top of the pile. The fan of ashy pages beneath collapsed with a whisper like feet on snow. It blew a wave of heat from the stove and made the embers glow red again for a moment.

Hiro tapped the book but found it too hot to hold so he turned the tongs to examine the other side. The cover was cracked and black with soot, and the edges of the pages had burned away, but the interior pages seemed mostly intact. As soon as the book had cooled enough for handling, Hiro lifted the cover. Heat had destroyed or obscured the ink on almost all the entries. The few pages that still showed visible writing seemed close to illegible.

Hiro hoped they would prove more readable in better light.

He pulled the best-preserved pages from the book and tucked them into his sleeve. He hoped they held enough information to tell him what Mayuri had risked injury to conceal and destroy.

Chapter 13

"Did you find what you were looking for?" Father Mateo asked. "And why on earth did you ask where to find Nobuhide? He's the last person I thought you would want to see."

They walked north along the west bank of the Kamo River. Two-story houses and merchant shops crowded the path.

"Because we're going to see him," Hiro said. "Right now."

"Now? Why?"

"Hideyoshi's killer might try to kill Nobuhide too," Hiro said, "and he deserves a warning."

"How did you . . ." Father Mateo's eyes widened. "You said the other women heard nothing."

"I said they heard no intruders," Hiro said. "They may have entertained an assassin without knowing it."

"Why warn Nobuhide?" Father Mateo asked. "Do you really think he's in danger?"

"Possibly," Hiro said. "Until we know for certain, we can't assume anything."

Father Mateo stopped in the middle of the path. Hiro

took two more steps before he realized the Jesuit wasn't following.

"What's wrong?" Hiro asked.

"You don't normally show such regard for your enemies."

"Nobuhide is not my friend, but he's not my enemy, either. Arrogance is not a capital crime. It's hardly fair to condemn a man based on his reaction to his father's mutilated corpse." Hiro gave the priest a sideways glance. "Isn't that what you would say?"

"Close enough," Father Mateo said. "But why are you concerned for his safety now? What did you learn at the teahouse?"

"Do you know the name Oda Nobunaga?" Hiro asked.

They had reached Marutamachi Road, but instead of turning right, toward home, Hiro made a left into one of the expensive residential wards that lay southeast of the shogun's fortress and the imperial palace.

"Lord Oda controls Owari Province, to the southeast." Father Mateo thought a moment and added, "He's a retainer of the shogun, isn't he?"

"Nominally, yes," Hiro said, "like all the other daimyo, but some people think Lord Oda plans to kill Ashikaga Yoshiteru and claim the shogunate for himself."

"Can he do that?" The Jesuit sounded surprised. "Doesn't the emperor pick the shogun?"

Hiro laughed. "The emperor says so, and the shogun doesn't dispute it in public, but in reality the shogun rules by strength alone. If another daimyo seized Kyoto, the emperor would appoint him shogun in Yoshiteru's place."

"What does that have to do with Nobuhide?"

"A stranger visited the teahouse last night. He claimed to be a rice merchant from Nagoya, which lies in Owari Province.

"If the man who killed Hideyoshi acted at Lord Oda's command, this murder could represent the start of an attack on the shogun's retainers and their families. To weaken the shogun's support.

"It's what I would do if I wanted to seize the shogunate."

"But Hideyoshi was retired."

"A perfect test of the shogun's vigilance. Assassinate a retired general and his family, and see if anyone notices."

Hiro paused outside the door of a large wooden house with a peaked roof and sprawling veranda surrounded by well-kept gardens. A latrine and storehouse were just visible at the back of the yard, along with a larger building that looked like a stable. Hoof prints marked the worn dirt track that ran along the outer edge of the property, and a gravel path led from the street to the door.

Trees dotted the property, but someone had trimmed all the branches so nothing grew within four feet of the sloping roof. Pruning scars suggested they had been kept that way for some time. Someone was very cautious, and also ignorant. Four feet might stop the average man, but trained shinobi could jump at least twice that far, even from the branches of a tree.

Father Mateo looked at the house. "I thought *yoriki* lived at the police barracks."

"Most of them do," Hiro said. "The *dōshin* said Nobuhide had permission to live at his father's home."

As Hiro approached the house he caught a whiff of cedar. Only the wealthy built houses of cedar instead of the less-expensive pine.

The carved front door swung open as they approached.

Nobuhide scowled at them from the doorway. "What do you want?"

Hiro and Father Mateo bowed. Nobuhide didn't return it.

"What are you doing here?" he demanded. "This is a house of mourning!"

A second samurai appeared in the doorway.

He was older than Nobuhide, and slightly taller. They shared the same slender build and narrow features, though the newcomer had no mustache. He wore a blue-gray kimono emblazoned with the Akechi crest and a pair of swords stuck through a dark gray girdle. When he bowed, Hiro noticed strands of silver in his hair.

Something about the newcomer looked odd, but Hiro couldn't place it.

"May I help you?" the stranger asked.

As the samurai spoke, Hiro realized why the man seemed strange.

The traditional samurai topknot, or *chonmage,* required shaving the forehead and pulling the remaining hair into a tail atop the head. The hair was folded over, sometimes more than once, and fastened with a band just behind the shaven area.

This samurai didn't have a shaven pate. He also had a melodic voice, and Hiro suddenly recognized that the newcomer was a woman, though dressed in a masculine style.

Hiro bowed again. "We have come to offer condolences and a caution—Akechi Hideyoshi's assassin may have reason to target the rest of the family too."

Nobuhide's eyes narrowed. "We do not want your condolences. Go away!"

"Nobuhide!" The woman's voice held more than a hint of warning.

"No foreign ghost will desecrate my father's corpse!" Nobuhide blocked the doorway and laid his hand on the hilt of his katana. "I forbid you to enter my home!"

"Fortunately, it is not yet your home." The woman turned to face the visitors and bowed. "I am Akechi Yoshiko, eldest child of Akechi Hideyoshi. Please come inside."

Nobuhide did not move.

Yoshiko stepped forward until she stood directly behind her brother, with her mouth only inches from his ear. Her lips barely moved as she whispered, "Do not make me embarrass you in front of strangers."

Nobuhide tensed as if preparing for a fight.

Chapter 14

The moment passed. Nobuhide removed his hand from his sword.

"I was going out anyway," he said. "Make sure they are gone when I return."

He slipped his sock-clad feet into a pair of sandals that sat beside the door and stalked off in the direction of the stable.

Nobuhide's shoulder brushed Hiro as he passed. On any other day the insult would have required a fight, but Hiro chose to ignore it. If Nobuhide wanted a confrontation he could have one, in two days' time. Until then Hiro was focused on the killer.

Three more pairs of sandals sat beside the door with their toes pointed neatly toward the house. The smallest looked barely large enough for a school-age child. The pair beside them was covered in drying mud. The sandals closest to the door were made of straw and falling apart from age. At least three people remained in the house.

Yoshiko bowed. "I apologize for my brother. He is devastated by our father's death."

"You are not?" Hiro asked.

"Of course, but rudeness dishonors his memory more than tears."

Father Mateo bowed. "I am Father Mateo Ávila de Santos, and this is Matsui Hiro, my translator. We are trying to find the man responsible for your father's death."

The hint of a smile flashed over Yoshiko's face. It vanished just as quickly. "Yes. Nobuhide mentioned you. Please come inside."

The men removed their shoes and stepped up into the house. Yoshiko led them through the entry and into the large central room beyond. The square room had a high ceiling and tatami on the floor, like the common room in Father Mateo's home, except that this *oe* measured thirteen mats in size. The scent of lingering woodsmoke dulled the odor of cedar emanating from the pillars and beams. A tokonoma in the southern wall, opposite the entrance, displayed a landscape scroll in shades of black and gray. Sliding doors separated the room from five adjacent chambers. All but one of the doors was closed, but the door beside the tokonoma was open, revealing a second, smaller common room beyond.

Yoshiko walked to the host's seat at the south end of the hearth. As she knelt, she gestured for the guests to join her.

Hiro and Father Mateo knelt to her right, with their backs to the eastern wall.

"Under the circumstances," Yoshiko said, "you will forgive me for dispensing with formalities."

She waited for them to nod assent before continuing. "You mentioned a warning, but Nobuhide claims to have the killer under guard. Please explain."

To Hiro's surprise, she looked at Father Mateo for the answer.

Few samurai treated the priest with such respect, despite the fact that the Jesuit had a samurai as his translator.

"We do not believe Sayuri . . . the entertainer . . ." Father Mateo paused as if uncertain what to say.

Hiro didn't share the Jesuit's concern for delicacy, particularly with a woman who looked and acted so thoroughly like a man.

"The girl may not be responsible," Hiro said, "or at least not entirely. A man claiming to be from Nagoya visited the Sakura Teahouse last night."

He paused to see if Yoshiko caught the reference and understood the threat.

Her eyebrows drew together. "Lord Oda has no reason to kill my father."

"We think he may be planning an attack on the shogunate," Father Mateo said.

Yoshiko's face became a mask.

Hiro sat very still. He didn't trust himself to move, or even blink, without revealing his frustration with the priest. Yoshiko hadn't asked the expected questions—what the stranger did, or if he was a samurai—but the Jesuit's comment had put her on guard before she could explain her reaction, and she seemed disinclined to say anything more.

"If so," the priest continued, "the assassin might try to kill your brother too."

"Nobuhide?" Yoshiko's eyes crinkled with restrained laughter. Her smile faded almost immediately but her amusement remained. "*Yoriki* can't even enter the shogun's presence, and they're never promoted to any higher position. You do not kill a flea to scare a dog."

"It could be a test of the shogun's vigilance," Father Mateo said. "Your whole family could be in danger."

"Such a test would not extend to a powerless son and an aged wife." Yoshiko didn't look concerned. "Still, I will take precautions. Thank you for the warning."

Hiro wasn't quite ready to leave. The priest had ruined his chance of obtaining much information from Yoshiko, but the house itself might contain other useful clues. "May we pay our respects to your father?"

Yoshiko looked surprised.

"Father Mateo's religion has special prayers for the dead." Hiro doubted the woman had ever met a Christian, but he gambled that she would abide by the samurai code of hospitality, which required respect for all faiths. "He did not have opportunity or permission to say them earlier but would like to do so now."

Yoshiko stood up. "Very well, my father lies this way."

She led them to a sliding door in the eastern wall and opened it without kneeling. The six-mat room beyond had latticed doors on three sides and white tatami on the floor. Cedar panels covered the wall opposite the entrance, and weapons of every size and description hung from hooks embedded in the planks.

Hiro counted no less than twenty swords—roughly split between long katana and the shorter *wakizashi*. A pair of halberds hung near the ceiling, just out of reach, though Hiro doubted they ever saw much use. Only monks used *naginata* regularly.

Three unstrung bows, a dozen daggers of various sizes,

and several *tessen*, or bladed fighting fans, hung between the swords. An arquebus perched at eye level in the center of the wall. Based on its polished, pristine appearance the weapon had never been fired.

Empty hooks suggested a pair of missing swords, one large and one small. Hiro had no trouble finding them. They lay in the wooden coffin on the floor.

Akechi Hideyoshi lay faceup in a cedar box with his hands folded over the hilt of his katana. His *wakizashi* was sheathed at his side. The body had been dressed in a lamellar breast-plate and decorative armor with white lacing that stood out brightly against the new, dark leather and metal fittings. Even if Hiro hadn't known that white *odoshi* was only used for the dead, the smell of fresh leather and untarnished metal plates would have told him the armor was purchased specifically for the dead man's funeral.

Hideyoshi's topknot emerged from a hole at the peak of his helmet and lay across his shoulder, brushed and oiled until it gleamed like silk. The dark oil almost concealed the gray in his hair. A scowling *mempo* mask covered his face and hid the wounds in his neck.

Although Hiro had hoped for a second glance at the wounds, he appreciated the care and respect inherent in the arrange-ment of the body. Hideyoshi almost looked as if he died of natural causes.

Hiro wondered who had prepared the body for burial or, more likely, for cremation. The careful arrangement of the hair suggested a man, but only a woman would have dressed the body in new ceremonial armor instead of the set Hideyo-shi had worn in life.

The samurai's real armor hung on a wooden dummy in

the corner of the room. The scuffed leather plates showed years of use, and the dark-blue *odoshi* lacing was stained and frayed at the ends. That set, not the new one, would have been Hideyoshi's choice.

Father Mateo approached the corpse and bowed to show respect. As he clasped his hands in prayer, Yoshiko backed away and disappeared. Hiro wondered what prayers a Christian priest could say for the soul of a dead man who did not share his faith and whether Father Mateo was really praying or merely feigning to give Hiro an opportunity to look around the room.

In addition to the unusual display, a tokonoma in the southern wall held a large *tessen* with elaborate paper panels at both ends. When folded, the paper and wooden ribs concealed the row of shining blades that transformed the delicate fan into a vicious concealed weapon.

A semicircle of wooden pegs sat in front of the fan. Each peg held a small leather sheath with a metal blade protruding from the tip. The bladed sheaths slipped over a person's fingertip and first knuckle to imitate the claws of a giant cat. Female shinobi, also known as *kunoichi*, considered the claws a weapon of choice, but *neko-te* were extremely rare and never put on display. Hiro had not seen any since leaving Iga, though three parallel scars on his shoulder and four more on his upper leg gave him more than passing familiarity with the weapon and its use.

The memory of Hideyoshi's mutilated body flashed through Hiro's mind. *Neko-te* usually inflicted stabbing wounds, but the sharpened claws could also rip and slice, particularly when assassins stood above or behind the victim.

Hiro stepped to the tokonoma for a closer look.

Six of the ten claws sat askew on their pegs, and one had something wrong with its blade. It looked as if someone had replaced the claw with a piece of a broken dagger, and the blade was only lightly attached to the sheath. It might not even be attached at all. Hiro couldn't tell without touching the blade.

As he stifled the urge to reach out and examine what appeared to be the murder weapon, a female voice behind him said, "You have seen *neko-te* before."

Chapter 15

Yoshiko stood in the doorway.

Hiro turned his head and straightened, grateful for the instinct that stayed his hand.

"No." Father Mateo walked to the tokonoma and pointed at the fan. "Is that the proper name? I thought it was called *tessen*."

Yoshiko joined them at the alcove. "I meant the little blades. Assassins wear them like claws." She raised a hand and hooked her fingers. "These belonged to a *kunoichi* who attempted to assassinate the shogun shortly after he came to power, almost twenty years ago. My father learned of the plot and killed her. The shogun gave him the weapon as a prize."

Father Mateo pointed to the claw with the strange-looking blade. "That one looks broken. Did it happen in the fight?"

"No." Yoshiko blushed. "That happened later."

"Recently?" Hiro asked.

"Many years ago." She smiled in memory. "I was playing, and disobeying, as children do."

"She sneaked the weapon out and caught a blade in a tree," said another voice.

Hiro turned. A miniscule woman stood in the doorway. Her head barely reached her daughter's shoulder, and her hands looked as small and delicate as a child's. Her white hair framed a face that reminded Hiro of a dying blossom, once beautiful but wrinkled and dried with age. A black kimono and obi enhanced her fragility, though her straight back and quick-moving eyes revealed both intelligence and strength. The hem of her inner kimono peeked out from beneath the outer one, in customary style. That kimono, too, was black.

Hiro and Father Mateo bowed. The woman bowed in turn. As she rose, she tucked a necklace back inside her kimono, but not before Hiro noticed the tiny silver ornament at the end.

Yoshiko extended a hand. "Mother, these men are Father Mateo and his translator, Matsui Hiro, the men of whom Nobuhide spoke." She paused. "My mother, Akechi Sato."

Sato reminded Hiro of his own grandmother, down to the possibility of a dagger in her sleeve. The widow's delicate appearance seemed too carefully cultivated for truth, though he suspected she used it more for self-defense than for deception.

"I replaced the broken claw with a piece of dagger," Sato said. "You have good eyes. My husband didn't notice it for years."

Or pretended not to, Hiro thought, though that truth no longer mattered.

"Thank you for honoring my husband," the elderly woman continued, "I am grateful for your prayers. They bring me comfort."

"I apologize for disturbing you," the Jesuit said.

Sato shook her head. "I hoped you would come so I could thank you. I mourn my husband's death, but I do not want an innocent girl to die if she is not to blame."

"Do you know anyone who would want to hurt your husband?" Hiro asked.

"He had no enemies." Sato looked past them at the body. "He didn't even have many relatives. He served the shogun honorably until his retirement five years ago."

"And since then?" Hiro asked.

"The shogun granted him a stipend, ten koku a year."

"Koku?" Father Mateo asked.

Hiro wondered at the question. The priest already knew that word.

"One koku is the amount of rice that will feed a person for one year," Yoshiko explained. "It is the measure by which samurai salaries are calculated."

Father Mateo nodded as though learning something new. Then he asked, "Will you keep the koku, now that your husband has died?"

The inquiry suddenly made sense. Samurai didn't talk about money, but ignorant foreigners could, at least under the guise of education. Hiro was impressed. Perhaps the priest had become more Japanese than the shinobi gave him credit for.

"I don't know," Sato replied. "It will depend on the shogun."

"I'm afraid I must ask an indelicate question," Father Mateo said. "Were you both . . . home last night?"

"Yes," Sato said.

"I went for a ride in the early evening," Yoshiko corrected gently.

"But you came home before dark, and we went to sleep early." Sato raised her chin. "Despite her unusual appearance, my daughter knows how to behave."

Hiro wondered if the slight emphasis on "daughter" was intentional or merely coincidental.

He bowed. "Thank you for your courtesy. We have bothered you long enough in your day of mourning."

They exchanged bows again and Yoshiko escorted them to the door.

"Can you think of anything else we should know?" Father Mateo asked as they slipped their sandals on. "Anything at all that might help us find your father's killer?"

"No," Yoshiko said. "He was a retired samurai with little income and no political connections. His only relative was his brother, Hidetaro, who depended on Father's income to survive. I am glad you care about the truth, but in the end I think you will find Nobuhide is right. The girl is to blame."

Father Mateo said nothing until they reached the road. Then he turned to Hiro and said, "Well, I'm more confused now than when we started."

"Puzzles often grow more complicated as you solve them," Hiro said.

"Are we solving this one? I'm not sure."

"Five hours ago we had no suspects," Hiro said, "now we have at least three."

"Which three?"

"The merchant from Nagoya, Mayuri, and Akechi Hidetaro."

"The merchant I understand," the Jesuit said, "but why the others?"

"Mayuri burned her ledgers this morning. I retrieved some pages from the bathhouse fire."

"Is that why you made me use the latrine? And what made you look there? Why not in the kitchen stove?"

"A teahouse kitchen is too public—too much chance that someone would see her do it."

"What do the pages say?"

Hiro raised an eyebrow. "I didn't have time to study them in the bathhouse."

"If not, why consider her a suspect?"

"She owns the teahouse where Hideyoshi was murdered. She burned her records the morning after his death. She prevented the other women from helping when Sayuri screamed, and she's too nervous to leave us alone with Sayuri for any length of time. Those reasons are sufficient even without the pages."

"Why Hidetaro, though? Nobody considers him a threat, and he depended upon Hideyoshi for his livelihood."

"Did you see Sayuri's eyes light up at the mention of his name?" Hiro asked. "That's enough to keep him on the list, at least until we talk with him in person.

"And from now on, let me do the talking. Yoshiko might have said something useful if you hadn't given everything away."

"I thought we went to warn her. You never said you suspected her of anything." Father Mateo frowned. "I came to Kyoto to help people find the truth. I cannot fulfill that mission in silence."

"As I can't fulfill mine if you get yourself killed," Hiro countered. "You must not assume that anyone is innocent."

"She's Hideyoshi's daughter!"

"The fact that she shares his blood does not bar her from spilling it," Hiro said, "though I agree that an assassin seems more likely."

"Do you think we can find the man from Nagoya?" Father Mateo asked. "He may have left the city in the night."

"More likely early this morning," Hiro said. "We need to talk with Luis."

Chapter 16

A samurai paced the road in front of the Jesuit's house as though trying to summon the courage to knock on the door. He walked with a minor limp, perhaps from a long-healed wound to a thigh or knee. Drying mud stained the hem of his faded blue robe and clung to the edges of his sandals. His *tabi* socks, though clean that morning, already showed transfer stains.

By contrast, his topknot was freshly oiled, with every hair in place.

He turned at the sound of Hiro's and Father Mateo's approaching footsteps. Hiro didn't recognize the stranger's face, but the five-petaled bellflower *mon* on the man's kimono symbolized the Akechi clan.

The samurai bowed as they reached him. Several days' stubble dotted his shaven pate.

"Are you the foreign priest?" he asked, "Matto-san?"

"I am Father Mateo," the Jesuit said as he returned the bow, "and this is my interpreter, Matsui Hiro. May we help you?"

"I am Akechi Hidetaro. Hideyoshi was my brother."

Father Mateo waited for the stranger to continue.

Hidetaro said nothing.

Silence hung in the air and the pause grew awkward.

"Invite him inside," Hiro said in Portuguese. "Samurai do not talk in the street like merchants."

"Please come in," the Jesuit said. "May we offer you tea?"

A relieved smile lit Hidetaro's face. "Yes, thank you."

Ana was cleaning the floor when the three men entered the house. When she saw the visitor she sprang to her feet and scurried toward the kitchen without a word.

Father Mateo escorted the visitor to the hearth. Hiro followed them, noting the way Hidetaro raised his right leg carefully to ensure that his foot didn't drag against the tatami. Even so, his right sock made a whispering sound as it moved across the floor.

The men had barely seated themselves around the hearth when Ana returned with tea and a plate of sweet rice balls. She set down the refreshments and returned to the kitchen, pausing just long enough to scoop up the curious kitten that had poked its nose from Hiro's room.

Hidetaro looked around as he sipped his tea. "This looks almost like a Japanese home." He looked at Hiro. "Can foreigners live like Japanese?"

"Father Mateo does," Hiro said. "He even speaks a little Japanese."

Hidetaro took the hint. "Can you drink tea?" he asked the priest. "What about Japanese food? Can your stomach handle it?"

Father Mateo smiled. "Yes, in fact I prefer Japanese food."

It was not the first time he had heard the question or seen the surprised reaction to his response.

"Really?" Hidetaro asked. "I have never met a foreigner before."

"There are only a few of us in Kyoto," Father Mateo said, "though my superiors hope to build a permanent temple soon."

Hiro noted the substitution of "temple" for "church," a deliberate choice on Father Mateo's part, and one the shinobi had not taught him, though Hiro approved of it more each time he heard it. Kyoto had hundreds of temples dedicated to many deities. One more caused neither confusion nor concern.

"That would be very nice," Hidetaro said politely. "Every god should have a temple."

They sipped their tea. Hidetaro sampled a rice ball and made a surprised sound. "These are good!"

The compliment seemed genuine but the comment sounded forced. Hiro suspected Hidetaro wanted to explain the point of his visit, though convention prevented him from speaking directly until the host invited him to do so.

Hiro raised his eyebrows at Father Mateo.

"My condolences on your brother's death," the Jesuit said. "Can I do anything to help you in this difficult time?"

Hiro noted with approval that the priest didn't ask why Hidetaro had come, or how the samurai learned about their involvement in the murder. He was learning subtlety after all.

Hidetaro looked at Hiro, "Can I trust the foreigner's discretion?"

"His religion forbids repetition of information told in confidence," Hiro said. "If he reveals a secret, his god will banish him to the Hell of Everburning Flames forever."

Hidetaro leaned back and blinked in surprise at the mention of eternity. Buddhist hells were only temporary. After a brief pause he blurted out, "Sayuri is not responsible for Hideyoshi's death."

Hiro gave him a sideways look. "Why do you say that?"

Hidetaro's gaze flickered to the hearth and back. "I just know. She would not kill him."

"Was she in love with him?" Hiro watched Hidetaro's reaction carefully.

"No." The samurai's face revealed nothing. His posture did not change.

"She entertained him often," Hiro said. "Perhaps she was."

"No," Hidetaro repeated. He seemed to be struggling with something.

Just before Hiro asked another pressing question Hidetaro said, "I am the one she loves. In fact, I had made arrangements to buy her contract and marry her."

Hidetaro's words sounded genuine and he met Hiro's eyes when he spoke, but his shabby clothes and aging face made the claim improbable at best. Hiro saw another problem too, but etiquette didn't allow him to broach that subject.

"Hideyoshi didn't mind?" Father Mateo asked. "After all, he visited her often."

Hiro almost choked on his tea. It was precisely the question he never would have asked. He wondered whether the Jesuit was relying on his foreignness to excuse the indelicate question or whether the priest was really so socially ignorant. He suspected the former, but a glance at the priest revealed nothing. As always, Father Mateo's face wore a pleasant and honest smile.

"No more than I minded his visits to her," Hidetaro said.

The ambiguous response was worthy of a shinobi. Hiro hadn't expected such facility from a samurai.

"Hideyoshi enjoyed Sayuri's company," Hidetaro contin-ued, "but he wanted me to buy her contract. He thought she deserved a better life than a teahouse."

"He didn't mind his brother marrying an entertainer?" Hiro asked. Samurai honor forbade most marriages to people outside the samurai class.

Hidetaro shifted slightly. "Until a few months ago, I wanted to become a Buddhist monk. In Yoshi's eyes, any marriage was preferable to that."

Samurai did not discuss family issues in public. The hint alone ended the conversation and made the ensuing silence awkward.

At last, Father Mateo said, "His death must have come as a terrible shock."

"Yes," Hidetaro said. "I learned of it this morning, at the teahouse. Mayuri would not take my payment. She said she could not accept it because Nobuhide intends to execute Say-uri. She also told me about your investigation and that you hoped to prove Sayuri innocent."

"Did you see Sayuri?" Hiro asked.

"No. Mayuri would not allow it."

"When was the last time you saw her?" Hiro asked.

"A week ago, or possibly more. I can't afford teahouses—that is, I have to save my money for her contract. You must prove her innocent. She did not do this."

"We will do our best," Father Mateo said.

Hidetaro stood up. He moved slowly, as though his injured leg still hurt a little. "Thank you for the tea."

Hiro escorted the guest to the door. As they reached the entrance Hidetaro said, "This foreigner is a good man, I think. Do you find it strange to serve him?"

"He is a man, with good qualities and bad ones, like any other," Hiro said as Hidetaro slipped on his muddy sandals.

Hiro nodded at the shoes. "Last night's rain created a lot of mud."

"Did it?" Hidetaro asked. "I was asleep at home."

"Indeed." Hiro bowed. "Thank you for honoring us with your visit."

Hidetaro returned the bow and departed, walking slowly to prevent anyone from noticing his limp.

"Well, I guess we can take him off the suspect list," Father Mateo said as they watched the samurai walk away on the narrow road.

"Quite the opposite," Hiro said. "He just placed himself firmly on it."

Chapter 17

D o you really think Hidetaro killed his brother?" Father
Mateo asked.

"I think he's less than honest," Hiro said, "which merits investigation. Speaking of which—where's Luis?"

"Probably napping," Father Mateo said. "I think he finished his business for today."

"Exactly what we need to discuss." Hiro walked across the common room and rapped on the paneled door to the merchant's room. "Luis? Are you awake?"

He heard a rustling sound and a groan, followed by footsteps heading for the door. It rattled and Luis's face appeared in the opening. His eyes were misty with sleep and his long hair stood out around his face. "No. What do you want?"

"Information about the rice merchant you sold weapons to this morning. Was he from Nagoya, by chance?"

Luis blinked and the sleepy look left his face. "How did you know that?"

"I think you may have done business with a murderer."

"All of my clients are murderers. What Japanese isn't?"

"Luis." Father Mateo joined them at the door. "I think I understand what Hiro means. A rice merchant from Nagoya visited the Sakura Teahouse last night. We think he may have murdered Akechi Hideyoshi. If he's the same man you met this morning, you may be able to help us find him."

The door slid open further and Luis stepped into the common room. He wore the same white shirt as earlier and a clean pair of dark-colored breeches. He had taken off his tunic before his nap, and the end of his wrinkled shirt flapped loosely below his rounded belly. Hiro had rarely seen a less flattering costume.

"Akechi?" Luis repeated. "Is that the dead man's name?"

"Yes." Father Mateo nodded eagerly. "Do you know him?"

"It might just be a coincidence. These Japanese only have about twenty surnames between them."

"Anything you can tell us might help," Father Mateo said.

Luis scratched his chest while he thought. "A couple of months ago I sold a hundred arquebuses to a samurai named Akechi, but not Hideyoshi. The given name was different. Miso-something, I think. He was passing through Kyoto on his way to join some warlord in the south.

"The rice merchant from Nagoya mentioned Akechi's name when he contacted me. Apparently they're friends or something. He thought it would get him a discount." The merchant looked smug. "I raised all the prices by twenty percent and then gave him a ten percent markdown. He never knew the difference."

Hiro ignored his rising frustration and returned to the topic of interest. "Who introduced the samurai to you? The one from the Akechi clan."

"I don't remember," Luis said. "I know several of the

merchants, and most of them make introductions. It's a ridiculous samurai custom anyway, needing to know someone
personally before you can do business. Normal people just
find what they want and buy it."

"This is important," Hiro insisted. "Who made the introduction?"

Luis thought for a moment. "It must have been the tailor,
Yaso." After a pause he added, "Definitely Yaso. He set up this
morning's meeting too."

"Did either man tell you where he was staying?" Hiro
asked. "Did they have relatives in Kyoto?"

Luis sneered and shook his head. "We only talked about
muskets. I could care less about their personal lives."

"Do you have records of the sales?"

"I keep detailed ledgers, but you won't find what you're
looking for. I list names, but no addresses or other information about the buyer."

"Good enough," Hiro said. "Have you got the ledgers here?"

Luis turned back to his room and returned a moment later
with a ledger, leather-bound in the Portuguese style. He flipped
through the pages until he found the transaction he wanted.

"There." He pointed to the page. "That's the first one, the
samurai."

It took Hiro a moment to find the entry, and not only
because it was written in Portuguese. The lines and columns
made no sense until he realized that the merchant orga-
nized the pages horizontally, not vertically like a Japanese
ledger.

Hiro examined the line Luis indicated. Everything except
for the customer's name was written in the Portuguese merchant's even script. Hiro found it difficult to read but enjoyed

the effort. Despite his irritating nature, Luis had beautiful handwriting.

The customer's name was far more legible, because that wasn't written by hand. Samurai and many merchants used a carved seal, or *inkan*, in place of a formal signature. The seals discouraged forgery and eliminated the need to carry a writing brush or ink. When pressed into a paste-like ink and then on a document or page, the seal displayed the characters representing the bearer's name.

The characters on this one read "Akechi Mitsuhide."

"And the other?" Hiro asked. "The man you met this morning?"

The merchant flipped two more leaves and ran his finger down the page until he came to the final entry. "Well, that's interesting."

He tipped the book toward Hiro and Father Mateo. The column for the customer's seal contained an illegible smudge. "He must have rushed the impression."

"Or deliberately marred it to obscure his name," Hiro said.

Luis shrugged. "That's going to make it difficult to track him, not that he's still here anyway. He left Kyoto as soon as he picked up his weapons and wanted to start early to get ahead of the traffic on the road. That's why I had to get up at such an abominable hour."

"Do you think this Akechi is related to your dead samurai?"

"It would astonish me to learn otherwise," Hiro said.

"Interesting that no one mentioned a relative in Lord Oda's service," Father Mateo mused.

"But not surprising," Hiro said. "This also means Yoshiko was mistaken, or lied. Both Lord Oda and the shogun have reasons to want Hideyoshi dead."

"Mateo." Luis's face grew red. "You need to leave Kyoto now. Don't martyr yourself for a prostitute."

"I became a priest because I believe in the truth," Father Mateo said. "I will not run away to save myself and abandon an innocent woman to die. I fear God's judgment far more than any death."

Hiro excused himself and returned to his room. The priest would not leave Kyoto until the facts freed Sayuri or condemned her, no matter what Luis said. But the merchant's ledger reminded Hiro of the pages hidden in his sleeve, and he wanted to see what further clues they revealed.

Chapter 18

Hiro knelt before the writing alcove in the south wall of his room and slipped the burned pages from his sleeve. He laid them in a row on the low wooden desk. After studying them for a while he reached for the narrow box that sat at the far end of the desk.

The cedar box had several compartments. One held parchments, another ink sticks. A third held various papers, including the scrap Hiro retrieved from Mayuri's kimono. He removed the paper from the box and added it to the others.

The pages looked identical in thickness, but accounting books all looked similar and the scorch marks made it impossible to tell for sure.

Father Mateo entered the room and knelt beside Hiro.

"I don't understand," he said. "Why would one page be ripped and others burned?"

"She might have tried to rip out the incriminating pages and then realized torn ledgers looked suspicious."

"It is a ledger, then?"

"Several of them." Hiro explained what he had seen in the fire room.

"But what was Mayuri trying to hide?" Father Mateo asked. A few seconds later his mouth fell open in surprise. "Do you think she's using one brother's death to defraud the other?"

"What?" Hiro pulled his gaze from the scraps. "What are you talking about?"

"Won't Mayuri have to give Hidetaro's money back if Sayuri is executed? But if there's no record of the payments . . ."

"That's not a bad theory," Hiro said, "although, if you're right, Hidetaro has known Sayuri longer than either of them admits."

"Businesses start a new ledger every year on New Year's Day. Whatever Mayuri is trying to hide goes back at least three years."

"And Sayuri only had her debut this spring," Father Mateo said.

"Exactly," Hiro said. He continued, thinking aloud. "An apprentice spends at least four years in training, so it's possible Hidetaro saw Sayuri before her debut. I didn't think to ask if Hideyoshi visited another girl before Sayuri caught his eye."

Father Mateo picked up one of the burned pages. He examined both sides and handed it to Hiro. "Do you see anything useful? I don't recognize anything but numbers."

Impeccable calligraphy ran down both sides of the paper in straight vertical lines. Fire and ash rendered most of the figures illegible, but Hiro could tell the numbers were high. That didn't surprise him. Cedar floors and fancy kimonos weren't cheap.

Most ledger pages had headings at the top of every column,

but the top and sides of the page in question had perished in the fire. The others looked the same.

Hiro laid the scrap on the desk. "It's too badly burned. Without the headings I can't tell whose accounts the columns contain, or even what the numbers stand for. It was a slim chance anyway. Accounts alone won't explain what Mayuri is hiding."

Father Mateo pointed at the unburned page. "Now that we know it's a ledger, can you tell anything from that one?"

Hiro picked up the original jagged scrap. It had come from the top of a page and contained one intact column heading and part of a column on either side.

"The center column has a name." Hiro pointed. "Tanaka Ichiro."

"Do you know him?"

Hiro cocked an eyebrow at the priest. "Tanaka is a popular clan name in Kyoto, and Ichiro means 'first son.' We could find a thousand men in Kyoto by that name.

"More importantly," he continued, "only nobles have two names, and the Bushido code disapproves of samurai patronizing teahouses. Even if we found the right Tanaka Ichiro, he won't admit it."

The priest looked disappointed.

"It wouldn't help anyway," Hiro continued. "We can't track down every visitor to the Sakura in the hope that someone will know what Mayuri might want to hide. Her secret might not relate to the murder at all. The opposite seems more likely—this was just a convenient excuse to cover up an embarrassment."

"Or another crime," Father Mateo said. "Can you read any more of the page?"

Hiro looked at the scrap. "The numbers don't start at zero, which suggests a running tally. The figures are large, but that's hardly unexpected." He squinted at the torn column to the right of Ichiro's name. "The next column heading might say 'Akechi,' but it's ripped in the middle and the given name is missing."

"Then it could be either Hideyoshi or Hidetaro."

"Or someone else entirely. We can't tell without a given name."

"Could Hidetaro have killed his brother to ruin the teahouse's reputation and lower Sayuri's price?"

Hiro looked up, impressed. "For a priest, you think of some intricate schemes."

"I was a man before I was a priest, and the Bible describes some very ingenuous sinners. It might even teach you a thing or two, if you read it."

As usual, Hiro ignored the invitation. "Hidetaro wouldn't kill his brother in the teahouse." He turned the ripped page over in his fingers while he thought. "Too much chance Sayuri would take the blame."

"Was it a shinobi after all?"

Hiro set the scrap on the desk. "Perhaps a hired killer. Not a shinobi or *kunoichi*—at least, not an experienced one."

"Why not?"

"The wounds. Hideyoshi's throat was slashed from behind, which suggests an assassin, but the execution showed a re-markable lack of skill. His throat looked ripped as well as cut, so the killer was strong—probably a man, though a woman might have done it. No one creates that many wounds with a knife, which means *neko-te*, but the jagged cuts indicate an inexperienced user."

Hiro raised his hand and hooked his fingers in imitation of claws. "*Kunoichi* use *neko-te* to stab or cut, but rarely both at once." He pantomimed stabbing himself in the heart and then slitting his own throat. "It takes too much time. A professional would have known that."

"Maybe the killer wanted to be sure he was dead?"

"Again, a sign of a novice," Hiro said. "The stab wounds barely bled, which means Hideyoshi was already dead or so close that it made no difference."

"How do you know all this?" A hint of suspicion crept into the Jesuit's voice.

"I'll show you." Hiro stood up and positioned himself behind the priest. "You're Hideyoshi, kneeling on the floor in front of the alcove."

Father Mateo twisted around with a concerned frown on his face. "Wait a minute."

Hiro pointed at the desk. "Trust me. Look there."

He waited until the priest complied.

"Now," Hiro continued, "while you're looking at a mediocre flower arrangement—which probably looks slightly better because you're drunk—the killer sneaks up behind you and slashes your throat with *neko-te*."

Hiro's right hand hovered over the Jesuit's hair while his left snaked around the priest's neck and then pulled away with violent speed. Father Mateo jerked backward, startled, though the shinobi had not touched him.

"Your blood spurts out on the wall as the killer attacks again," Hiro pantomimed a second, slower cut across the priest's throat, "and again. That's when the ripping happens. The blades get stuck in the grooves from previous cuts. One blade also comes loose."

"How?" Father Mateo asked. "Weren't they sewn into the finger cuffs?"

"Yes, but it's hard to sew a blade into leather securely. That's why the weapon is normally used to stab instead of slice. The blade must have caught on Hideyoshi's collarbone or in the sinews of his neck. Either way, it came loose during the attack."

Hiro put his hands on the priest's shoulders. "Back to the killing.

"You slump forward, nearing death, but the killer doesn't leave as a shinobi or *kunoichi* would have. He, or she, pulls you onto your back to finish the job."

Father Mateo let Hiro lower him backward to the floor. The shinobi extended his fingers, still hooked like claws. "The killer stabs you in the eyes and then in the chest, where the loosened blade pulls free. An experienced assassin would have noticed and removed it from the scene, but this killer leaves it behind."

"So that's why you didn't suspect a shinobi." Father Mateo pushed himself back to a kneeling position.

Hiro nodded. "Also, shinobi and *kunoichi* rarely stab a victim in the eyes. Defiling the dead invites retribution on the assassin's clan."

Father Mateo looked surprised. "Divine retribution? I thought you didn't believe in superstition."

"Not all retribution is divine."

"A shinobi would never defile a corpse?"

"A professional will do anything if the price is right," Hiro said, "but shinobi or not, the person responsible for the killing must have hated Hideyoshi."

"Or hated the look of his dead eyes," Father Mateo said.

Hiro turned to the priest in surprise. "I hadn't thought of that, but I think you're right. Shinobi are trained not to mind a dead man's eyes, but it does take training and fortitude. I didn't like it the first time I saw it myself.

"If this wasn't a professional with orders to desecrate, our killer is probably someone who's never seen a freshly slaughtered corpse."

Chapter 19

Hiro looked back at the papers, trying to decide what Mayuri would want to hide. As he stared at the scraps and wished for an answer, a tiny black and orange paw slipped over the side of the desk and edged toward the ledger pages.

Hiro looked under the desk. The tiny kitten sat at the edge of the alcove, ears flattened and foreleg fully extended as if reaching for the papers. She froze when Hiro's face appeared, then whipped her paw away and dashed from the room.

Hiro shook his head. "So much for spiders."

"I don't think Sayuri could have done it," Father Mateo said, too absorbed in the problem to notice the kitten's antics. "She's far too gentle to stab a man in the eyes. Besides, she's become a Christian."

"I've heard you talk about the heroes of your Bible, your David and Joshua and the rest. Your Scriptures prove that accepting your faith doesn't stop a person from killing." Before the priest could reply Hiro continued. "However, Sayuri would have to be much stronger than she looks to overpower a samurai from behind."

Father Mateo took a deep breath and released it with nearly the force of a sigh. "Then you finally agree she's innocent."

"I agree she may not have held the *neko-te*," Hiro corrected. "I won't go as far as innocence."

Father Mateo scratched his nose and then shook his head. "I can't believe you really train women as assassins."

"Why does it surprise you?" Hiro asked. "Women are far more vicious than men."

"I just can't imagine a woman sneaking around with a dagger in her hand."

"*Kunoichi* don't sneak. They pose as priestesses, or prostitutes . . . or entertainers. I'm not convinced this was a *kunoichi*, though, or even a woman. We can't make any assumptions. Only facts provide answers."

Hiro cast a glance at the sliding door in the western wall, which led to the porch and yard. The panels glowed crimson with the light of the setting sun.

He stood up and straightened his kimono. "I think I'll go have a drink."

Father Mateo hid a frown. "Sake?"

"Did you think I gave it up?"

The Jesuit's shrug indicated yes.

"Ana dumping the last flask in the koi pond cured me of bringing it home," Hiro said, "but you should both give up the idea that I will stop drinking it elsewhere. Don't men drink together in Portugal?"

"There are other things to drink."

"True enough," Hiro said, "but there's one problem with all of them. They are not sake."

Father Mateo accompanied the shinobi to the door.

Hiro started toward the road, turned back, and asked, "Do

you want to come along? I promise to drink enough that Ginjiro won't mind if you don't indulge."

"No thank you." Father Mateo's lip twitched. "I have a prayer meeting tonight."

Hiro concealed his amusement behind a nod. The Jesuit wouldn't have fooled a five-year-old, let alone a shinobi trained to read men's faces. Still, he respected the effort. The priest was trying to act like a samurai and a friend.

As he walked toward the river he imagined how surprised the priest would be if he ever learned that Hiro hated sake. The brewery, and Hiro's drinking, served a very different purpose.

Hiro reached the Kamo River just as a rider on a dark brown horse approached the bridge from the opposite side. The mare's hide glowed crimson in the setting sun and her hooves seemed to disappear in the shadows near the road.

Only samurai had the legal right to ride, so the equestrian's twin swords did not surprise Hiro, though the rider's dark *hakama* trousers and matching silk surcoat made the shinobi take a closer look. Men almost always chose contrasting colors.

The rider was a woman, though dressed like a samurai, and even across the river Hiro recognized her face.

Akechi Yoshiko reined her horse to the right and trotted southward along the narrow dirt road on the west side of the river. She ducked to avoid a tree branch that grew over the path and spurred the mare to a canter. As she rode away, she glanced over her shoulder as though making certain no one followed her.

But for that gesture, Hiro might have dismissed it as just an evening ride for pleasure or exercise, but Yoshiko's concern made him curious. He decided to forego his original plans for a little while and turned south along the parallel path that followed the eastern bank. As he hurried along, he wished he could have worn his shinobi trousers in public instead of the bulky kimono and swords his alleged occupation required. Kimonos made it hard to run without attracting notice and even harder to scale rooftops and climb trees for a secret view. He consoled himself with the knowledge that the kimono reduced the need for explanations if Yoshiko noticed him following. This close to Pontocho, Hiro could claim an appointment in the pleasure quarters.

The sun slipped beneath the horizon and the sky darkened from red and gold to lavender and indigo. Puffy clouds glowed like embers and then faded like dying coals.

Hiro lost sight of the horse in the fading light. The sound of its hooves died away. He slowed his pace and balled his fist in frustration, though he doubted he had missed any useful clue. A woman on horseback attracted attention even in busy Kyoto, and he doubted Yoshiko would take the horse on any suspicious mission.

For a moment, though, he had felt almost like a real shinobi again. He had missed that feeling since his arrival in Kyoto. Clandestine practice kept his skills sharp but didn't produce the excitement of tracking real prey.

A few minutes later Hiro reached the bridge at Sanjō Road. Darkness had fallen but glowing lanterns beckoned from the commercial ward on the opposite side of the river. As Hiro stepped onto the bridge to cross, he heard a faint neigh from somewhere behind him.

He turned and looked down the road toward the Sakura Teahouse. It wasn't difficult to spot the establishment at night.

Lanterns hanging from the eaves lit the building as brightly as day. Hiro saw figures in the yard and on a hunch, he walked toward the teahouse.

A horse-shaped shadow stood in the road in front of the Sakura. A dark figure in trousers held its reins, but it didn't look like Yoshiko. More likely, a *dōshin* held the reins while the woman met with someone inside the house. Nobuhide's men would not refuse a request from the *yoriki*'s sister, even if it made them act like grooms. At least, the older ones would not refuse. Hiro doubted the arrogant younger man would sacrifice his pride for any woman.

As Hiro reached the space between the first and second houses, he conquered his curiosity and stopped. A closer approach would only work to his disadvantage. The *dōshin* wouldn't explain Yoshiko's presence even if they knew the reason, and Hiro couldn't scale rooftops wearing a kimono and swords. He could stop Yoshiko when she left, but she had no reason to tell the truth or even respond to his inquiry. His presence would only inform her that he knew what she was doing, and Hiro disliked unequal exchanges of information that didn't weigh in his favor.

He retreated as far as the bridge and looked for a place to hide. He wouldn't confront Yoshiko, but he had no intention of leaving before she did. He wanted to know the length of her visit and whether she left alone.

The sakura trees along the road provided no cover for someone on the ground. Leaves and branches would camouflage a climber in a hood, but a man without a mask would stand out like snow on a mountaintop.

Wide verandas circled the houses on both sides of the road. The porches were dark and shadowed by eaves, but candles flickered behind the paneled screens and Hiro didn't relish the thought of explaining his presence to a resident who stepped out for a breath of air.

He turned to the bridge. The arched wooden structure was built on pilings of wood and stone that curved above and across the river. The riverbed was fairly steep, but the sheltered space where the bridge met the bank created an artificial cave just large enough to hide a man. Hiro moved around the end of the bridge and eased himself toward the bottom of the structure.

He had almost reached the shadowed space when a voice yelled, "Help! Murder!!"

Chapter 20

Hiro spun toward the road, then realized that the yell came from under the bridge.

A lumpy shadow emerged from the deeper darkness beneath the pilings. The sharp smell of urine wafted toward him, followed by a blast of rancid breath as the shadow screamed, "Help! Help! Murder!"

"Shh." Hiro hushed the figure and waved his hands palm up to demonstrate he held no sword. "I'm not going to hurt you."

He listened for footsteps on the road but heard nothing. The yells had not alarmed the *dōshin* yet.

"Help!" the shadow called, more feebly this time. The odiferous figure canted to one side as though looking at Hiro from another angle. It did not yell again. Instead it asked, "Are you the police, or a murderer come to kill me?"

"Neither," Hiro hissed. "I'm . . . lost. I wanted a place to sleep."

"Lost? With those swords?" The shadow cackled with laughter. "Try again."

The scent of long-dead fish and rotting teeth assailed Hiro's nostrils.

"All right," he confessed, crouching low and dropping his voice to a whisper. The shadow crouched a foot away and leaned forward conspiratorially. Ancient sweat and the odor of greasy hair joined the assault on Hiro's senses. He tried to ignore them and stifled a cough of disgust.

"My wife is up there," Hiro whispered, "with another man. I don't want her to know I followed her."

The shadow cackled again, more softly this time. "Are you going to kill him? Do you want me to help? I would, you know, for a silver coin."

"Not tonight." Hiro thought quickly. "I think she has a second lover also, and I want to find him too."

"Then give me the silver anyway. If you don't, I'll yell again."

"If I do, will you stay quiet until I leave?"

The beggar's shadowy head tipped from side to side as he considered the offer. "All right."

Hiro pulled a coin from the purse inside his kimono and placed it in the beggar's outstretched palm. He had no trouble finding the proffered hand despite the darkness. The beggar almost poked Hiro in the eye in his eagerness to grab the coin.

The moment metal met palm the beggar snatched the silver away with a cackle and shuffled back under the bridge. Hiro crouched beside the piling and waited. He tried not to breathe through his nose.

A few minutes later a horse approached from the direction of the teahouse. Hooves thudded on the bridge. When Hiro judged the rider had reached mid-river he crept to the end of the bridge and looked across. Lanterns in the commercial ward backlit the horse, but Hiro could tell the rider was dressed like a samurai and had a full head of hair.

Yoshiko had spent about half an hour in the teahouse, too long just to pick up her father's belongings and far too short to conduct an interrogation. Hiro considered following her but decided against it. In the dark and on foot was no way to track a rider.

Instead, he set off across the bridge. On the other side of the river he headed west along Sanjō Road. Plinking music and women's laughter floated out of Pontocho, along with the muffled conversation of men and women walking in the narrow alley. He glanced toward the House of the Floating Plums but couldn't distinguish Umeha's house from the other gaily lit establishments. He smelled rice cakes and grilling meat from a nearby shop and a whisper of sake from the breath of a man passing by in the road.

He left the alley behind without a second look and continued down the road. He turned left at the next thoroughfare, a commercial street filled with restaurants and sake shops. Hiro thought their familiar lights glared less and welcomed more than Pontocho's.

A little way down the street, a vendor had set up a noodle stall in front of a sake shop. The stall was only a charcoal brazier standing beside the vendor's crates of supplies, but the smell of noodles and thick fishy sauce made Hiro's stomach growl. He stopped and ordered the largest bowl available.

The vendor pulled fresh noodles from a box and dangled them in boiling water for little more than a minute before swirling them into a bowl and pouring a ladle of fishy soy sauce over the top. A sprinkle of dried bonito flakes finished it off, and Hiro handed the vendor a copper coin in return for the heaping bowl and a pair of chopsticks. He ate the noodles standing in the road and returned the empty bowl with a speed that surprised and pleased the vendor.

"Thank you," Hiro said, "very tasty."

The vendor bowed and continued bowing as Hiro turned south on the unpaved road.

A couple of minutes later Hiro arrived at Ginjiro's sake brewery. Like many brewers, Ginjiro's had an open storefront with a raised floor that sat almost waist level above the street. Patrons knelt at the edge of the floor to enter, and once inside they could sit, drink sake, and watch passersby in the road. Hiro liked Ginjiro's because it was small, and also because the shop offered better food than most.

Ginjiro's opened at noon and closed when the last patron left or the sun came up, which usually meant the shop stayed open until dawn. Ginjiro served the sake himself, from barrels kept behind the wooden counter that ran the length of the establishment at the back of the shop. The floor of the service area sat at ground level, so only half of Ginjiro was visible over the top of the counter.

Hiro surveyed the storefront as he approached. Two samurai sat by the left end of the bar, drinking sake from tiny cups the size and shape of half an eggshell. An earthenware flask marked with Ginjiro's seal sat on the tatami before them. It looked much like the flask Hiro used as a decoy until Ana's wrath relieved him of that unpleasant portion of his cover. Most sake drinkers had a personal flask for taking sake home. Hiro was glad to have an excuse for its omission.

The customer on the right raised the flask and filled his companion's cup and then his own. They raised the cups to each other and resumed their conversation.

An ancient monk sat alone at the opposite end of the brewery. His cross-legged form teetered on the edge, as if about to
tumble into the street. Liver spots covered his balding head,
an almost-perfect match to the color of his tattered robe,
which was itself spotted with the remnants of meals long
eaten and other things best forgotten.

When the monk saw Hiro, his wet lips parted in a grin that
revealed his last remaining lower tooth.

"Ai! Hiro!"

The monk raised a hand in a wave that would have tipped
him to the ground if Hiro hadn't stepped up and caught his
arm.

"Good evening, Suke." Hiro steadied the monk and withdrew his hands carefully to ensure the elderly cleric did not
fall.

With the monk settled, Hiro drew his katana from its sheath
and laid it on the raised floor while he slipped off his sandals
and climbed into the brewery. Then he carried the sword to
the bar. Ginjiro accepted the weapon with a bow and placed it
in a wooden holder at the far end of the room, beside three
other katana. Two would belong to the other patrons. The
third must have been left by drunken mistake.

Hiro raised two fingers to Ginjiro.

The proprietor frowned. "Don't buy him sake. You know I
don't like him here."

"Then run him off," Hiro said, well aware that the brewer
would not.

"You know I can't. Not without risking bad karma."

"And the abbot of his temple complaining to the magistrate," Hiro added. The brewer feared the judge's wrath far
more than any gods.

"He's bad for business," Ginjiro complained.

"I don't like to drink alone," Hiro countered, "so it seems to me that makes him good for business—if you want mine, anyway."

Ginjiro frowned as he reached beneath the counter and clapped two ceramic sake cups on the wooden countertop. He sighed and moved away to draw a flask of sake.

When the brewer returned Hiro took the cups and the flask of liquor across the room to Suke.

"Very kind of you, very kind," the monk said as Hiro knelt and set the cups and flask on the floor between them. "Amida Buddha have mercy on your soul."

Hiro filled Suke's cup and then his own.

The monk raised the cup in both hands. "Infinite blessings upon you."

He downed the sake in a single gulp and lowered the cup. Suke's tongue passed over his lips to catch every drop and his eyes locked on the sake flask like a thin dog watching a butcher.

Hiro refilled Suke's cup and didn't bother to set down the flask. The monk drained the cup twice more in quick succession, but after the fourth cup he sipped at the liquor instead of bolting it down.

Hiro set down the flask and raised his own cup to his lips. They sipped in silence. Every time the shinobi refilled Suke's cup, the monk offered happy blessings that never quite lost their edge of surprise, as though Suke didn't remember the oft-repeated ritual.

Hiro didn't believe his kindness bought eternal merit as Suke claimed, but the shinobi liked to see the old man happy, and the monk gave Hiro a good reason to buy sake and a better excuse not to drink it.

As he filled Suke's cup for the seventh time and gestured for Ginjiro to bring another flask, Hiro asked, "Have you seen Kazu lately?"

"It's not so late." Suke pondered his sake cup, drained it in one swallow, and placed the cup on the tatami for a refill. Hiro upended the empty flask over the cup.

Suke sighed and looked anxiously toward the counter, as though uncertain whether Ginjiro would bring them more sake. Only after the second flask arrived and the cup was full did the monk seem to remember Hiro's question. "Not today. Yesterday he bought me a cup of sake."

Knowing the monk, it was probably more like a flask.

"Kazu is a good man," Suke said, "though not as good as you are, Hiro, Amida Buddha bless you."

The words had barely left his mouth when a samurai approached the sake shop. He wore an expensive black kimono that bore the shogun's crest, and his swords cost more than most shopkeepers made in a year. He wore his hair in a perfect topknot, oiled and shining like moonlight on a midnight lake. His narrow face and black almond-shaped eyes stopped women in the street, but he exuded a humility that belied his twenty years. His careful movements and friendly demeanor made men trust him and consider him no threat.

Most men, anyway.

Hiro knew Kazu better than that.

Chapter 21

The samurai drew his katana, climbed into the shop, and handed the sword to the brewer. As he turned away from the counter with his cup and flask in hand, he noticed Hiro sitting beside the monk. A smile spread over the young man's face and he swept a graceful bow.

"Hiro," he said in the eloquent accent favored by the shogunate and the imperial court. "What brings you to Ginjiro's? Avoiding another prayer meeting with your foreign priest?"

Hiro smiled at the flawless speech. Kazu had done nothing but complain while learning it, yet, all these years later, no one would guess the polished young man had grown up in the wilds of Iga.

"He needs someone to pray for other than you, Kazu," Hiro retorted with a grin.

Kazu laughed and knelt between Hiro and the monk. He looked around the room as he settled himself. He opened his mouth to ask a question but Hiro cut him off.

"Haven't seen her."

A flash of disappointment crossed Kazu's face. Hiro knew the reason. Kazu had taken a fancy to Ginjiro's daughter, Tomiko, who helped the brewer in the shop on certain nights.

Samurai did not intermarry with merchants, but that knowledge had done little to curb Kazu's ardor, and, although Hiro doubted the young man would act on the impulse, he did all he could to discourage the foolish crush.

"You know better," Hiro said.

"We are the only ones here," Kazu protested, misunderstanding Hiro's objection. He picked up the empty sake flask on the floor and shook it meaningfully. "Suke won't remember anything tomorrow."

"I'll remember your generosity forever," Suke slurred as he helped himself to a cup from Kazu's flask. "A thousand Amida blessings on your house."

He drained the cup and leered at Kazu over the rim.

"See?" Kazu said.

The brewer brought a third flask of sake for Hiro and also a plate of pickled vegetable snacks. When the monk reached for a radish, Ginjiro swept the plate away and placed it between the samurai, just out of Suke's reach. The brewer glared at Hiro as though daring him to feed the offending monk before returning to his place behind the counter.

Suke looked from the samurai to the food with a pleading expression that turned to a drunken grin as Hiro pushed the plate in the monk's direction. The vegetables disappeared in less than two minutes, followed by most of Hiro's third flask.

Kazu shook his head. "All that sake isn't good for him."

"When did you develop a conscience?"

Kazu lowered his head and gave Hiro a practiced glare. "If you want him here to drink with you, it behooves you to consider his well-being."

Hiro nodded, accepting the chastisement, and asked Suke, "Have you eaten rice today?"

"Rice?" Suke's question sent bits of pickled radish all over the front of his robe. Kazu leaned back to avoid the spray. The monk shook his head emphatically. "Not today."

Hiro caught Ginjiro's eye, cupped his hands in a bowl, and mouthed the word "rice."

Ginjiro shook his head, but when Hiro held up two silver coins the merchant sighed and disappeared through the indigo curtain that separated the storefront from the living quarters and brewery beyond.

Hiro took a sip from his sake cup, which was still half full from his initial pouring. The fermented rice liquor smelled sweet but burned like poison in his throat. Hiro found few things more unpleasant than pretending to enjoy it.

Hiro and Kazu sipped at their cups while the monk finished off Hiro's liquor and started on Kazu's. When the rice arrived Hiro gave Ginjiro the silver coins, plus another for the sake. It was more than twice the total bill, but Hiro didn't mind. The extra money ensured that Suke would have a place to sleep off the drink later on.

As the monk shoveled down his rice, Kazu asked, "Have you had a busy week?"

"More than usual," Hiro said, "but I need to go. Shall I tell you on the way?"

Kazu nodded assent to the coded request. "We can walk together."

They said farewell to Suke, retrieved their swords, and stepped down into their sandals. Hiro stepped to the center of the street and started north.

Kazu waited until they had left the brewery behind before asking, "What do you need?"

He kept his voice low to ensure they were not overheard, but as always he retained his polished accent. Kazu never dropped his elaborate shogunate façade.

"Did you hear about the murder east of Pontocho this morning?" Hiro asked.

Kazu shook his head. "Not your work, I assume."

"Nor yours?" Hiro asked.

"You know I don't take those assignments. I am too valuable at the shogunate." After a pause he added, "What happened?"

"A samurai, murdered in a teahouse."

"Why are you asking me about it?"

"The corpse is named Akechi Hideyoshi."

The startled look on Kazu's handsome face made Hiro's next question unnecessary.

"The general?" Kazu asked. "Akechi Mitsuhide's cousin?"

It was Hiro's turn to look startled. "How do you know that name?"

"Everyone at the shogunate knows that name," Kazu said, "and I would be a pretty poor scribe if I forgot, considering that I wrote the order condemning him to die if he sets foot in Kyoto again. At the shogun's instruction, of course. He was furious when Mitsuhide defected to Lord Oda's command."

"Does the death sentence extend to the rest of the family?" Hiro asked.

"Of course not. The last thing the shogun wants is a blood

feud with the Akechi clan, especially with Lord Oda threatening to seize the shogunate."

"Has he threatened the shogun publicly?"

"Not yet," Kazu said, "but it's only a matter of time, and when the fight comes the shogun needs every loyal sword he can get."

"Does he believe the Akechi are loyal?" Hiro asked. "I heard that Akechi Mitsuhide visited Kyoto on his way to Nagoya."

"To buy weapons, if I'm not mistaken." Kazu gave a knowing smile. "A hundred and fifty arquebuses to arm Lord Oda's troops. Why do you think the shogun was so angry?"

"All right, All-Knowing One," Hiro said, "let's see how you fare with this riddle. How many merchants from Nagoya sold rice to the shogun this week?"

Kazu's grin disappeared in an instant. "If that's a joke, it isn't funny."

"A man claiming to be a Nagoya rice merchant visited the Sakura Teahouse last night," Hiro said.

Kazu's delicate eyebrows knitted with concern. "A spy?"

"That's what I want to know," Hiro said. "If he killed Hideyoshi, Lord Oda may be testing the shogun's defenses."

Kazu nodded. "I will see what I can find."

"Tonight," Hiro said. "I need an answer by morning."

"Why in such a hurry? The corpse can't get any colder."

"If I don't find the killer in two days, Hideyoshi's son will kill the Jesuit priest."

Kazu stared at Hiro as though the shinobi had suggested they should kill the foreigner themselves. "You cannot let that happen."

"I hardly need you to tell me that my life depends on the priest's survival. Hanzo made that clear when he sent me here."

"I'm not talking about your life." Kazu looked like someone had kicked him in the stomach. "The shogun's spies in Nagoya report that Lord Oda has told the Portuguese Kyoto is not safe. He granted permission for them to build a church in his capital and promised safety for every trader who locates his warehouse there.

"For now, the Portuguese merchants have stayed in Kyoto, and elsewhere. They know that more cities mean more sales. But if your priest dies . . ." He trailed off.

"Oda will have all the warehouses, all the firearms," Hiro said.

Kazu shook his head. "Worse than that. Lord Oda will march on Kyoto and the Portuguese will help him take it."

Chapter 22

"Father Mateo isn't going to die," Hiro said with more confidence than he felt, "but I need to know who wanted Akechi Hideyoshi dead. If it's not Lord Oda, or the shogun seeking vengeance, I'll know I need to look for someone else."

"I do not think the shogun is involved," Kazu said, "but I will look at the records and meet you at Ginjiro's tomorrow evening."

"That's too late," Hiro said. "I only have until noon the day after tomorrow."

"I could check tonight and meet you in the morning. An hour after dawn, at our usual sparring ground just north of Tofuku-ji?"

"Excellent," Hiro said. "It's been a while since I taught you a thing or two."

They had reached Shijō Road. Hiro started to turn right, toward the river, and paused. "One more thing."

Kazu arched an eyebrow.

"Don't do that," Hiro said. "People might think we're related."

"We are related."

"Not in public," Hiro growled.

Kazu's second eyebrow joined the first.

"Why didn't Hideyoshi's son follow him into the shogun's army?" Hiro asked. "Wouldn't a general's son normally receive a commission?"

"Normally," Kazu replied. Then, "Akechi Hideyoshi had a son?"

"Has a son. A *yoriki* named Nobuhide."

"Unfortunate choice," Kazu said. "He will not win the shogun's favor with a name so close to Nobunaga's."

"Do you think that might have affected his status?"

"I doubt it, but I can look. If he has a record it should be next to his father's."

They parted for the second time and Hiro turned back again. "Kazu."

The younger man looked back over his shoulder.

"Be careful," Hiro warned. "I doubt the shogun ordered this murder, but, if he did, a man who starts asking questions could find himself in danger."

The next morning Hiro woke before dawn. A gentle but unexpected weight pressed down on his feet and ankles. He raised his head and saw the tortoiseshell kitten curled in a ball at the end of the futon, directly atop his feet. She had her tail tucked under her nose and her eyes screwed shut in sleep. When Hiro stirred she raised her head and gave him a sleepy look, then closed her eyes and laid her head down with a sigh.

Hiro slipped out from under the kitten and into his practice clothes, a dark blue tunic and surcoat that belted at the waist and a pair of baggy black *hakama* that almost reached the ground. He slipped on a pair of socks with a separate section for the toe and special soles designed for outside wear without sandals, opened the sliding door to the garden, and knelt on the veranda.

He spent several minutes in silent meditation, eyes closed and listening to his surroundings. He heard a breeze in the cherry tree and a koi break the surface of the pond. Leaves rustled, a shutter creaked, and a bird made a sleepy chirp on the far side of the garden wall. Hiro isolated each sound and imprinted it in his memory.

When he finished Hiro went back inside and went through a series of katas. The practice forms kept his body limber and his muscles familiar with fighting stances. Most mornings he practiced in the yard or on the roof, but that morning he worked inside to practice stealth on the raised wooden floor that often creaked underfoot. Hiro completed his exercises without a sound.

He didn't even wake the sleeping kitten.

Half an hour before sunrise Hiro changed to his usual gray kimono, fastened his swords to his obi, and left the room. He left the kitten dozing on the futon.

Candlelight flickered in Father Mateo's room. Hiro saw the Jesuit's shadow against the paper panels of the dividing wall. As he expected, the priest was kneeling in prayer.

Hiro slipped to the front door using *nuki-ashi*, a secret step that prevented floorboards from creaking. He had several errands to run that morning and intended to accomplish them alone.

He walked west to the river, crossed the bridge, and continued on toward the Nishijin district, which lay in the northwest corner of the city. He reached the silk and embroiderers' ward as the sun began to rise.

Hiro took his time as he walked along the unpaved street. Two-story buildings rose on both sides of the narrow thoroughfare. The merchants lived on the second floor, above their street-level workshops and storefronts. Hiro often wondered if they found the close quarters stifling. He couldn't imagine living where the neighbors could see from their windows into his own.

In an hour or two the street would bustle with shoppers and ring with merchants' voices announcing their fabulous wares, but at dawn the road was empty and the stores were shuttered tight. Here and there turtledoves strolled in the road. The birds' rolling gait and bobbing heads made them look like drunken samurai heading home from an overnight binge.

The shop Hiro wanted stood on a corner beside a famous silk emporium. He didn't expect to find it open, but as he approached the corner he saw an indigo *noren* hanging in the doorway of the store, announcing that the tailor had already opened his shop for business.

White letters on the indigo banner read YASO KIMONO AND SILKS.

A girl of eight or nine stood in front of the door and swept the edge of the street with a homemade broom. Her braid hung past her waist, and her glossy black hair shone in the morning sun. She wore a kimono of pink silk, exactly the shade of cherry blossoms in bloom. Although the color was slightly out of season, the cut and fashion were of the latest style. A contrasting obi bound her waist and trailed to the ground behind her.

The girl looked up at the sound of Hiro's footsteps and her face glowed with delighted recognition. She bowed but did not greet him. Well-bred little girls from the merchant class did not speak until spoken to, especially when addressing samurai.

Hiro returned the bow, and the girl blushed red at the compliment.

"Good morning Akiko," he said. "Is your father in?"

She nodded.

"Would you ask him if he will see me? Please tell him I am sorry about the hour."

Akiko bowed and disappeared into the shop. A couple of minutes later a man emerged. He wore a brown kimono and no sword, and he had a rolled-up piece of silk behind his ear. A glint of metal in the silk suggested a needle, or possibly several. The man had a thin mustache that made him look older than his thirty-three years, and his eyes had a permanent squint from sewing without enough light.

He bowed to Hiro with a mixture of curiosity and familiarity.

Hiro returned the bow. "Good morning, Yaso. I hope I did not disturb you."

The tailor smiled. "Only samurai sleep late." He gave Hiro's kimono an appraising look. "Is there a problem with your kimono? I don't see any tears or stains."

"I'm afraid not. I have a question about one of your other clients."

Yaso leaned forward eagerly. "A fashion you'd like to copy?"

"Not exactly. The man is dead."

Yaso nodded. "Akechi Hideyoshi. That design might be bad luck."

"How did you know who I meant?" Hiro asked.

"My clients don't die every day. His son, Nobuhide, was here yesterday.

"I'm not in the habit of divulging private information," the tailor added. "It's not good business."

"The question is actually about Hideyoshi's cousin."

Yaso's expression turned grim. He didn't answer.

"I know what you helped him do," Hiro said, "but if you help me I might forget to mention it to the shogun."

It was a gamble. Hiro remembered that Luis wasn't certain who had made the introduction. But sometimes, gambles paid off.

Yaso pressed his lips together until the color bled away. After a very long moment he asked, "I know the man you mean. What help do you need?"

Chapter 23

"How did you meet Akechi Mitsuhide?" Hiro asked.

"I never actually met him in person. He wanted to buy some goods from the foreign trader, Luis. Hideyoshi knew that I make clothes for the Portuguese and asked me to make the introduction."

Hiro raised an eyebrow at the lie. Yaso blushed. "Well, I do make kimonos for the priest, and I might have let a few people think I make Luis's clothes too. I repair them when they tear, you know."

Hiro doubted Luis had ever worn a patched garment but had the manners not to say so.

"So you made the introduction?" Hiro asked.

"I set up a meeting," Yaso said, "but I swear I thought the firearms were for the shogun's service. I didn't know Mitsuhide would take them to Lord Oda. I swear it."

"I believe you," Hiro said, and meant it. The tailor looked him in the eye and didn't fidget. His movements didn't indicate dishonesty, and Hiro doubted the tailor had the training or constitution to lie well.

"Did you hear from Hideyoshi's cousin again? Or anyone else in Lord Oda's service?" Hiro asked.

"No," Yaso said slowly, "but two days ago a stranger came to the shop and asked me to introduce him to the Portuguese merchant. He said he was a rice merchant from outside Kyoto and that bandits were raiding his shipments and his warehouses. He wanted firearms to protect the rice.

"At first I refused. I didn't know him, and had no reason to make the introduction. But then he said he was a friend of Akechi Hideyoshi's. He claimed they were meeting at a teahouse later that night, and that Hideyoshi told him I could introduce him to the Portuguese trader."

"So you did," Hiro said.

Yaso nodded. "I arranged a meeting." He paused. "Did I help one of Lord Oda's spies?"

"It's possible," Hiro said. "Did you tell Nobuhide about this?"

Yaso looked at the ground. "I was frightened. He might have held me responsible."

"You are not responsible," Hiro said, "but I understand your concern, and I will keep our conversation to myself."

Hiro left the relieved tailor and retraced his steps as far as Higashioji Dori, where he turned south and followed the road toward Tofuku-ji. The temple lay almost an hour's walk away, at the very southern edge of Kyoto, but Hiro didn't mind the exercise. He walked briskly down the empty street and considered the possibility that the merchant from Nagoya had killed Hideyoshi, either on orders from Lord Oda or for some other unknown reason.

In some ways it made sense and in other ways none at all. If Lord Oda sent a spy to Kyoto expecting Hideyoshi's cooperation, but the retired general refused, the "rice merchant" might have killed him to keep him silent. On the other hand, a daimyo like Lord Oda should know whose assistance he could count on. A man didn't seize whole provinces by acting on unverified assumptions. Hiro wished he had learned about the stranger before the man left Kyoto, but put the thought out of his mind. A man who dwelled on past problems often missed the ones that stood ahead in the path.

When Hiro reached the entrance to the Tofuku-ji grounds, he found Kazu standing in the middle of the road. The young samurai wore a robe of jet-black silk emblazoned with the shogun's *mon*, a circle with five horizontal black and white bars, and he scowled at Hiro like a *tengu* demon from a children's tale. He bowed as the shinobi approached, and the moment Hiro returned the bow Kazu drew his katana and leaped forward with a yell that sent birds flying from a nearby pine.

Hiro's katana left its scabbard with a hiss and met Kazu's blade with a crash of steel on steel. For ten full minutes they fought, advancing and retreating along the road as the blades rang like cymbals in the silent morning air. From the moment Kazu struck, Hiro thought of nothing but the swords, and he barely thought of those. He fought by instinct as much as will, his world consisting only of a tiny sphere of ground and air and steel.

Slowly, Hiro backed his opponent toward the river that bordered the northern edge of the temple grounds. Kazu shifted sideways to avoid falling off the bank, but failed to see a fist-sized rock behind his foot. His geta slipped and he fell.

Hiro pounced for the kill, but Kazu rolled away and jumped to his feet. His sword deflected Hiro's blade with a clang, but Hiro reversed his momentum without slowing and whirled around with the speed of a striking snake. His blade stopped less than an inch from Kazu's side.

Kazu's face fell. He shook his head and raised his blade to his opponent, then lowered it and bowed—a deep and respectful bow that admitted defeat. Hiro answered with a lesser bow of his own and resheathed his sword.

The fight was over. As always, Hiro won.

A group of monks stood on a nearby bridge, where they had gathered to watch the fight. Hiro glanced in their direction. The older ones nodded respectfully. The youngest one even bowed. Then, one at a time, they turned and shuffled off toward various buildings on the expansive temple grounds.

Hiro and Kazu walked south along one of the many gravel paths that connected the various buildings and twenty-four subtemples in the compound. Here and there monks walked around or knelt in meditation. A small group stood by the river practicing katas with wooden swords. The Rinzai sect of Buddhism had no objection to martial pursuits.

Hiro led Kazu across the Tsuten-kyo, a covered wooden bridge that spanned a deep, natural ravine between the northern temple entrance and the abbot's quarters to the south. In the middle of the bridge Hiro looked out over the tops of the myriad maple trees that covered the defile. A sea of feathery leaves spread out beneath the walkway as far as he could see. In autumn, when the leaves changed color, the bridge would look out on a sea of maple fire.

At the south end of the bridge, Kazu slowed his pace and said, "I looked through the records and found no sign that the shogun wanted Akechi Hideyoshi dead. He didn't blame Hideyoshi for his cousin's defection. In fact, there's a note in Hideyoshi's file specifically stating that the shogun does not hold him responsible."

"I think Nobunaga did send a spy." Hiro related his conversation with Yaso.

Kazu frowned. "You have to get the priest to leave Kyoto. This morning, if you can."

"I don't think he will go," Hiro said.

"Persuade him," Kazu insisted.

Hiro narrowed his eyes at the younger man.

"I apologize." Kazu blushed, remembering how substantially Hiro outranked him. "But many lives are at stake if the foreigner dies."

"Did you learn anything else of interest?" Hiro changed the subject to let Kazu know he forgave the breach.

"Did you know Hideyoshi had a brother?"

"Hidetaro?" Hiro stopped and looked around. There was no one else in sight. He stood with his back to the abbot's house, facing Kazu and the bridge. "Does he have a record with the shogunate?"

Kazu stopped too. "He was a high-ranking courier. He delivered secret messages for the shogun."

"A spy?" Hiro remembered Hidetaro's faded robe and minor limp.

"Not shinobi," Kazu said, "just a trusted courier with a little training in disguise and sleight of hand to help him pass through enemy territory safely. He retired—"

"After an injury," Hiro finished.

Kazu's nose wrinkled. "He was never injured. He retired after his father died."

A flicker of movement behind Kazu caught Hiro's eye.

Someone had turned onto the bridge, and, despite the distance that separated them, Hiro thought he recognized the approaching samurai's face.

Hiro grabbed the shoulder of Kazu's tunic and dragged the young samurai into a cluster of pine and maple trees by the side of the road.

"Hey!" Kazu began, but fell silent at the look on Hiro's face.

Hiro crouched behind the wide trunk of an ancient pine. Kazu did the same. A screen of low-hanging maple branches between the pines and the path completed their camouflage.

A moment later they heard footsteps on the bridge. A samurai in a faded blue kimono emerged from the covered passage and walked south toward the abbot's residence. His muddy geta crunched on the gravel path.

The even footsteps made Hiro wonder if he had mistaken the man for someone else. He glanced around the tree as the samurai passed.

It was Akechi Hidetaro, and he wasn't limping.

Hiro waited until the samurai passed the near end of the abbot's house and then whispered, "That's Hidetaro. I'm going to follow him."

"Why?" Kazu asked. "It's clear the merchant killed Hideyoshi."

"Never rely on assumptions," Hiro said. "The last one always kills you."

"Follow him if you want to," Kazu said, "but please try to get the priest to leave. Nobuhide isn't reasonable, and he will kill the Jesuit if he can."

Hiro had started toward the path, but he turned back at Kazu's comment. "I thought you didn't know Hideyoshi's son?"

Kazu straightened. "The shogun has a record on Nobuhide

too. He tried to join the shogunate but the reviewing general called him too stupid and shortsighted for command."

"The record says that?" Hiro's right eyebrow crept up just enough to show disbelief.

"The official report reads 'best suited for duty as a *yoriki.*' Read between the lines. No competent man is appointed to the police. It's a service of last resort. The explanatory comments say Nobuhide refuses to accept direction or admit mistakes. If he decides the priest should die, you won't dissuade him."

Hiro started after Hidetaro. "Then I'll just have to persuade him that someone else deserves it more."

Chapter 24

Hiro reached the gravel path just as Hidetaro disappeared around the far end of the abbot's residence. Hiro followed but didn't hurry. A large, open yard lay beyond and he had no desire for Hidetaro to notice him at once.

Whitewashed brick and wooden walls surrounded the distinguished gardens that lay on all sides of the abbot's house. Hiro left the path and walked beside the wall to minimize his visibility as he rounded the end of the building.

The square open yard had crushed gravel on the ground. The long wall of the abbot's southern garden formed the northern boundary of the yard. At the eastern end of the white-painted wall stood the *kuri*, the temple kitchen. The building stood at least four stories high at the peak of its sloping roof, but most of the height was attributable to the giant eaves that ran from the ridge of the roof to the top of the ground floor wall. A gentle, concave curve ensured that snow would not gather on the roof.

On the ground floor, a pair of swinging entrance doors sat directly in the middle of the western wall. Three wide wooden steps led up to the doors from the ground. The *kuri* had no other windows or entrances that Hiro could see from his end of the yard, and he didn't waste any time looking. Hidetaro was just disappearing around the far corner of the *kuri,* on the path that led to the lesser temple of Ryogin-an.

Hiro waited until Hidetaro disappeared from view before crossing the wide gravel yard. Ryogin-an lay across a short covered bridge that spanned the same ravine as Tsuten-kyo, though the little canyon was shallower here and not as wide.

Wooden walls and tall trees surrounded the temple and its gardens. The path provided the only way in or out.

Hiro took his time crossing the wooden bridge. Birds chirped and squawked in the maples and a squirrel chattered in the ravine. The air was filled with the pleasant smells of new growth and drying leaves, scents that reminded Hiro of Iga, of home.

At the far end of the bridge an elderly monk cleared leaves from the path with a wooden rake. Hiro approached him and bowed.

The monk bowed politely in return. "May I help you?"

"I thought I saw my friend from across the yard. His name is Akechi Hidetaro."

Hiro didn't expect the monk to know the name. Thousands of samurai visited the temple and meditated in its various gardens.

To his surprise, the man nodded. "Hidetaro just went by a minute ago."

He pointed a wrinkled finger at the wooden wall that surrounded the temple building and its gardens.

Hiro bowed in thanks and continued along the short gravel path. He spied Hidetaro kneeling before a dry garden on the eastern side of the temple.

Like many Zen landscapes, the eastern garden consisted of a gravel bed studded with small rocks and boulders of various shapes and sizes. Some stood upright but most were placed at angles to the ground. The gravel was clear of debris and freshly raked into geometric patterns. Straight lines ran the length of the bed, broken by circles surrounding the larger stones.

Hidetaro's gaze focused on a slanting stone that sat near the center of the garden. He didn't look up when Hiro arrived. Hiro didn't expect him to. Zen Buddhism taught a form of meditation that shut out the world and focused on an object, space, or thought. The rest of the world existed only when the practitioner decided it could return to his consciousness.

Hiro knelt to Hidetaro's left and practiced his own meditation, opening himself and his thoughts to the surroundings that other forms of meditation tried so hard to ignore. His eyes and ears found each bird that sang in the maple trees. A falling leaf tapped against the garden wall and scratched the wood with its points as it fell to earth. When he ran out of new sounds, Hiro considered the spaces between the stones. In that, his shinobi training overlapped with the principles of Zen, though Hiro's study of negative space focused on discovering usefulness rather than mere understanding of their existence.

As Hidetaro returned from his meditative peace, he looked to his left and startled. Hiro kept his gaze on the garden and pretended not to notice. Hidetaro stood up and turned to leave.

"Good morning," Hiro said.

Hidetaro turned back. "Good morning. I apologize if I interrupted your meditation."

Hiro gestured for the other man to sit and then turned to look at the stones. "Actually, I came to talk with you."

Hidetaro knelt beside the shinobi and faced the garden. "Has the foreign priest found my brother's killer?"

"Perhaps."

Both men studied the rocks again. Without Father Mateo to feign ignorance, Hiro had to comply with the samurai social conventions that forbade a direct approach.

"This is a peaceful garden," Hiro said. "Do you meditate here often?"

"Do you like it?" Hidetaro's wistful smile suggested a familiarity with polite but not heartfelt compliments. "Many people do not appreciate these dry landscapes, but then, few people really understand Zen meditation."

"Have you studied long?" Hiro asked.

Hidetaro's gaze flickered across the stones. "I wanted to become a monk."

An unusual ambition for a samurai's son.

"Your father did not agree?" Hiro guessed.

"He naturally expected his eldest son to become a warrior, not a priest."

"So you did."

"Of course. I followed him into the service of the Ashikaga clan and practiced Zen on my own, mostly here at Tofuku-ji. I preferred this subtemple—Ryogin-an—because few people come here. Less chance of anyone telling my father that I had not abandoned my spiritual life."

A thin smile crept over Hidetaro's face, suggesting an unpleasant memory.

Hiro took a guess. "Your father found out anyway."

Hidetaro didn't seem surprised. "Yes, and he disinherited me, though I did not know he had done it until he died."

"Yet you did not become a monk." Etiquette wouldn't let

Hiro ask the reason, but it didn't prevent him from pointing out the obvious.

"Not for want of effort. I requested release from the shogun, renounced my stipend, but the monastery refused to let me join the order." The thin smile flickered away. "The abbot believed the shogun sent me to spy on the monks' activities."

"How strange," Hiro said. It didn't really seem strange at all, given Hidetaro's training and the monks' tendency to riot when displeased with the shogunate.

"To this day the abbot refuses to let me take the vows, though I have permission to meditate here as often as I wish."

Hidetaro told the story without emotion, like a man recounting cities he had lived in or the food he ate for lunch. Hiro couldn't help contrasting the current detachment with the previous day's concern. Unfortunately, he didn't know Hidetaro well enough to judge which persona was truthful and which a mask. He decided to find out.

"By the way," Hiro said, "your limp seems much better this morning."

Chapter 25

Hiro watched Hidetaro. Hidetaro watched the rocks. The samurai's right hand clenched into a fist and then gradually relaxed, but otherwise he did not move.

After almost two minutes, he turned his face to Hiro and said, "The limp was an act, put on to make you believe I did not murder my brother."

Hiro narrowed his eyes. "Why would you need a limp for that?"

"A dragging foot leaves different prints from one that lifts normally," Hidetaro said.

Hiro wondered how he knew about the footprints if he hadn't seen Sayuri, but decided to take an indirect path to the answer.

"What made you consider yourself a suspect?"

"I am the older brother, but Hideyoshi had more success. I depended upon his goodwill for everything from my clothes to the food I eat. I had the good fortune to fall in love with a woman, and the misfortune to have my brother favor her too.

"Any one of those could provide a motive for murder. Only

a fool would not consider me a suspect, particularly when no other comes easily to mind."

Hiro turned to face Hidetaro. "Shall I ask the obvious question, or would you prefer to answer without my asking?"

"I did not kill him." The samurai's eyes remained on the stones and his posture did not change.

"And the next, also obvious, question?" Hiro asked.

"I do not know who killed him. Our cousin Mitsuhide recently swore allegiance to Lord Oda, but I doubt the shogun would kill a friend for the acts of a distant relative. In addition, I am still alive and so is Nobuhide. If the shogun wanted vengeance, he wouldn't have stopped with Yoshi."

Mention of Nobuhide gave Hiro an opening. "Have you seen your brother's family since his death?"

"Yesterday morning. I tried to persuade Nobuhide of Sayuri's innocence, but he would not believe me. That is why I went to see Matto-san."

Hiro ignored the mispronunciation of Father Mateo's name. "How long have you known Sayuri?"

"Yoshi invited me to the Sakura at cherry blossom season, to see the girl's debut. I didn't expect much. My brother was always bragging about some beauty from the Sakura. They rarely amounted to anything. Sayuri was the exception.

"I never thought I would care for a woman." Hidetaro's gaze lost its sharpness as emotion took hold. "But Sayuri is not like any other woman."

Hidetaro fell silent as if struggling for an explanation. At last he said, "She laughs at my feeble jokes, and when she smiles at me she means it."

It was a strange compliment, but one that suggested honesty. Hiro would have discounted comparisons to birdsong or the moon, but Hidetaro's simple phrasing rang true.

It also gave Hiro an opportunity to learn more about the samurai. "What do you mean?"

Hidetaro raised a hand to his face. "When most women smile, their faces become masks. The smile doesn't reach their eyes."

He demonstrated. His lips turned up and his eyes glittered with feeling but their edges didn't crinkle with real joy. Then he smiled a second time, in earnest.

"You see?" he asked. "A true smile begins in the eyes."

"I never noticed," Hiro lied. "Is that why you wanted to marry her?"

It wasn't a normal choice. Most samurai would never marry a commoner, let alone a woman in the entertainment trade. Hidetaro's monastic tendencies made the decision even more unusual. Few men would allow a woman to change the course of an ascetic life.

"That, and the fact that she returned my affection." Hidetaro gave an uncomfortable smile. "You may see the difference in our ages, but Sayuri did not mind it."

Hiro found that surprising too, especially since the girl had talents to match her looks. Young, beautiful women rarely fell in love with substantially older men.

Unlike Hidetaro, the shinobi sought a deeper, and probably financial, explanation. He wondered where a destitute samurai found the money to buy a performer's contract and whether Sayuri believed Hidetaro had silver hidden in his purse as well as his hair. Social convention prevented him from asking.

"Did Mayuri negotiate much on the contract price?" Hiro wondered aloud.

Hidetaro's cheek twitched. "Not as much as I would have liked."

"Perhaps she will reduce it more because of all the blood."

Hiro realized a moment too late that his effort to flush out a useful response had overstepped the boundaries of politeness.

Hidetaro stood up. "I'm afraid I have an appointment. Please excuse my rudeness, but I must leave."

Hiro stood up and bowed. "Thank you for speaking with me. I apologize if my words have offended."

They left the temple together. When they reached the abbot's quarters Hidetaro paused and reached down to adjust his katana.

He gave Hiro an apologetic smile. "Go on without me. This will take a minute."

Hiro started up the path toward Tsuten-kyo, stifling a smile at the samurai's clumsy attempt at deception. Such an awkward effort might fool the guards at provincial border stations but they would never mislead a shinobi.

Hiro suspected where Hidetaro was going. He was tempted to follow and see whether Hidetaro managed to see Sayuri, but the knowledge would not help his investigation, so he decided to check on Father Mateo instead.

At the church Hiro found Ana on her hands and knees, polishing the floor and grumbling to herself. She looked up as the shinobi's shadow fell across the doorway. Her ancient face condensed into a scowl.

"Of all the cats in the world," she said, shaking her cleaning cloth in his direction, "I should have known you would pick the defective one."

Hiro stopped. "What?"

Ana pointed at Father Mateo's room. The sliding door stood open. Hiro heard a rustling, like silk rubbing against tatami mats.

Ana rose up on her knees and rested her fists on her hips. "That cat ate Father Mateo's Bible!"

Hiro started toward the room. Behind him, Ana went back to her work.

"Hm," she sniffed, "ten thousand cats in Kyoto. He picks the one that eats paper instead of mice."

Hiro paused in the doorway of the little room. Father Mateo sat cross-legged on the tatami, scrubbing at a dark splotch on the floor. He held a wet rag marked with stains that looked like ink.

A sheet of blank parchment lay on the floor at his side, with a dirty but empty inkwell on top of it. Remnants of glistening liquid clung to the bottom and a black swatch over the side suggested a spill.

The priest's beloved leather-bound Bible lay open in the writing alcove. The upper right corner of the open page was missing, along with the first few words in the right-hand column. At a distance it looked torn, but Hiro suspected the kitten was to blame.

He felt terrible and didn't know what to say. After trying several options in his mind, he settled on a statement of the obvious.

"Did my kitten do that?"

It was the first time Hiro referred to the cat as his own, and he did it intentionally. He had brought the animal into the house. That made it his, and he was responsible for it.

Father Mateo nodded and set the rag on top of the stained tatami. "I went to the kitchen to add more water to my ink, and when I returned she was eating Paul's letter to the Romans. I dropped the inkwell trying to shoo her off."

"I am sorry. Can the book be fixed?"

"Only one verse is missing," Father Mateo said, "and under the circumstances I'm not likely to forget it." He paused and then recited, " 'For all have sinned and come short of the glory of God'—kittens included."

Hiro would have felt relief, but the Jesuit's smile seemed forced.

"I am sorry," he repeated.

"God will forgive the kitten, and you, and I would never presume to hold a grudge on His behalf," Father Mateo said. "Besides, we have a more serious problem. Luis has disappeared."

Chapter 26

W hat do you mean, disappeared?" Hiro asked.

"When I woke this morning, Luis was gone," Father Mateo explained. "At first I thought he was sleeping, but when he didn't get up for breakfast I checked his room. He wasn't there, and his horse isn't in the stable."

"Did he go to the warehouse?" Hiro would not have saddled a horse for the ten-minute walk to the Portuguese shop, but Luis never walked when he could ride.

"The travel papers are also gone. The imperial ones, that grant access beyond Kyoto."

"Your pass?" Hiro's stomach clenched.

"The pass," Father Mateo corrected. "The emperor granted only one for my household. I think he believed we would always travel together."

"More likely he wanted to keep you from going to two different places at once," Hiro said, "to track your movements more easily. If Luis took the pass you can't leave Kyoto."

Father Mateo frowned at the implication. "I wasn't leaving. I'm more concerned about where Luis has gone."

"Isn't it obvious?" Hiro was furious. "He's run off to save his cowardly life at the cost of yours and mine."

Father Mateo started to object, but then sighed. "It does look that way. He's never left the city without telling me in advance."

Hiro turned back to the common room. "Ana!"

"You don't have to yell," the housekeeper declared. She put down her rag and stood up. "I'm old, not deaf."

"Do you know when Luis left or where he was going?"

"I heard a horse just after dark last night," she said. "I assumed it was Luis, since you don't ride and Father Mateo's congregation was arriving for prayer."

"Fourteen hours," Hiro said. "We'll never catch him. He's past the shogun's second barricade, no matter which direction he went."

The shogun and most warlords erected barricades at intervals along the highways and at the borders of the lands that they controlled. There taxes were charged, goods inspected, and travelers' papers viewed. Anyone without a pass or a good excuse would be turned back or restrained, but the emperor's seal guaranteed that Luis would pass quickly and unmolested.

"Perhaps he'll come back on his own," Father Mateo suggested.

"He'd better," Hiro said, "because if he doesn't and Nobuhide kills you, I will hunt that Portuguese traitor down and make him beg to die."

"Hiro," the priest said, "don't say that. I do not want Luis to die and I do not want you to kill him. Vengeance belongs to God alone.

"Promise me you will not harm Luis, no matter what happens."

Hiro didn't answer.

"Hiro," Father Mateo warned.

"Perhaps it won't be necessary. I have new evidence that suggests Lord Oda is responsible for Hideyoshi's death."

"Really?" Father Mateo stood up and wiped his hands on his kimono.

Ana saw the rag on the tatami and bustled into the room. She knelt and shook her head at the ink spot on the floor. "Hm."

Father Mateo gave Hiro a worried look and left the room. Hiro followed him out.

"So," the Jesuit said, "who killed Akechi Hideyoshi?"

Hiro had already started toward the swinging door. "I'll tell you a theory on the way."

As they walked, Hiro explained what he had learned from the tailor, though he did not mention Yaso's name. He also omitted Kazu and the shogunate.

"So the merchant from Nagoya was really a spy who killed Hideyoshi to avoid discovery," Father Mateo said. "Do you think Nobuhide will believe it?"

"No," Hiro said. "This solution relies on two assumptions, and I cannot reveal my informant's name. More importantly, I'm not convinced the murder happened that way."

"Then why are we going to see Nobuhide?" Father Mateo asked.

"That is an assumption too," Hiro said with a smile.

"A safe one, based on the fact that his house is directly ahead of us." Father Mateo pointed at the Akechi home, directly ahead on the left-hand side of the road.

"An incorrect one," Hiro said. "We are going to see Akechi Sato.

"I need more time to solve this murder. Nobuhide won't agree, and this theory won't convince him, but it might be strong enough to persuade his mother."

"Or his sister," Father Mateo agreed.

Hiro gave the priest an incredulous look. "Yoshiko? We have a better chance of teaching my cat to sing."

"She's a woman too."

"In body only," Hiro said, "and barely that. No, our best chance lies with Hideyoshi's wife."

They walked up the path to the house. Three pairs of shoes sat outside the entrance, the tiny pair that could only belong to Akechi Sato, a pair of mud-spattered geta, and the decrepit servant's sandals Hiro had seen on their previous visit.

The shinobi knocked on the door. Shuffling steps approached from the other side, and the door swung open to reveal an elderly manservant. He wore a brown kimono with no crest and his well-worn *tabi* showed evidence of repair. He bowed and waited for the samurai to speak.

"Good morning," Hiro said. "We have come to see Akechi Sato."

The servant nodded. "I will see if my mistress is available."

He disappeared into the house.

Hiro leaned toward Father Mateo and whispered, "Agree with everything I say."

Soft footsteps heralded Sato's arrival. She wore a black kimono with no decoration and matching black obi. The hem of her inner kimono showed at the neckline. In defiance of tradition, that too was black. She wore no makeup and no visible jewelry except for the silver pins that held her hair in place. Her eyes showed no redness or puffiness, but she looked older than the day before and bent down, like a lily after a thunderstorm. Hiro suspected that, like the lily, Sato's brokenness was not permanent. A strong woman's spirit was not easily crushed.

Hiro and Father Mateo bowed. When they rose, Yoshiko had joined her mother in the doorway. Hiro blinked in surprise. He had not heard the samurai woman approach.

Like her mother, Yoshiko had shed her colored robes for black, but the daughter's kimono was cut in male lines and she wore a samurai's obi instead of the larger one women preferred. Her hair was freshly oiled and pulled into a topknot. Even in mourning, Yoshiko remained a samurai.

The women bowed politely but not deeply.

"May we help you?" Yoshiko asked.

"We have identified your father's killer," Hiro said. "Sayuri is innocent."

"I don't believe you." Yoshiko narrowed her eyes. "Nobuhide told me what happened. The woman was alone with my father all night and in the morning he was dead. No one else entered the room. My father did not kill himself. No one else could have done it."

Hiro's mind prickled in warning. Leaving guests outside violated the samurai code, and the day before Yoshiko had invited them in at once. Something had caused her hospitality to vanish without a trace.

Sato peered from behind her daughter. She looked at Father Mateo with longing, as though she wanted to invite him in.

Hiro took a chance. "One of Lord Oda's spies came to Kyoto to purchase weapons from the Portuguese. We believe he asked your father for assistance and killed Hideyoshi when he refused to cooperate."

"A spy who conveniently disappeared before you could capture him?" Yoshiko asked with disdain. "You shame yourself, trying to persuade my mother with a lie. Go away."

She stepped back and closed the door in Hiro's face.

Chapter 27

A moment later the door swung open again.

"Are you still here?" Yoshiko asked.

"We have hardly had time to leave," Hiro said.

Yoshiko sighed and opened the door. "My mother wishes to offer you tea. She wants to hear more of your explanation, though I warn you that I will not forgive an attempt to defraud her."

She gestured toward the interior of the house. "Come inside."

Sato stood at the far end of the entry chamber. As the visitors stepped into the house, she bowed and led them into the common room.

A haze of pale blue smoke hung in the air, and the perfume of sandalwood incense overwhelmed even the scent of the cedar beams. Hiro loathed the cloying odor, though it was common in houses of mourning. In addition to its religious significance, incense masked the smell of a corpse in decay.

He saw other signs of mourning too. The common room hearth had no fire, and the tokonoma sat empty in recognition of the patriarch's recent death. The empty alcove reminded Hiro of his own, although his remained perpetually vacant by choice.

When they were seated and the manservant brought tea, Yoshiko said, "Why should we believe your tale? Lord Oda had no reason to kill my father."

"Wasn't he a traitor like his cousin Mitsuhide?" Hiro asked the question bluntly, in violation of every social rule but also knowing that Yoshiko could not take offense because of her own rudeness. He hoped his abruptness would provoke a useful admission.

Father Mateo looked shocked. Akechi Sato gasped and raised her hands to her mouth. Yoshiko narrowed her eyes and clenched her jaw, but recovered much more quickly than Hiro expected. Within moments her face had resumed its samurai stillness.

"I see you have learned about our clan's embarrassment," she said. "My father was not a traitor. He tried to convince Mitsuhide to change his mind, but the fool would not be dissuaded.

"If you know about Mitsuhide, however, you also understand why Lord Oda would not harm my father, or any other member of my clan."

"On the contrary," Hiro said, "killing your father would prove the defection was real."

As the words left Hiro's mouth he had a sudden flash of insight. He opened his mouth to speak but closed it quickly with the words unspoken. It was only an assumption, not a fact. At least until he could find the facts to support it.

"Killing my father was more difficult than you believe," Yoshiko said.

Father Mateo gave Hiro an alarmed look, and the shinobi realized the priest had taken Yoshiko's words for a confession. Hiro shook his head slightly and the priest relaxed, though he looked both nervous and confused.

"As I told you before, my father has killed *kunoichi*," Yoshiko continued. "Not only the one who tried to assassinate the shogun but also another, sent to take my father's life. It happened five years ago in the very teahouse where he died. My father disarmed her and killed her with her own poisoned dagger. He should have done the same to this assassin.

"Which leads me to believe that my father knew his killer."

"Do you have evidence of that?" Hiro asked.

"Someone slit my father's throat while he waited for Sayuri to return from the latrine," Yoshiko said. "He would have heard the killer coming, yet he allowed that person to approach him from behind. He must have recognized the killer's voice, or perhaps her gait."

A strange gleam entered her eye as she looked at Hiro. "Surely you could recognize a woman's gait?"

Hiro ignored the comment and the unexpected implication. "So you believe Nobuhide is correct, that Sayuri killed him?"

"If the woman didn't do it she was involved. How else could a killer have entered his room, slain him, and left without being seen?"

"Do you agree?" Father Mateo asked Sato.

She smiled sadly. "I do not know who killed my husband, nor do I worry about the dead. I may go to him, but he will not return to me."

"You know King David?" Father Mateo asked.

"Should I not? After all, I am a Christian."

The Jesuit's face broke into a smile of delight. "How did you become a Christian?"

Sato shook her head and looked at her hands, which lay folded in her lap. "I do not want to bore you with an elderly woman's tales."

"Please," Father Mateo said, "I would like to hear it."

Hiro did not want to hear it. He wanted to leave and prove his new theory correct, preferably after obtaining a few extra days to investigate.

He tried to catch the Jesuit's eye, but the priest refused to look in his direction. Hiro realized with frustration that his friend was being deliberately obtuse.

"I married very young," Sato said, "but for years I bore no children. It was embarrassing. A samurai wife has one duty—to provide her husband with an heir. Yoshi was patient and did not send me away, but I grew desperate. I prayed to Buddhist gods, Shinto *kami*, and every other spirit I could find. Mostly I prayed to Kannon, the goddess of mercy. I promised that if she gave me a child I would put a statue of her in my home and pray to it every day as long as I lived."

"But Kannon did not help you," Father Mateo said in his most understanding tone.

"No." An impish grin came over Sato's face. Her eyes glittered with delight at having fooled the foreign priest. "Kannon gave me a daughter, Yoshiko."

Mother and daughter exchanged a smile. It was the first real emotion Hiro had seen on Yoshiko's face, but the expression disappeared almost at once.

"Your husband must have been pleased," Father Mateo said.

"Most men would prefer a son," Sato said, "but Kannon

helped there too. Yoshi loved Yoshiko from the moment she was born. He raised her as a samurai, exactly like a boy." She paused. "I didn't like that much at first, but they seemed so happy that in time I grew happy too. Now I am very glad it worked out this way."

She glanced at Yoshiko like a child who reveals a family secret and doesn't know what to do. Hiro wondered which part of the story Sato wished she hadn't told.

Just before the silence grew awkward, Yoshiko prompted, "You were telling them about the foreign god."

Sato nodded. "The year Yoshiko turned thirteen she had her *genpuku*." She wrinkled her brow in concern and looked at the priest. "Do you know this word?"

"The ceremony when a samurai becomes a man." Father Mateo glanced at Yoshiko and added, "That is, an adult, with the right to wear two swords."

Sato nodded, pleased that she didn't have to explain. "Yoshiko—her name was Chiko before *genpuku*—learned very fast. She had her ceremony at thirteen. Her father gave her a pair of heirloom swords."

"So he didn't mind that he had a daughter and no son." Father Mateo said.

"He was satisfied," Sato agreed, "but I felt like a failure. Just before the *genpuku* I heard that strangers from across the sea had brought a new god to Japan. I thought perhaps this foreign god might give me another child, so I asked Hideyoshi to take me to see the foreigners.

"He didn't believe your God would hear me, or even speak Japanese, but he agreed because he wanted one of the foreign weapons for his collection."

"Did you meet Francis Xavier?" Father Mateo asked.

"No, a foreigner called Pinto-san," Sato said. "He was not a priest, though he said he intended to become one when he returned to his land across the sea. He was tall, with skin like a ghost and a nose the size of a rice bowl. I felt badly for him, because he smelled terrible and the stink made his big nose red and runny."

Hiro suspected the running nose was red from alcohol rather than stink, but interrupting would only delay their departure even more.

"Pinto-san told me the Jesus god walked on earth like a man. That gave me hope. A god who had a mother might have pity on a woman who wanted a son. Pinto-san taught me a prayer and said I could ask this Jesus god for anything, but he also said that the Jesus god would only give me things if his father, the Almighty God, wanted me to have them. He said this many times, that Jesus could always hear me but only granted prayers when his father allowed him to."

"Yes," Father Mateo said. "That's how it works with Jesus."

"No different than our Japanese *kami*," Sato said, "except that *kami* don't even listen unless they want to."

Hiro's foot went to sleep. Ordinarily he would have suffered through the prickling irritation, but his patience with Sato's story was at an end. He wiggled first his foot and then his leg, hoping the widow would notice and conclude her recitation.

Yoshiko gave him a look that hovered between disbelief and understanding. He raised his eyebrows a fraction in return. Yoshiko started to speak but Sato continued. "I promised your Jesus the same thing I promised Kannon. Within a month I was pregnant with Taromaru—that is, Nobuhide." Sato smiled apologetically. "We called him Taromaru as a child."

Yoshiko leaned back and frowned at her mother. Sato did not notice or did not care.

Hiro suspected the latter.

"When I became pregnant," Sato continued, "I tried to have a statue made for God, but then I learned that He prefers to be worshipped as a cross."

"Not exactly," Father Mateo said. "The cross is a symbol to remind us of His sacrifice. We don't worship the image itself."

"Just like *kami*," Sato agreed. "The god is in the tree, except that the *kami* is the tree and Jesus is not the cross."

Hiro smothered a smile. He could see theology struggling with pragmatism in Father Mateo's thoughts. Pragmatism won.

"I am glad you know Jesus," the priest said. "I hope you continue to pray to Him."

Sato looked offended. "I promised, didn't I?"

Yoshiko stood up and bowed. "Thank you for your visit."

"Thank you for listening to us," Hiro said.

"Please tell Akechi-sama that we are sorry to have missed him," Father Mateo added.

Hiro was just about to use that opening to ask for additional time when Yoshiko narrowed her eyes and said, "You may refer to my brother as Akechi-san, not -sama."

"I apologize for my imperfect Japanese," Father Mateo said. "I thought an heir was addressed with the highest honorific."

"Your Japanese and your understanding are correct," Sato said, "but Nobuhide is not my husband's heir. Yoshiko is."

Chapter 28

Hiro found it difficult to hide his surprise. "Yoshiko is the heir?"

"Yes," Yoshiko said, "since before Nobuhide was born."

"Does the law recognize a female heir?" Father Mateo asked.

"Only if the patriarch leaves a will that names her specifically," Hiro said.

"Which my husband did," Sato said. "He wrote it years ago."

"Before Nobuhide's birth?" Hiro asked.

"No," Sato replied. "Fortunately he wrote it after that, so no one can claim an accident or omission."

Hiro wanted to see that will, but needed a reason that wouldn't sound suspicious. He glanced at Father Mateo and tilted his head slightly, hoping without real hope that the Jesuit would understand and find a reason to ask.

"How fascinating," Father Mateo said. "I have never seen a Japanese will. I wonder if they differ much from the Portuguese tradition."

Months of teaching the Jesuit to understand coded looks and unspoken signals finally paid off in earnest.

"Would you like to see it?" Yoshiko asked.

"I would be honored."

"Please sit down," Yoshiko said. "I will retrieve it for you."

She left the room as the guests returned to their positions by the hearth. Sato accompanied them with a pleasant smile, though her forehead wrinkled with something that looked like sorrow.

Yoshiko returned, carrying a weathered but expensive bamboo case. She knelt by the hearth, opened the cap at the end of the case, and shook a parchment scroll from the bamboo cylinder. The scroll held its shape, expanding only a little when released.

Yoshiko extended the scroll to Father Mateo, using two hands. He accepted it the same way and unrolled it carefully.

"May I ask Hiro to translate?" he asked. "I do not read your language well enough to comprehend such an important document."

"Of course." Yoshiko dipped her head in consent.

Hiro took the scroll and read it quickly to himself. It was written in tiny characters composed of fine, narrow strokes. The calligraphy showed both native skill and years of careful study. Not a single misplaced brush mark marred the scroll.

Akechi Hideyoshi's personal seal was stamped at the bottom in vermillion ink to verify the will. The pasty ink was glossy and slightly raised, as required for a documentary seal. Hiro saw no deficits in construction or execution.

He traced his finger down the page as he read the scroll aloud.

" 'I, Akechi Hideyoshi, set these words to parchment in the seventh year of the Shogunate of Ashikaga Yoshifuji.' " Hiro paused and looked at the priest. "Yoshifuji was the Shogun's childhood name. He took the name Yoshiteru in adulthood."

"Thank you." Father Mateo gave a little laugh. "Does that explain when the will was written? I'm still not very good with the Japanese calendar."

"It means this was written twelve years ago." Hiro looked down and continued reading. " 'It is my will that upon my death, my daughter, Akechi Yoshiko, will inherit my entire estate, including all money, lands, and property owned by me or to which I am entitled. If my stipend continues beyond my death, it should transfer to her in its entirety.

" 'I wish for Yoshiko to provide financial support for her mother, Akechi Sato, and for my brother, Akechi Hidetaro, as long as they live. She should permit my son, Akechi No-buhide, to continue to reside in the family home. In all matters affecting the clan, Yoshiko's decision is final. I trust her judgment as though she were my son.

" 'Life is short and sorrowful. A wise samurai spends his life prepared to die. When I leave this life, know that I was prepared.' "

Hiro's right finger grazed the seal. "Akechi Hideyoshi."

He rubbed the finger against his thumb but felt no waxy transfer. The seal was not soft or wet.

"It is very well drafted," Father Mateo said.

Yoshiko laughed. "I agree, but my brother did not think so."

"Was he angry?" the priest asked.

"Extremely. Nobuhide expected the will would name him as our father's heir."

"Can he challenge it?" Father Mateo wondered.

"No," Sato said. Her voice was firm. "That is my husband's

will. I knew when he wrote it and where he stored it, and I retrieved it after his death."

Hiro explained. "A wife's testimony is final if she saw the will and knew its contents before her husband died."

Sato nodded. "I did, and that is Hideyoshi's will."

Hiro returned the scroll to Yoshiko. She rolled it tightly and returned it to its case. As she laid the bamboo cylinder on the tatami she asked, "Did you have any other questions?"

"We had hoped you might persuade Nobuhide to give us a few more days to find Hideyoshi's killer." Hiro answered Yoshiko but his eyes met Sato's as he spoke. "It would be most unfortunate if an innocent woman died tomorrow just for lack of time."

Sato nodded agreement. She looked at Yoshiko, eyebrows raised in a silent request.

"I am sorry," Yoshiko said, "but I cannot grant your request. Not without further evidence. If, by tomorrow, you have found this spy or have proof that he killed my father I will reconsider."

"Thank you." It was the only response Hiro could give.

"May I ask another question?" Father Mateo asked.

Yoshiko looked at the priest with interest.

"I apologize for my presumptuousness," he said, "but I am curious about Japanese laws and customs. Will your father's stipend continue after his death?"

"They usually do not," Yoshiko said.

"Did he have other income?" the priest asked. "Business interests, or an inheritance?"

Yoshiko and Sato exchanged a look.

The older woman answered. "Hideyoshi was his father's

heir, but that money has been gone for many years. We are hopeful that the shogun will show mercy and allow us to retain his stipend."

"How do Japanese address the issue of creditors?" Father Mateo asked.

Yoshiko tilted her head to the side. "I do not know what you mean."

"Did your father owe anyone money when he died? Like rice merchants or tailors? Take the teahouse, for example. How will his final bill be paid? Will there even be a bill, since he died there?"

Hiro was impressed with Father Mateo's unexpected subtlety. The shinobi had wondered how Hideyoshi managed to afford the Sakura on a subsistence-level stipend, but convention prohibited him from asking. He hadn't thought to address the topic as a legal issue, not that the tactic would not have worked. Only a foreigner could ask such intrusive questions without causing serious offense.

"I would be . . . disappointed if Mayuri expected payment for the night my father died."

"Did he have other debts?" Father Mateo asked. "How would they be paid?"

"We have a little savings," Sato said, "and Nobuhide's income."

"The will mentioned support for Akechi Hidetaro," Father Mateo said. "Will you still provide that support if the stipend is revoked?"

"It was my father's wish," Yoshiko said.

"Did your father support his brother during his lifetime?" the priest asked.

"It was his duty as the Akechi heir."

"Did Hidetaro request more money recently?" Hiro asked.

Yoshiko seemed to realize that an informative conversation had just become an interrogation. She thought longer than usual before responding. "Yes, he did. He did not say why, but he came here the night my father died to ask for money. My father refused."

"Do you know why he wanted it?" Hiro asked.

Yoshiko shook her head as she looked him in the eye. "No."

"Did they argue about it?"

"No. Where there is no money, there is no point in argument." Yoshiko leaned backward. "But your questions suggest that you suspect my uncle as well as an unknown spy."

Chapter 29

I apologize if my question held an inappropriate implication." Hiro dipped his head in humility. "That was not my intention."

Yoshiko nodded acceptance, but her eyes narrowed suspiciously.

Father Mateo stood up and bowed. "Thank you for teaching me about your customs. May I pray again for your father before I leave?"

"I would like that," Sato said quickly. Yoshiko's lips pursed in objection but she said nothing.

Sato led them across the room and slid open the paneled door to Hideyoshi's armory. The room looked almost exactly as it had the previous day, except that a bowl of cooked rice sat on the floor outside the coffin at the end nearest Hideyoshi's head. A single chopstick stood upright in the rice. As Hiro entered the room he noticed a second object beside the bowl. A thin vase held a single hydrangea blossom, the same type and color as the ones in the room where Hideyoshi died.

The coincidence seemed too great for an accident. Hiro's new theory about the spy gained momentum in his head.

Father Mateo knelt beside Hideyoshi and bowed his head in prayer. Hiro stood just inside the doorway and studied the room for anything out of place. He saw nothing else new or different.

His gaze lingered on the tokonoma. The *neko-te* seemed to mock him from their semicircle of pegs. He couldn't shake the conviction that those claws had murdered their owner, despite Sato's explanation for the broken blade.

The priest finished his prayer. As Yoshiko led them to the door Hiro said, "Your mother selected a fine set of funeral armor."

The samurai woman glanced at him from the corner of her eye. "My mother did not select the armor. Nobuhide did."

"Well, you have done a fine job preparing him for . . ." Father Mateo's voice trailed off uncertainly.

"Cremation," Yoshiko said. "My mother requested a Christian burial but Nobuhide insisted our father should not decay in the ground. I agree with that disposition, though not with the way my father appears."

She paused as if consumed by an inner struggle. Hiro wondered what she wanted to say but felt that she should not.

"My father should have worn the armor he wore in battle," she said at last, "not the ceremonial breastplate my brother chose."

At last Hiro understood. A samurai did not criticize family members, but Yoshiko wanted him to know that the inappropriate armor was not her fault. He wondered why she cared what he believed. Given her earlier comment about women's gaits, he sincerely hoped she didn't have an interest in him beyond the investigation.

"By the time I returned from my morning ride and learned about Father's death, Nobuhide had already washed and dressed the body," she continued. "It was too late to change it."

Hiro nodded. There was no point in platitudes or false re-assurances. They both knew Nobuhide had chosen wrong, and that further handling would only dishonor the corpse. Some things could not be changed.

In the entry they exchanged bows.

"If I may ask," Hiro said, "who knew about your father's will before he died?"

"Only my mother," Yoshiko said. "She was there when he wrote it. I saw it for the first time yesterday."

"Yet you knew you were his heir?"

Yoshiko smiled. "My father has always favored me. I didn't need a will to tell me his intentions."

"Who knows about the will now?"

"Nobuhide, of course, and my uncle Hidetaro."

"Who told Hidetaro?"

"I did, yesterday, when he came to pay his respects and to pray for my father's soul. I do not believe in gods myself, though I understand that some people find comfort in faith."

"How long did he pray?"

She looked up at the door frame, thinking. "Half an hour, perhaps? He may not have prayed the entire time. I left him alone with my father and saw him only when he left."

Hiro bowed. "Thank you again for your courtesy."

As they approached the Kamo River bridge, Nobuhide rode toward them on a dappled gray gelding. He appeared to be heading home, but when he saw the foreigner he pulled his horse to a halt and glared.

"What are you doing here?" he demanded.

"This is a public road," Hiro said. "We are walking on it."

"You are walking away from my house," Nobuhide accused. "The magistrate's order gives you no right to harass my mother."

"Or your sister," Hiro added.

Nobuhide snorted. "That fox spirit can take care of herself. I suppose she told you how she cheated me out of my inheritance."

"She showed us your father's will," Hiro said. "Have you reason to suspect a trick?"

"Not a new one." Nobuhide scowled. "She has always been his favorite, but I never suspected he would give her the inheritance too. No wonder he kept his will a secret."

He pointed at the priest. "But I still have the right of vengeance, and I intend to carry it out. Tomorrow your head will roll."

"Not if we find the real killer first," Hiro said.

"I'll help you out," Nobuhide replied. "The killer is at the teahouse, under guard."

"Perhaps," Hiro said. "Perhaps not. Did you know a man from Nagoya visited the Sakura the night your father died?"

Nobuhide looked startled. "What are you talking about?"

"And when was the last time you saw your father's brother?"

"Hidetaro?" Nobuhide's nose wrinkled as though the name carried an odor. "Do you think he had something to do with my father's death?"

"We are investigating several possibilities. The point is that the answer is far from clear."

"It seems clear enough to me."

"What about your sister?" Hiro asked. "Do you know where she was the night your father died?"

"At home, as usual." Nobuhide paused. "She said she told you that yesterday."

"She did. I was just making sure you didn't have something to tell us, since she isn't here now."

"Do you think I'm afraid of a woman?" Nobuhide's scowl returned with a vengeance. "I would have no problem calling her a liar. That is, if she ever lied."

"And where were you, exactly, two nights ago?"

Nobuhide's left hand released the reins and went to the hilt of his katana. "I am a *yoriki*, assistant to Magistrate Ishimaki, and a servant of the shogun. How dare you imply that I would kill my father."

"I merely asked your whereabouts. I intended no implication."

Nobuhide sniffed. "If you must know, I was at the House of the Floating Plums all night. I stayed with a girl named Umeha. Speak with her if you wish."

Hiro bowed. "That will not be necessary."

Nobuhide smiled without humor or goodwill. "Make sure the priest shows up at the teahouse tomorrow. I will kill you both if I have to chase him down."

After Nobuhide rode away Hiro turned south along the Kamo River road.

"We're not going home?" Father Mateo asked.

"No time," Hiro said. "I need to talk with Sayuri."

"Sayuri? Why?"

"I need to know more about her relationship with Hidetaro. Our Nagoya spy might not have left town after all."

Chapter 30

"Is Hidetaro the spy?" Father Mateo sounded incredulous. "What made you think of that?"

"I'm not certain what I think," Hiro said, "but this murder is more complex than it seems. Yoshiko claims she was home that night but her geta are covered in mud. Hidetaro had mud on his sandals and on his kimono. A man from Nagoya shows up and then disappears, and Mayuri burns her ledgers the next morning. I'd say that something is not what it seems, but that doesn't begin to describe the situation."

They walked down the river a little way and Father Mateo asked, "Did you know Sato was a Christian?"

Hiro nodded. "That's why I thought she might give us the extra time."

"How did you know? I had no idea."

"Her clothing gave the first clue. Some Japanese wear black in mourning but no woman wears a kimono and obi that match. The colors always contrast, and the inner kimono must be a third color since the inner hem shows above the neckline of the outer one. Yesterday, and again today, Akechi Sato wore all black, like a crow . . . or a Christian in mourning.

"Her reaction to you reinforced that initial impression. She showed no fear or wonder. She didn't startle or stare, and she showed no concern that your presence might defile her husband's body. On the contrary, she thanked you for your prayers.

"Only a woman comfortable with foreigners would react to you that way, and since samurai women don't engage in outside business she had to have experience with priests."

"She could have seen me in the road," Father Mateo pointed out, "or heard about me from Nobuhide."

"Who no doubt praised you in the highest possible terms."

Father Mateo laughed. "Probably not, at that. Still, it was a very good guess on your part. I thought you didn't deal in assumptions."

"I don't. Sato also wears a Christian cross on a chain around her neck. I saw it when she bowed."

Father Mateo lifted his head as though he had an interesting thought. "What if Sato killed Hideyoshi?"

Hiro blinked. "You don't think Sayuri could kill because she's a Christian, but you believe that elderly woman could? How do you reconcile that?"

"Christians believe in monogamy. Sato might have been jealous of Sayuri, and she didn't have to hold the knife."

"*Neko-te*," Hiro corrected. "I'm sure that's the type of weapon that killed him."

"Sato could have given the claws to whoever impersonated the spy."

"Possible but doubtful. From what I could tell, she actually believes in gods and wouldn't want to anger them. And if I remember correctly, your Jesus isn't very big on murder."

"But her husband was involved with another woman!"

Hiro laughed. "You don't know much about Japanese wives."

Father Mateo looked offended. "I know enough about women to know that they don't like being replaced."

"Entertainers are not replacements for wives. A wife bears children and keeps the household accounts. No one expects her to display any skill at singing or conversation. Wives provide security. Entertainers offer social interaction. They fill completely different roles."

"All women are good at conversation," Father Mateo argued, "Japanese men just don't listen to most of them."

Hiro cocked an eyebrow at the priest. "Forgive me, but I hardly consider a celibate priest an authority on women.

"Akechi Sato is not responsible for her husband's death. She doesn't have the strength to ride a horse or to walk all the way to the Sakura. Her sandals showed no hint of mud, so she wasn't out in the rain. She couldn't have wielded the weapon that killed her husband, either. *Neko-te* require hand strength she doesn't possess."

The priest looked relieved. "I'm glad you think so. I agree, but I took the other side because I wanted to hear you say it."

The four *dōshin* remained on guard outside the Sakura Teahouse, but they sat in a circle under one of the cherry trees instead of lurking by the path. As Hiro and Father Mateo approached, the youngest man startled and scooped something into his kimono sleeve. Dice, or possibly gambling sticks, unless Hiro missed his guess. Something to pass the time after the initial excitement of guarding a murderer died away, leaving only another routine wait.

Faint chanting emanated from the house. It came from the direction of the garden, most likely due to an open veranda door.

"Are the priests still here?" Father Mateo asked.

Hiro nodded. "The purification will take almost a week, and Mayuri can't use the room until it's finished."

"That must be expensive," the priest said.

"You have no idea."

Hiro knocked on the teahouse door. The chanting increased slightly as Mayuri opened the door. She looked irritated to see them, or possibly just irritated with all the inconvenience.

"We have come to see Sayuri," Hiro said.

Mayuri gave him a cold smile. "There is nothing new for you to discover here and your presence makes the girls nervous."

"Are you refusing us admittance?" Hiro asked.

Mayuri's smile widened and she opened the door a little more. "Of course not. The Sakura is pleased to cooperate with your investigation. Please come in."

They found Sayuri in the same front room, wearing the same kimono she had changed into the day before. Her eyes seemed hollower, perhaps from lack of sleep, but she smiled when she saw the priest.

Father Mateo started across the floor.

Hiro turned to Mayuri. "Thank you. We will let you know when we have finished."

She nodded and closed the door without a word.

Sayuri looked from Father Mateo to Hiro. "Have you found the killer? Will Nobuhide let me go?"

"Not yet," Hiro said. "May I see your dagger?"

She looked surprised. "I don't carry a *tanto*."

Hiro wasn't fooled and he was finished playing. "If you're an entertainer and not a prostitute, you have a weapon under that kimono. Produce it for me or I will find it myself."

She looked at him for a long moment, then reached her right hand into her left sleeve and withdrew a long, slender sheath. She snapped it open to reveal a painted fan with metal ribs connected by hand-painted paper panels that showed a city scene.

Sayuri closed the fan with a click and took the blades in her left hand. Her right hand drew the concealed dagger from the bottom of the sheath. The five-inch blade fit snugly in the largest rib of the fan. Its length and diameter were closer to a throwing knife than a *tanto*, or more properly a *menhari-gata* since it was concealed in a fan. Sayuri spun the knife in her hand so the blade lay across her palm and offered the hilt to Hiro.

He accepted the weapon and examined it carefully, paying special attention to the grooves where the blade met the handle and where the handle fitted the sheath. He saw no blood or suspicious marks. The polished metal shone like new, though the blade was not newly forged.

"Very nice," he said as he handed it back. "A family heirloom?"

Sayuri shook her head as she resheathed the dagger and returned it to her kimono. "It was a gift from Mayuri. She carried it when she was an entertainer."

"Tell us again what happened the night Hideyoshi died," Hiro said. "The truth this time."

"I told you the truth yesterday."

Hiro gestured to Father Mateo. "Let's go. We can be halfway to Nagasaki by evening." He glanced at Sayuri as he started for the door. "Good luck with Nobuhide tomorrow. I am sure Father Mateo will pray for your soul."

Sayuri grabbed the Jesuit's arm as he began to rise. "No, wait. I'll tell you everything."

Chapter 31

"A kechi-san visited almost every night since my debut," Sayuri said, "but he was a regular client of the teahouse even before I started as an apprentice.

"Two nights ago, he arrived shortly after sunset. I served him dinner and sake, and afterward I sang and danced. He got very drunk and stayed very late. I wanted him to leave, but he refused to go. He started telling me that he intended to become my exclusive patron." She gave Father Mateo a side-long glance.

"An exclusive patron has rights not available to other men," Hiro explained.

Father Mateo raised a hand and ran it through his hair.

"I hoped it was a lie," Sayuri said. "Mayuri hadn't mentioned it to me. He became insistent, trying to touch me, and I grew scared. That's when I told him I needed to use the latrine and went to see Mayuri. She told me to return to the room and entertain my guest. She did not agree to intervene.

"I went to the latrine and hid there a very long time. Hideyo-shi was so drunk, I didn't think he could stay awake very much longer. When I did return to the room he had fallen asleep. I stayed with him because Mayuri would be angry if I left a guest alone. I fell asleep too, and when I woke up he was dead."

With the exception of the comments about patronage, which Hiro suspected had their roots in honesty, Sayuri told the story without emotion.

"Did you move Hideyoshi's body from where you found him?" he asked.

She shook her head and looked at the floor. "I wouldn't defile myself that way."

"I thought Christians didn't believe in ritual defilement," Hiro said.

She raised her head and met his eye. "I am Japanese as well as Christian, and my clients do not share my faith. I would not ruin my career by touching a corpse."

"Then how did your kimono get so much blood on it?" When Sayuri didn't answer Hiro added, "Perhaps I did not make myself sufficiently clear. I ask, you answer. If you lie, the priest and I go to Nagasaki and you face Nobuhide alone."

Her face crumpled. "I touched him but I didn't move him."

She gestured to the hearth at the center of the room as though she could still see the corpse laid out beside it. This time, the horror on her face was very real. "I saw Akechi-san lying there, covered in blood, and at first I didn't realize he was dead. I shook him and tried to revive him. I swear, I didn't move his body."

"When was the last time you saw Akechi Hidetaro?" Hiro asked.

She flushed and looked at her hands. "I don't remember. Weeks ago."

"How many more lies do you think I will listen to?" Hiro

demanded. "I know he was buying your contract. He was here yesterday—did you see him?"

"Yesterday?" She looked up suddenly. Her lip trembled. "Mayuri didn't tell me."

"When was the last time you saw him?"

Her shoulders slumped. "Two days ago, in the morning. He argued with Mayuri, and left, and then sneaked around the side of the house and told me what had happened." She bit her lower lip. "Mayuri changed the price. She wanted more money and he couldn't afford it, so she told him to go away."

"What changed her mind?" Hiro asked.

Sayuri clasped her hands and rubbed the thumbs together. "I don't know, but I can guess." She looked miserable.

"Then guess," Hiro said.

"I think Hideyoshi did want to become my patron, and he offered Mayuri money to break her contract with Hidetaro. Hideyoshi was rich." She looked up with sudden fire in her eyes. "But Hidetaro is a better man. I'd rather be his wife, and poor, than a rich man's mistress."

"Did Akechi Hideyoshi know about your feelings for his brother?" Hiro asked.

"Yes, but I don't know how. I didn't tell him. He teased me about it the night he died. He said I should be nice to him instead of Hidetaro."

Her eyebrows drew together and her lips pursed at the memory. She gave a little shiver as though trying to forget what she could not unsee.

"Do you think Hidetaro sneaked in here and killed his brother while you slept?"

Sayuri gripped her hands so tightly the knuckles whitened. "No."

"You know your story makes him look guilty," Hiro said.

"No," she repeated. Her chest heaved. "He wouldn't do that. Hidetaro isn't violent, and, more importantly, he wouldn't kill his brother when the blame might fall on me."

"Did anyone else join Hideyoshi in the room the night he died?" Hiro asked.

"Anyone else?" Sayuri repeated. "What do you mean?"

"Visitors, other clients, entertainers . . . anyone at all."

"No." She shook her head. "It was just him and me."

"Did he leave the room at all? To visit the latrine?"

She looked up. "He did visit the latrine. That was early in the evening. He went twice, one short visit and the second time longer." She paused. "The second time was after dinner."

"Was he injured when he returned?" Father Mateo asked. He sounded eager to hear the answer, as though it might provide an important piece of the puzzle.

Hiro wished the priest would reveal less about the expected responses, especially when asking leading questions.

"Not that I noticed," Sayuri said. "Certainly not the way he was later on. That didn't happen in the latrine."

Based on her tone, she wished it had.

"I'm sure you would like to spend some time in prayer," Hiro said.

Father Mateo looked offended. "I was going to suggest that," he said in Portuguese, "but my religion is not a cover act."

"Not for you," Hiro replied in Portuguese, "but I need it to cover me for a little while. Ten minutes should be sufficient."

He slipped out of the room as the priest and Sayuri began to pray. The common room was empty, as was the smaller family room beyond. The women must be upstairs, sleeping or doing whatever they did in the morning hours.

Hiro crossed the smaller common room and entered the narrow hall that led to the stairs and the yard. The little sliding door to the left beckoned as it had on his earlier visit. If Hiro guessed correctly, that door led to Mayuri's office. At least, he hoped it led to the office and not a storeroom or other useless space. His task would be much harder if he had to infiltrate the second floor.

He had wanted to check the office since he discovered that Mayuri had burned her ledgers. The woman might have destroyed all evidence of whatever act she wanted to conceal, but he wouldn't know until he looked for himself.

Hiro crept to the opposite end of the hall and listened. He heard voices upstairs, at least four and all female. They spoke too quietly for him to hear more than simple sounds, but the tones suggested an ongoing conversation rather than one about to end.

He returned to the opposite end of the hall and pressed his ear to the door. He heard nothing. He closed his eyes and opened his lips a fraction to increase his hearing and focus his attention.

Still nothing.

He took a deep breath and slid the paneled door. It whispered open with barely a sound.

As he stepped across the threshold a frigid female voice asked, "What are you doing here?"

Chapter 32

Hiro straightened his shoulders. "Looking for you, Mayuri."

The woman sat at a low, movable desk in the center of the room. Although smaller than the guest rooms at the front of the house, the office was finely apportioned with white tatami of the highest grade and cedar paneling covering two of the walls. A tokonoma just to right of the entrance held an expensive vase, and beyond the alcove cedar doors indicated a floor-to-ceiling storage closet. A cedar chest to the right of the desk most likely held both money and record books, but it was closed, obscuring its contents.

Mayuri's eyebrows knit together in a frown. "This is my private office. You have no right to be here."

Hiro stepped into the room and slid the door closed behind him. He looked at the single, long-stemmed orchid stalk in the decorative vase.

"A lovely arrangement," he said.

Mayuri sniffed. "Riko might amount to something if she

tried, but she doesn't apply herself to flower arrangement. That vase should hold two stalks, not one."

She tilted her head slightly. "But we were not discussing flowers. What is your purpose here? My cooperation does not extend to you creeping around my teahouse and listening at doors."

"Does it extend to explaining your activities on the night of Hideyoshi's murder?" Hiro paused. "I wanted to ask you privately, in deference to your status as the owner of this establishment. If you prefer, we can conduct this interview publicly."

Mayuri raised a hand and patted the back of her elaborately coiffed hair. She forced an embarrassed smile. "This will do, thank you, though I find your question both objectionable and foolish. Why would I have a man killed in my own teahouse?"

"I haven't accused you," Hiro said. "I just asked where you were that night."

"As I believe I mentioned yesterday, I was in this office all evening. I settle each month's accounts on the middle day of the following month. On another night I might have been anywhere, but, since the night in question was the middle of the month, I was here with my ledgers all night."

Hiro found that suspiciously convenient.

"Do you always do your accounting here?" he asked.

"Yes." She gestured to the box beside the writing desk. "I keep all of my records in one place."

"Were you alone all night?"

"Okiya brought me tea and rice before she went upstairs. She can attest that I was here all evening. The only time I left this room was when Sayuri asked me to speak with Hideyoshi."

"Did you speak with him?" Hiro wondered which version of Sayuri's tale Mayuri would confirm.

"I did not." She paused. "When Sayuri came to me, I told her we could not force a paying customer to leave. I intended to leave her to handle the situation, but I heard her crying as she passed the window on her way to the latrine."

Mayuri gestured toward the slatted window near the roofline.

"I decided to speak with Hideyoshi, but I finished totaling a column first so I wouldn't lose my place in the ledger. It took several minutes longer than I expected.

"When I reached Sayuri's room I saw a pair of silhouettes on the door."

She fluttered her fingers in imitation of the flickering shadows cast by a candle flame.

"Hideyoshi was lying on the floor and Sayuri was kneeling over him. She wasn't struggling or complaining, and he was . . . moaning." She tilted her head knowingly. "I left at once, without opening the door. I didn't want to disturb them."

"Was Hideyoshi Sayuri's patron?" Hiro asked. "She claims he was not."

Mayuri stared at him. "Do you know the purchase price of a high-ranked artist's favors?" A slow smile crept over her face. "The price is even higher when patronage is not negotiated in advance."

Her greedy smile reinforced Hiro's silent condemnation of her character. The shinobi had no issue with a voluntary trade of money for sexual favors. Teahouses and the women who worked there played a vital social role. But a woman who saw her entertainers as mere commodities, who would knowingly abandon a girl Sayuri's age to a lecherous patron when another man wanted her as a wife—such a woman could easily commit murder, though Hiro doubted she would wield the blade herself. Hiro considered her callousness the lowest kind of crime. Lower, because it was not a crime at all.

"I see your displeasure," Mayuri said, "but you do not understand our world. Hideyoshi was a good customer and he had the money to pay for what he wanted."

"And his brother?" Hiro asked.

"I thought Hidetaro might plead his case to you," Mayuri said. "This would not be the first time a poor man failed to obtain what he could not afford."

"Indeed, it would not." Hiro bobbed his head. "Thank you for your time."

"What now?" Father Mateo asked as they left the teahouse. "Every time we try to eliminate a potential murderer, we add someone else to the list."

"Two more," Hiro said. "I spoke with Mayuri also."

When they reached the bridge, Hiro started across the river. Father Mateo followed.

"We're not going home?" the Jesuit asked.

"No. We're going to find out why Hidetaro lied about staying home the night his brother died."

Father Mateo looked confused.

"He claimed he was home alone all night, but Yoshiko says he visited with her father in the evening and the mud on his sandals says he was out in the rain."

"He could have walked in mud the following morning," the priest said.

"It rained hard at midnight, but not for long. The ground

had absorbed the water by morning and most of the puddles had dried. Hidetaro might have found a deep one that left some mud on his sandals, but the hem of his robe was soaked with dirty water too. That had to happen at night when the streets were wet."

"Why didn't you mention that to him before?"

"Several reasons. Until a short time ago, I thought the assassin was a spy for Lord Oda. Now I wonder if that spy exists at all."

"Several people saw him," Father Mateo said. "Including the entertainers, who would have known Hidetaro on sight."

"Unless he wore a disguise," Hiro pointed out. "Hidetaro served as a courier for the shogun. His training would have included the use of disguises."

"But the spy bought weapons from Luis. Where did Hidetaro get the money?"

"I haven't worked that piece out yet," Hiro admitted.

"Besides, murdering his brother would make Hidetaro a pauper."

"Would it? Yoshiko intends to obey her father's will, which instructs her to continue her uncle's support."

"But he loved Sayuri," Father Mateo insisted. "Even if you're correct about the rest, why would Hidetaro murder his brother under circumstances that made the girl a suspect?"

"What if he didn't?" Hiro asked. "What if we have the timing wrong?"

"I don't understand." Father Mateo shook his head and shrugged.

"I believe Hideyoshi was dead when Sayuri returned from the latrine."

Chapter 33

"Sayuri said Hideyoshi was alive when she returned to the room," Father Mateo protested. "Why would she lie?"

"Because she knows Hidetaro killed him," Hiro explained.

"But why would Hidetaro kill his brother?" Father Mateo said.

"Yoshiko said they argued about money earlier that evening. I think they did, but they also fought about Sayuri. Hidetaro asked his brother for money to pay off the contract, not realizing Mayuri raised the price because Hideyoshi wanted Sayuri too. When Hideyoshi refused his brother's request, he also explained exactly what he intended to do with the girl Hidetaro loved."

"So Hidetaro followed him to the teahouse and killed him."

"Something very much like that, yes."

A monk at Tofuku-ji told them how to find Hidetaro's house, which lay just north of the temple compound and east of the

Kamo River, at the end of an unpaved earthen road studded with fist-sized stones.

The tiny wooden house sat on a raised foundation with a veranda of split bamboo that had long ago lost its shine. The walls were clean but aging, and where the original timbers had rotted through, replacement boards shone unnaturally bright beside their weathered neighbors.

The buildings on either side were similarly small but in worse repair, likely the homes of servants who worked too hard in their masters' houses to spend much time on their own. It was not the sort of neighborhood where Hiro expected to find a samurai. That, combined with Hidetaro's courier training, reminded Hiro again to make no assumptions.

A pair of nicely pruned cherry trees stood in the yard of Hidetaro's home and framed the front steps with their branches. A worn dirt path connected the road to the house, though instead of a lawn or a garden the front yard was covered with knee-high thistles and weeds.

Hiro was surprised by the disarray. He would have expected a would-be monk to keep the yard tidy and neat.

The priest and the shinobi walked up the path and knocked on the wooden door. Hidetaro opened it almost at once. He must have seen them coming.

"Have you identified Yoshi's killer?" he asked.

"We hope to, if you will help us," Hiro said.

Hidetaro stepped back from the door. "Of course, please come inside."

As they stepped up into the house he asked, "Would you like some tea?"

"No thank you," Hiro said. "We won't be long."

The house was too small to have a separate entry. The

front door opened directly into the central and only room. An alcove in the east corner held a large wooden chest that probably contained Hidetaro's bedding, while his futon would be folded and stored in the built-in closet immediately to the right. The north wall had a combination writing alcove and tokonoma, and the hearth sat almost in the center of the room. In all, the entire house measured barely six mats in size, little larger than Hiro's bedroom at the church.

The house smelled of pine boards and the smoke of pine-fueled fires. A hint of incense lingered in the air, probably brought in on Hidetaro's clothes when he returned from meditation. Hiro inhaled deeply but caught no scent of food or grease or decay, no uncleanliness at all.

The smell reminded Hiro of the training house at Iga that young shinobi used to practice stealth and infiltration. The house was not inhabited by people or permeated by human smells. Hiro had often sneaked inside to sleep there as a child, surrounded by the comforting scents of cedar, paper, and pine.

It was not the way he expected a murderer's house to smell.

Hidetaro led them to the hearth. Hiro deferred to Father Mateo, and the priest took the seat of honor directly to Hidetaro's right. Hiro knelt on the far side of the priest.

"How can I help you?" Hidetaro asked.

Hiro's eyebrows raised at his host's directness.

"Sayuri's time is running out," Hidetaro said. "This is not the time for manners."

"Very well," Hiro said. "When did you learn Hideyoshi intended to become Sayuri's exclusive patron?"

Hidetaro blinked. "I don't know what you're talking about."

Hiro knew he could not learn the truth through questions.

The shogunate had trained Hidetaro to dissemble when his life was on the line. The samurai would expect politeness.

Hiro gave him the opposite.

"I think you do," Hiro said. "I know you argued with Hideyoshi the night he died, and your stained robe says you were out in the rain, not home asleep as you claimed. I know that you wanted Sayuri for your wife and that Mayuri changed the contract price the very day your brother died. She changed it because Hideyoshi wanted Sayuri for himself, but not as a wife—he already had one of those. He wanted her for his whore, and that made you furious, even more because he only wanted her to injure you."

Hidetaro clenched his jaw, inhaled deeply, and released the tension as he exhaled.

"How much more proof would Nobuhide need to find you guilty?" Hiro asked. "Or would you rather let Sayuri take the blame?"

"Tell Nobuhide what you know," Hidetaro said, as calmly as if responding to an inquiry about the weather. "Sayuri will live. I am prepared to die."

Hiro felt a flash of victory that instantly changed to doubt. Hidetaro intended to take responsibility, but his confession was not made in earnest. Guilty men rarely welcomed death so stoically, particularly for crimes of passion, yet Hidetaro looked like one of Father Mateo's much-heralded martyrs marching to his pyre.

The priest apparently thought so too.

"I don't think you killed him," Father Mateo said. "What did you really do that night?"

"I killed my brother," Hidetaro said. "You caught me. In

the morning I will confess to Nobuhide, and Sayuri will live. Tonight, I have nothing more to say."

Hidetaro's confession would save Father Mateo, the Sakura, and perhaps even the shogunate, but the words made Hiro angry instead of pleased. Suspicion of Hidetaro's innocence chewed at Hiro's conscience like a dog at a butcher's bone, and for the first time in his life as a shinobi, Hiro found himself caring more about the truth than about success.

His chest burned with frustration, as much with himself as with Hidetaro. He wanted to accept the confession and walk away, successful as always. Hiro did not fail. He succeeded at any cost. No life, no expense, no principle ever stood in his way . . . except for one.

Hiro would not let an innocent life pay a guilty man's debt.

He realized with bitter irony that a similar choice had landed him in Kyoto, punished with an assignment to protect the foreign priest. It had been the only failure in his spectacular career—and that failure, too, had been spectacular in its way.

Hiro had agreed to help Sayuri only to save the Jesuit's life, but he had also agreed to help find Hideyoshi's killer. He had given his word. That goal was secondary to his oath to protect the priest, but once the shinobi accepted a mission, he did not and would not fail. He couldn't just find a person to take the blame. Until Hiro found Hideyoshi's murderer his conscience would not release him from his pledge.

That didn't keep him from hoping his instincts were wrong, and that Hidetaro really did kill Hideyoshi. Because if Hidetaro wasn't guilty, Hiro had less than eighteen hours to learn who did. And despite Hidetaro's noble offer to take

Sayuri's place, Hiro was not convinced that Nobuhide would accept his uncle's claims of responsibility.

In fact, he found it more likely that Hidetaro's "confession" would trigger the very executions the noble gesture was intended to prevent.

Chapter 34

"Tell us how you killed Hideyoshi," Hiro said.

Father Mateo glared. "Can't you tell he only confessed to save Sayuri's life?"

"If he wants to take the blame he can explain how he committed the crime." Hiro looked at Hidetaro. "Or, if he wants us to find the real murderer, he can explain what really happened the night his brother died."

Hidetaro breathed in and out at a measured pace that Hiro recognized as a Zen technique for reducing stress and clearing a cluttered mind. The samurai did not fidget, or even move, but the breathing revealed his internal conflict.

Hiro gave him time to make up his mind.

At last Hidetaro nodded. "I will help you for the remainder of today. Tomorrow, if you have not found the killer, I will confess in order to save Sayuri's life."

"You love her enough to die for her?" Hiro wondered what that felt like.

"All men die," Hidetaro said, "most, for no valid reason. At least this death will not be meaningless."

"But you may not need to die at all," Father Mateo said. "Tell us what happened the night your brother died."

"That story begins earlier in the day," Hidetaro said. "The day before yesterday, in the morning, I visited the Sakura Teahouse to make a payment on Sayuri's contract. It was the middle day of the month, and I always made my payments on the middle day and the last day."

He gave an embarrassed smile, like a little boy caught in a lie. "I originally told you that I made that payment the morning my brother died, which wasn't true, though I did go to the teahouse that morning. Mayuri told me about the murder—though it wasn't Mayuri I expected to see."

He paused. "It's better if I continue in proper order.

"On the morning before Hideyoshi died I went to the teahouse to make a payment. Mayuri would not accept my silver. She said another man had offered a much larger sum for patronage alone. Mayuri intended to keep the girl in the teahouse after all.

"I demanded to know the patron's identity and the amount he had offered to pay. She named an astronomical sum—a thousand gold koban."

Hiro's eyes widened in surprise. Father Mateo looked confused, so Hiro explained. "One koban is the equivalent of three koku of rice. A thousand koban would feed an army for a year."

"Mayuri had to be lying," Hidetaro said. "No man would pay so much for a woman's favors."

"I agree," Hiro said, "but why would Mayuri lie?"

"I think she needed to make the sum so high that I couldn't match it. Even so, I decided I had to try. I spent the day meditating in order to crush my pride, and in the evening I went to see Yoshi. We spoke in private, in his personal armory. I knelt before him and asked him to buy Sayuri's contract for me. I swore that if he granted this request I would never ask him for anything again, not even a grain of rice."

"But Hideyoshi didn't have that kind of wealth," Father Mateo said.

Hidetaro drew back in surprise. "He must have had it. He was the patron whose name Mayuri wouldn't mention."

"How did you learn that?" Hiro asked.

"Yoshi didn't just deny my request for help. He laughed in my face and called me a fool for falling in love with a prostitute.

"That was his word," Hidetaro added quickly, "not ever mine."

Father Mateo nodded in understanding as the samurai continued. "Yoshi told me he had bought Sayuri's favors for himself. He said he would think of me when he deflowered her."

Hidetaro's fists clenched at his sides. He closed his eyes and slowed his breathing again. He did not speak until his demeanor and voice were calm.

"When Yoshi finished laughing he handed me a dagger from his collection. He suggested I use it to commit seppuku, since it was the last thing I would ever receive from his hand."

"Did you find a better use for it than ritual suicide?" Hiro asked.

"I wanted to, and if Yoshi were not my brother I would have killed him on the spot, but I didn't. I threw the knife away as hard as I could.

"It struck the tokonoma and knocked over the display." Hidetaro gave a bitter laugh at the memory. "The *neko-te* flew everywhere and the *tessen* fell to the floor. Yoshi started cursing and I heard Nobuhide laugh, but I left the room and didn't look back."

"Nobuhide saw you throw the knife?" Hiro asked.

Hidetaro nodded. "He came into the room to ridicule me about my choice of wife. He must have overheard."

The conversation lagged for a moment. Hiro waited for the samurai to continue, but decided not to prompt. He wanted to know where Hidetaro would pick up the tale.

"On the way home I thought about killing Yoshi. I wanted to, and almost decided to, but then I had a better idea, one that would give me Sayuri and revenge on Yoshi too." He smiled. "I would persuade Sayuri to run away with me."

"With no money?" Hiro asked.

Hidetaro shrugged. "I have a shogunate travel pass, a permanent one from my courier days. There are plenty of daimyo in need of retainers, and I suspect you already know how easily a ronin can find work if his pride doesn't get in the way.

"No offense intended."

Hiro nodded. "None taken. Please continue."

"I waited at home until dark and went to the teahouse. I sneaked around the veranda to Sayuri's room, but Hideyoshi had already arrived. I listened to them from the shadows and waited for an opportunity.

"Twice I had to hide around the corner while Hideyoshi went to the latrine. I considered approaching Sayuri then, but I couldn't risk Yoshi catching us before we could get away.

"As the evening grew late, Hideyoshi got drunk and tried to persuade Sayuri to undress. It didn't take her long to understand what he had in mind. She sounded frightened—I almost ran into the room and killed him after all.

"If he had forced himself on her I would have."

Hidetaro fell silent. Father Mateo opened his mouth to speak but caught himself and said nothing.

A moment later Hidetaro continued. "I heard Sayuri mention the latrine, so I ran into the yard and hid behind the latrine to wait, but she didn't come outside for several minutes."

That matched Hiro's understanding of the events. Sayuri spoke with Mayuri before visiting the latrine.

"When she finally arrived, I revealed myself and asked her to run away with me."

"But she refused to go," Hiro said.

"Actually, she said she would, but she was afraid of Yoshi. She was terrified that he would follow us and kill us. She also said that Yoshi claimed to own her contract already. I told her that wasn't true, and a magistrate would uphold my claim because I had been making payments for several months. I told her I would see Mayuri immediately and force her to accept my claim."

"You knew she wouldn't," Hiro said.

"It was late. Sayuri was crying. I had to do something. Sayuri wouldn't let me talk with Mayuri. She said she had already tried, to no avail. But then she said something very strange. She said that Yoshi claimed he could have any girl in the Sakura, any time, and as often as he wanted."

"If Sayuri was so scared, why didn't she leave with you?" Hiro asked.

"She was afraid Yoshi would sound the alarm and catch us. Also, her kimono belonged to the teahouse, and Mayuri could have her arrested as a thief if she ran away wearing it.

"We decided Sayuri would hide in the latrine until Yoshi fell asleep and then run away with me in the morning, after he left."

"Where did you go after that?" Hiro asked.

"I walked home. It took over an hour. The rainstorm

started shortly after I left the Sakura, so I took shelter under a tree and waited it out."

"Can anyone confirm your story?" Hiro asked.

"Actually, yes," Hidetaro said. "Just before the rain started I noticed a samurai following me. The figure stayed in the shadows, trying to avoid notice, which of course made his efforts that much more obvious. I pretended to turn a corner and ducked behind a wall. When the figure passed, I jumped out and grabbed him. Or, more properly, her—it was Yoshiko."

"Yoshiko?" Hiro asked.

"She overheard me arguing with her father and followed me to ensure I didn't harm him."

"Did she hear you talking with Sayuri?" Hiro asked.

"I worried about that at first," Hidetaro admitted, "but she said she didn't. She apparently hid just inside the garden wall. She saw me waiting outside the room and going to the latrine, but she didn't even know I had talked with Sayuri."

"How can that be?" Hiro asked.

Hidetaro thought aloud. "The latrine is partly hidden behind the teahouse, and Sayuri approached it from that side— she left the teahouse through the back door, not the veranda door that led directly to her room. I was hiding behind the latrine, and Sayuri joined me there for our conversation, so a person standing at the garden gate would not have seen us."

"But that person would have seen any shadows on the wall of Sayuri's room, or a killer on the veranda after the murder," Father Mateo offered.

Hidetaro shook his head. "Only if the murder occurred while Sayuri and I were talking. I left as soon as Sayuri entered the latrine, and Yoshiko followed."

Hiro stood up and bowed. "Thank you for your time and your honesty."

"When I thought Sayuri and I might escape together, I was prepared to say anything to convince you of our innocence," Hidetaro said as he walked them to the door. "If we cannot both escape Nobuhide's anger, I will say what I must to save her."

Chapter 35

Hiro and Father Mateo walked back through the city as the sky turned pale and the clouds glowed orange with sunset.

"Well, I guess Hidetaro wasn't disguised as the rice merchant after all," Father Mateo said, then added, "We can't let him take the blame if he isn't guilty."

"Don't worry," Hiro replied, "Nobuhide won't let him. Hidetaro wants to save Sayuri's life, but Nobuhide will see through his story at once. Only the real killer will divert his sword."

They crossed the Kamo River at Shijō Road, but Hiro did not turn north toward the church.

"Why are we going back to the teahouse?" Father Mateo asked. "Mayuri won't like it."

Hiro smiled. "I know."

When Mayuri answered the door she didn't even try to hide her irritation. "This is a place of business, not a Tokaido way station! How can I earn a living with you barging in and out?"

"This will all be over tomorrow, one way or another," Hiro said, "but we need to speak with Sayuri one more time."

"One time," Mayuri said, "and then no more."

She led them into the house.

A delicate smell of steaming rice and grilling meat lingered in Hiro's nostrils, where it mingled with the fainter scents of flowers and perfume—the smell of a teahouse preparing to welcome its guests.

Shamisen music floated through the air. Each note rose, wavered, and died away like a blossom blooming and falling from a tree. Hiro recognized this song too. It told of loss and death and endings, and the melody evoked those thoughts so perfectly that he didn't need to guess who played it or what inspired the choice.

Sayuri sat with her back to the door. She cradled her shamisen lovingly in her arms and did not bother to turn or look behind her when the door rustled open. Hiro and Father Mateo waited until she finished her song and laid the shamisen carefully on the floor.

Then she turned and her mouth fell open in surprise.

Mayuri closed the door with a gentle rattle, leaving them alone.

"Akechi Hidetaro sends his regards," Hiro said, "and best wishes for a happy future."

Sayuri scowled. "Why do you mock me?"

"I am not mocking," Hiro said. "His death will save you. You no longer have reason to fear."

"Death?" The word came out as a strangled whisper. "No. He didn't kill anyone."

"I doubt Nobuhide will find your words persuasive," Hiro lied, "particularly when he hears Hidetaro's confession."

"How could he confess? He didn't kill Hideyoshi."

"He claims he did, and his story sounds persuasive. He hated Hideyoshi, and Nobuhide knows they argued about you."

Sayuri raised her hand to her throat. "He didn't do it. I can prove his innocence."

"I do not believe you," Hiro said. "A woman's lies will not keep Hidetaro alive."

Sayuri looked down at her lap. When she looked up again, her eyes were full of tears. Her forehead wrinkled and her nose turned red in a futile effort to hold them back, but they ran down her cheeks as she spoke.

"Hideyoshi didn't just want me to sing the night he died. He wanted . . . everything. A patron's rights, even though he was not my patron. I didn't want to. I told him no, but he was so drunk and so strong. I knew I couldn't stop him. That's why I asked Mayuri to intervene."

"But she refused," Hiro said.

Sayuri raised a hand and wiped her cheek. "I was afraid, if Hideyoshi had his way, Hidetaro wouldn't want me anymore.

"When Mayuri wouldn't help I decided I would hide in the latrine until Hideyoshi fell asleep, but when I got there I found Hidetaro waiting. He wanted me to run away with him, but I was too scared to go. I thought Hideyoshi would follow us and kill Hidetaro. I couldn't let that happen. In the end, we decided that I would hide for the rest of the night and we would run away in the morning."

"How long did you hide in the latrine?" Hiro asked.

"I don't really know." Sayuri shook her head and wiped her cheek to stop a tear. Her crying had stopped except for a few stray droplets. "I stayed there as long as it took the moon to move a handsbreadth in the sky. I watched until it rose above the top of the slatted window, and then I waited a few more minutes."

She took a deep breath. "When I returned to the room, Hideyoshi was dead. His legs were still kneeling but his head and shoulders had fallen back onto the floor.

"There was so much blood . . ."

She paused and then continued. "I couldn't stand looking at his contorted body so I pulled it to the mattress. That's how the blood got on my kimono.

"I was frightened. I assumed Hidetaro killed Hideyoshi while I hid in the latrine. I went to the veranda, but no one was there. As I shut the door I realized I had Hideyoshi's blood all over my socks. I took them off and hid them in my kimono. I don't know why. I wasn't thinking very clearly."

"What did you do then?" Hiro asked.

"I sat in the corner, as far away from the body as I could get, and waited for morning. I made up the story about falling asleep to explain why I didn't call for help as soon as I found the body."

"Why didn't you call out?"

"I wanted to give Hidetaro time to get away."

"Yet now you claim he is innocent," Hiro said.

"I had time to think while I sat with Hideyoshi's body," Sayuri said. "I realized Hidetaro could not have done it. Well, wouldn't have anyway. Why would he murder his brother and risk someone blaming me when we intended to run away the following morning?"

Before Hiro could reply the door slid open.

"My guests are arriving," Mayuri said, "and I must ask you to leave. I apologize for the inconvenience."

Her smile negated the apology, but Hiro had finished questioning Sayuri anyway.

The men walked home in silence as the sky grew black and the stars appeared. As they approached the church Father Mateo asked, "Shouldn't we talk with Yoshiko? To see if she will confirm Hidetaro's story?"

"Not yet," Hiro said. "She had several chances to offer that information, but didn't, which suggests she has something to hide."

Before the priest could respond, the door to the church swung open. A backlit figure in a Portuguese doublet and leggings stood silhouetted in the entrance. The figure laid its hands on its hips in a show of exasperation.

"It's about time you got here," Luis fumed. "I found your missing spy."

Chapter 36

Luis led them into the house and pointed to the hearth.

A bald man with a long mustache sat cross-legged on the tatami, drinking tea from a porcelain cup. He wore no visible sword and his padded kimono was cut in provincial lines. A thin growth of stubble covered the back and sides of his head, but the new growth on his pate was slightly longer, suggesting more frequent shaving of that area over time.

The stranger didn't look up as Hiro and Father Mateo entered and said nothing as the other men joined him around the hearth.

Hiro arranged his kimono carefully to ensure it would not interfere if he had to jump to his feet. Lord Oda's spies had no reason to return to Kyoto unless they wanted to eliminate witnesses. Luis had made a colossally stupid decision in bringing the stranger home.

Hiro actually would have preferred it if the merchant ran away after all.

"May I introduce the missing spy from the teahouse," Luis said with a flamboyant gesture.

The bald stranger looked up. "I am Akechi Mitsuhide."

Hiro was stunned.

Father Mateo's mouth fell open. His lips flapped like a fish tossed on a riverbank.

Hiro recovered first. "How can this be?"

Luis waggled his shoulders and preened with a self-satisfaction that Hiro would find unbearable on any other day.

"I went after him, of course. There's only one major road between here and Nagoya, and he had four carts full of rice and weapons. It was easy to overtake him."

"How did you know who he was?" Father Mateo asked.

At the same time, Hiro said, "You actually went after a murderer?"

"Well, I didn't know he was a murderer," Luis said. "But if so, I could hardly let him get away, especially since it meant Mateo's life."

After a short, uncomfortable silence in which Luis seemed to realize he had done something more valiant than he intended, the merchant added, "It also would have ruined my business."

"How did you convince him to return?" Hiro asked.

"I offered," Mitsuhide said. "I owe my cousin that much at least."

"You didn't murder him," Hiro said. "If you had, you wouldn't be here."

"True, but I may have seen his killer. I will tell you what I know, on two conditions."

He paused. Father Mateo started to agree at once, but Hiro silenced the priest with a look and gave a noncommittal nod instead.

Mitsuhide apparently found that acceptable.

"I left Kyoto several months ago to join another daimyo," he said. "Men may call me a traitor for that, but my reasons are my own and not relevant to this discussion. I will say no more about it, and you will not ask. That is my first condition."

Mitsuhide's eyes held a challenge. Hiro gave a miniscule nod of assent.

"Second," Mitsuhide said, "I will not remain to speak with my brother's family. I will tell you what I know and leave at once. What you do with my information is your business, but I warn you that my name will earn you no friends, even among the Akechi clan. You will not follow me or try to stop me.

"That is the second condition."

"Assuming you tell the truth and do no harm to anyone in this house, those conditions are acceptable," Hiro said.

Mitsuhide nodded. "I returned to Kyoto two days ago to obtain additional weapons for Lord Oda. I shaved my head and disguised myself as a merchant to avoid discovery, but I decided to risk a meeting with Hideyoshi on the night before I left. It was foolish, but blood is blood." He paused. "Perhaps that was not the best choice of expression.

"I made an appointment at the Sakura Teahouse because I knew Hideyoshi spent his evenings there. I requested a girl whose name I did not recognize and gave her a gold koban, hoping the wealth would dazzle her so she wouldn't remember me well."

"It worked," Hiro said with a smile. "She found you boring."

Mitsuhide laughed. "As I intended. Boring men are difficult to remember.

"The girl entertained me in the front room on the west side of the teahouse. It shared a wall with Hideyoshi's room."

"Did you speak with him?" Hiro asked.

"Yes," Mitsuhide said, "in the latrine, after dinner. He was not pleased to see me. He told me to do what I had to do and go, and not to contact him or his family again."

"Not surprising," Father Mateo said.

"He understood my reasons for joining Lord Oda," Mitsuhide countered. "He only objected because I asked to take Nobuhide with me. The boy is wasted as a *yoriki*. I could have made him a real samurai. But Hideyoshi refused to let Nobuhide go, and I accepted his decision. I told him I would not ask again.

"I returned to my room and finished my sake. I intended to leave fairly early but the girl was attractive and sang moderately well, so I stayed later than intended. I left the teahouse shortly after midnight and headed for Pontocho, to find a sake shop where I could pass the hours until my meeting with the Portuguese merchant."

"Luis," Luis corrected. "Luis Álvares."

"As I left the Sakura, I noticed someone hiding in the shadows by the garden gate."

"In front of the gate or behind it?" Father Mateo asked.

Hiro approved of the question.

"In front," Mitsuhide said. "I pretended not to notice because I didn't want a fight."

Merchants didn't carry swords, but Hiro suspected Mitsuhide had other weapons concealed beneath his padded robe. Hiro would have too, in his place. He also would have been loathe to expose them or attract attention if he didn't have to.

"I walked a little way down the road," Mitsuhide said, "keeping my eye on the shadows in case I was followed, but as soon as I passed the woman went into the teahouse instead."

"Woman?" Father Mateo asked. "The person hiding in the bushes was a woman?"

"I only saw her from behind," Mitsuhide said, "and most of the lanterns were already out so I couldn't see her in detail, but she was wearing her kimono with the obi tied in front."

"A prostitute?" Hiro asked.

"No one else wears an obi that way," Mitsuhide confirmed. "That's why I noticed. At the time I thought she was sneaking in so no one would know she had strayed and stayed out so late. But when I heard about Hideyoshi's murder I wondered if she might have been the assassin, or at least another witness who might have seen something—if you can identify her."

"Quite possibly," Hiro said.

"Thank you for coming all this way back to tell us," Father Mateo said. "You may have saved two lives."

"I have one more question," Hiro asked. "Did Hideyoshi have a source of income other than his stipend from the shogun?"

"If he did, I never heard about it," Mitsuhide said, "though it wouldn't surprise me. Teahouses are expensive, and Hideyoshi spent a lot of time there. Then again, we didn't know each other well and I didn't visit often. We would hardly have discussed his financial status."

Mitsuhide stood up and stretched his legs. "Thank you for your hospitality. Now, as we agreed, I must go."

"Don't you want to rest?" Father Mateo asked. "We can give you a place to sleep."

Mitsuhide smiled like an indulgent parent trying not to laugh at a child's mistake. "I think I had better go. Any lives my information saved would be lost, and then some, if the shogun's retainers learn that I was here."

Chapter 37

Hiro walked Mitsuhide to the door and returned to the hearth just in time to hear Father Mateo ask, "Have you any idea how big a risk you took?"

"Hardly a risk." Luis sneered. "These Japanese know their emperor would cut off their heads in an instant if they harmed me. Besides, they all know I'm armed and I'm better with a firearm than they are."

Luis's eyes shifted from the priest to the fire as his hands fidgeted in his lap. Hiro was impressed by the merchant's unusually self-effacing attitude.

But the moment didn't last.

"Even you should be able to find the murderer now," Luis told Hiro, "since someone else has solved the hard parts for you."

"Perhaps I can," Hiro said drily. "One more question, though. What made you so certain the merchant was not the killer? You wouldn't have gone after him otherwise."

Not even Luis was that stupid, though Hiro kept that part to himself.

"He seemed too familiar," Luis said. "He claimed we had never met before, but he wasn't scared and he didn't stare like most of my customers do. At the time I just considered him a conniving, self-interested bastard, like any other merchant worth his salt, but when you pointed out the illegible seal and told me about the murder I realized I had seen him before. He looked different with his hair cut and wearing that moth-eaten robe, but yesterday evening I realized who he was—and guessed that he wouldn't have killed his cousin. Even samurai tempers have their limits."

"Why didn't you tell us before you left?" Father Mateo asked. "I thought . . ."

Luis sniffed. "You thought I fled for my life. Really, Mateo. I expect that of him"—he nodded at Hiro—"but not of you."

"You did take the imperial pass."

"I couldn't get through the barricades without it. I am sorry I didn't mention my departure but I didn't want to raise your hopes. I might not have found him, or he might have been the wrong man after all."

Someone knocked on the door. Ana bustled through from the kitchen, disappeared into the foyer, and returned a moment later.

"It's a fisherman, come to speak with Father Mateo." She sighed, tossed her hands, and returned to the kitchen muttering, "Hm. Come to pray at all hours, without even the decency to bring us a fish or two."

Father Mateo excused himself, and Hiro took the opportunity to leave the self-satisfied Luis preening by the hearth. The shinobi still didn't like the merchant, but he recognized the possibility of admirable qualities even in detestable individuals, and perhaps he also loathed Luis just a shade less than before.

Hiro went to his room and retrieved the scraps of paper from the teahouse ledgers. He set them on his writing desk and gazed at them idly as he considered what he knew about the murder. As his thoughts shifted from one fact to another, he suddenly found himself smiling. Despite the risk to himself and to Father Mateo, investigating the murder had let him use skills that he hadn't needed since coming to Kyoto, skills that had once defined him and kept him alive. He practiced every morning to keep his abilities sharp, but Hiro had missed the excitement of putting his life on the line.

As he sat lost in thought, a tiny black paw snaked onto the desk and snatched a ledger page.

"Hey!"

The theft brought Hiro back to the present in a flash. The tiny kitten streaked across the floor with the paper in her mouth. In the doorway she turned, rear legs swinging wide as her furry paws slipped on the highly polished floor, but she regained traction and disappeared in an instant.

Hiro jumped up and gave chase.

He reached the door as the kitten rounded the corner into Father Mateo's room. The door stood open, and Hiro barely had time to realize that the priest might have a parishioner with him before he, too, was standing in the doorway.

Fortunately, the room was empty except for the priest and the overexcited kitten, who gave a splay-legged leap across Father Mateo's futon before racing for the open veranda door. The priest sat cross-legged on the floor, looking out at the darkened garden with his back to the room, and did not see the kitten coming.

She leaped onto his shoulder, into his lap, and then pattered out into the night.

Hiro sighed. "Sorry. She had a paper. I guess it's gone."

"You mean this?" Father Mateo turned around and held up the scrap of paper. It was damp along one edge but still intact.

He chuckled, then sneezed. "She was too busy escaping from you to notice me, and it cost her the prize."

He extended the paper but Hiro shook his head slowly. "I don't need it anymore. I already know the answer."

Father Mateo frowned at the scrap. "Isn't this one of the ledger fragments from the Sakura?" He looked up, startled. "You know who the murderer is? When did you figure it out?"

Hiro smiled. "A minute ago. You gave me the final clue."

"I did? What was it?"

"I'll tell you in the morning. I have one more problem to solve tonight."

Father Mateo stood up. "Then let's get going."

"Not you," Hiro said. "I need to do this alone."

"You can't just leave me here to do nothing."

"Do you believe that god of yours answers prayers?" Hiro asked.

"He does. It isn't just a matter of belief."

"Then get on your knees and pray," Hiro said, "but wake me before you go to sleep."

Hiro returned to his room and lay down. He would not get much sleep that night, and years of training had taught him to rest when he could.

Hiro woke up the moment Father Mateo stepped through the door of the room.

The shinobi sat up, immediately alert. "Time?"

"An hour past midnight."

"Excellent. Thank you."

"I still think I should go with you."

"Impossible," Hiro said. "This is something I need to do alone."

"Are you going to assassinate Nobuhide?"

Hiro raised his eyebrows in mock surprise. "That's not a bad idea. Do you mind?"

"Of course I mind! You don't solve a murder by committing another one."

"I don't know," Hiro mused. "Eliminating Nobuhide would solve a lot of problems."

Father Mateo frowned. "Are you joking? I thought you were but suddenly I can't tell. I forbid you to kill Nobuhide."

"Calm down. I'm not planning to kill anyone tonight, though if my errand goes as planned, by noon tomorrow Nobuhide won't be a problem for us—or for Sayuri—anymore."

Chapter 38

Hiro changed from his kimono into a set of baggy black trousers and a dark blue hooded tunic that tied in the front like a kimono. Unlike a normal surcoat this one had narrow sleeves and was belted with a special girdle. Instead of his usual obi, he used a long piece of cloth sewn into a tube. Concealed inside the tube was a *kaginawa*, a small grappling hook on a length of cord. Hiro tucked a second length of cloth around his waist and fastened it to the obi. It would serve as a mask when he reached his destination.

Hiro tucked his hood into the back of the tunic, where it disappeared inside a special pocket designed for that purpose.

He opened a wooden chest beside his desk and carefully removed the papers stacked inside. When the chest was emptied he pressed on the false wooden bottom to reveal a secret compartment where he stored special weapons. Shinobi weapons. They glimmered in the candlelight as Hiro selected the ones he wanted.

Five *shuriken*, or throwing stars, could serve as either projectiles or a fist load in the case of hand-to-hand combat. They went into the inside pockets of his tunic sleeves. A handful of four-pronged *tetsubishi* caltrops joined the *shuriken,* along with a pair of *shuko,* three-pronged climbing claws that fitted over the wrists for scaling walls. As Hiro knew from other occasions, they were also useful weapons at close range.

He bypassed the other weapons and replaced the false bottom of the chest, seating it carefully to ensure a proper fit. He returned the papers to their places, retrieved his swords and a pair of daggers from the holder on the wall, and fastened a small leather pouch around his waist. The pouch held fire tools, a length of rope, and a *kairo,* a piece of treated bamboo Hiro used for holding coals, heating water, or anything else that came to mind.

He checked everything twice to make sure he hadn't overlooked anything he might need. As it happened, he doubted he would need the tools, but it was better to have them all than to die for want of any one of them.

Then it was time to go.

Outside, the moon looked like a giant golden koban, hanging high and full in the sky.

Hiro preferred to work in the dark of the moon, but he couldn't choose the timing of this assignment. He set off at the confident pace of a samurai on an evening errand.

He passed the temple, turned left at the Kamo River road, and walked south along the river toward Pontocho. He didn't see a single soul on the road, and only a few lights still glowed in the houses near the river. A breeze rippled the water and wafted a slightly fishy odor through the air. Hiro smelled the trees and some kind of night-blooming flower in the distance, along with a rancid undertone, probably from scrap and nightsoil buckets.

As he walked, he thought about Iga. Eighteen months was

not very long, and also an eternity. He missed his friends and relatives there, and until a couple of days ago he had wanted only to earn his way home. That hadn't changed, exactly, but for the first time he saw his current assignment as something other than a punishment. Had he not been shinobi, Father Mateo almost certainly would have died.

Half a mile north of Sanjō Road, Hiro left the path and disappeared into the shadows beneath the trees. Most of the houses on this side of the river had walled gardens, and Hiro walked close to the wall to avoid being seen. When he reached the last house before Sanjō Road, he removed the cloth from his obi and wrapped it around his face. He pulled up his hood and climbed up into a cherry tree that stood by the wall with its branches growing over into the yard.

Once up the tree, Hiro removed his katana and tied it carefully to a branch where no one would see it from the ground. Although necessary to his disguise, the longsword was a liability to stealth.

His hands found the hidden drawstrings inside his sleeves and drew the cuffs tight around his wrists. He did the same with the cuffs of his trousers.

With his clothes secured, Hiro continued up the tree until he perched about three feet above the eaves of the house adjacent to the tree. Unlike the Akechis', this house lacked a careful gardener, and the cherry tree's spreading branches extended several feet over the roof.

Hiro stretched himself along a branch and slithered away from the trunk. His weight lowered the branch until it rested against the roof. When the leaves touched the eaves, Hiro slowed his movements to ensure the limb would not rustle and alert the home's inhabitants.

He saw no lights, but that did not mean that everyone was asleep.

When he reached the roof, Hiro stepped from the branch without a sound and slowly eased the limb back up to its original position. He didn't dislodge a single leaf.

Hiro squatted on the roof and listened. He heard no sound from the house below and saw no lanterns or other light. After a couple of minutes, Hiro climbed to the peak of the sloping roof. He kept his body low to minimize his profile against the sky.

He saw no one in the street and no movement in the yard. The next house to the east had its shutters drawn. Its owners had also gone to bed.

Hiro jumped from the east side of the roof to a spreading pine in the neighbors' yard. The needles smelled sharp and fresh in his nose, and the bark felt reassuringly rough and stable under his hands after climbing the cherry tree. Pines were much easier to climb.

It took him only moments to traverse the pine and jump lightly to the roof of the second house. He moved more slowly up the ridge of the second roof because from its peak he would be able to see the Sakura Teahouse—and anyone in the teahouse yard would be able to see him too.

He crouched low behind the ridgepole that ran the length of the roof. Rough thatch poked at the soles of his slippers and jabbed at the knees of his trousers.

The continuing smell of pine told Hiro that he had touched or rubbed some sap onto his clothes. In Iga, that would mean failure, but fortunately this was not a training exercise. The flowers and perfumes of the Sakura would more than overwhelm a spot or two of pitch.

He eased himself over the ridge of the roof and looked down at the teahouse.

The shutters were open and lights shone brightly in the windows of every room on the lower floor, though the windows of the upper floor were dark.

Hiro moved along the roof toward the pair of large, spreading cherry trees that grew beside the teahouse latrine. As he remembered, their questing branches reached over the wall, not quite all the way to the neighboring roof but close enough for his purposes.

He crouched and sprang. The six-foot gap opened wide beneath him but he kept his eyes on his target and a moment later he felt the prickly bark beneath his fingers. He grabbed hold, relaxing his muscles to finish the fall without breaking the branch.

Less than a minute after he landed in the tree, a door slid open on the near side of the house and a portly samurai staggered onto the veranda. A tinkling female laugh followed him out into the night. It sounded like Riko, though Hiro couldn't tell for certain.

The samurai turned and laughed back into the room, then stepped off the porch and waddled toward the latrine. His gait wavered slightly, drunk but not quite beyond control. Hiro watched him pass beneath the other side of the tree and enter the latrine.

When the samurai had gone, Hiro moved silently through the branches until he reached a place where the leaves grew thick enough to hide in.

There he waited.

A few minutes later the drunken samurai finished in the latrine and returned to the teahouse. A feminine laugh greeted him and a kneeling figure slid the door closed behind him. Their shadows retreated farther into the room until Hiro saw only candlelight flickering on the paper panels.

The moon continued its circuit through the sky.

Some time later Hiro heard a murmur of voices on the front porch of the teahouse, or perhaps out in the street. A woman called "good night," and a lower male voice replied with indistinct words. Someone was leaving. The candles still burned in the samurai's room, so Hiro guessed another guest had departed for the night.

Moments later a light flickered in the upstairs rooms. It was pale at first, but grew, like someone bringing a lantern up a flight of stairs. It extinguished itself before it grew distinct, suggesting that the bearer had come upon a room of sleepers and didn't want to wake them. Hiro waited but the light did not reappear.

He leaned against his branch and watched the lights in the samurai's room. He had only until dawn, but the moon was still high. He could almost hear his father's voice reminding him that impatience was the enemy of stealth—a lesson the bullies of Iga had taught him all too well, and that he had repaid in full once he had learned to master patience and surprise.

Another hour passed and the final visitor departed. Hiro heard his drunken laughter in the street. He wondered what the neighbors thought about the teahouse's late-night revels and if they ever learned to ignore the raucous shouts of departing samurai.

A moment later the last candle went out in the downstairs room. The ground floor faded into darkness. A minute later, a light bobbed into the upstairs window. It disappeared as quickly as the one before. Hiro barely saw a woman's form silhouetted against the paper panels before the entire house went dark. Only the lanterns outside the latrine still burned.

Hiro waited. He watched the teahouse and the moon. He listened to crickets singing in chorus and a frog burping at the edge of an unseen pond. A brave cicada hissed in a tree, too early and out of season for the fourth month of the year.

A cloud slid across the sky. A second one joined it, and they combined into a single mass of gray. As the cloud approached the moon Hiro flexed his muscles, limbering them to move.

The moonlight dimmed, then faded as the cloud slipped over the pale disc. Hiro slithered down the tree trunk and scurried across the yard, keeping low and moving fast to avoid detection. By the time the moon reappeared, the shinobi was gone.

Hiro crouched at the edge of the wall beside the back door of the teahouse. The paper panels were dark and opaque with no movement or light within. He laid a hand on the door, lifted slightly to reduce its rumble against the wooden tracks, and pushed it open just far enough to slip through. Once inside, he closed the door without a sound.

To his left, the now-familiar hallway led to the staircase and the second floor. To the right lay his objective: Mayuri's office.

Chapter 39

Hiro glanced down the hallway toward the staircase. A faint, flickering light indicated a candle burning at the top of the stairs. Someone was still awake, which made his errand dangerous, but Hiro decided not to risk returning to the yard. With Nobuhide's guards on duty, and likely to use the latrine at any time, he didn't want to cross the yard again until he had to.

He turned to his right and walked to the office door, using the heel-up *nuki-ashi* step that prevented floors from creaking.

Once inside the office, he opened the chest where Mayuri kept her records. As he expected, several brand-new ledgers sat at the top of the pile. He pulled a candle, flint, and metal shield from his pouch, then lit the candle, and placed it inside the shield so that only a sliver of light remained. He lifted the first of the record books, held it before the light, and began to read.

The book recorded the business transactions of the Sakura Teahouse, mostly lists of names and fees, but the book was dated three years ago, and the numbers were much lower than the ones on the partly burned pages Hiro had rescued from the fire.

As he leafed through the pages, he noticed the heading "Akechi Hideyoshi" appeared on both the pages that tracked individual client accounts and also the ones where the teahouse's monthly receipts were tallied. Hiro's training in accounting was only rudimentary, but even he could tell what the columns meant.

Akechi Hideyoshi owned an interest in the teahouse.

Hiro paused. He had sensed the noise more than heard it, the slightest creak of a wooden step, like a house settling on its raised foundation. Or a stealthy foot on a staircase.

Hiro took no chances.

He replaced the book, closed the chest without a sound, and extinguished his candle. He stood in the darkness and listened.

A faint rustling reached his ears, barely audible in the sleeping silence of the house. He moved toward the built-in cupboard at the back of the room. The paneled door was exactly where he remembered and it slid open beneath his hand with barely a whisper. He squinted into the darkness, looking for a hiding place.

A wooden shelf divided the eight-foot closet in half horizontally. The upper compartment held shelves full of teapots and sake flasks. The lower one held thin futons and a number of quilted blankets. Fortunately, that compartment was only half full. It had just enough empty space for a person to squeeze inside.

Hiro tucked the candle and shield into his pouch, climbed into the cupboard, and slid the door closed behind him.

Not a minute later, the office door slid open. Light flickered under the cupboard door and flared in the cracks around the edges. Rustling silk suggested movement, but whoever entered the room moved almost as silently as a shinobi on the prowl.

Hiro heard nothing for a minute and then the wooden chest opened and closed with a click. A book thumped lightly on the desk and an ink stick scraped against the surface of a stone inkwell.

It was neither the middle day of the month nor the usual time for Mayuri to do accounting. Whatever she was working on, she wanted to do it in secret.

Hiro settled in for a wait, but not a tense one. Discovery was unlikely. If Mayuri had heard him in the room she would have opened the cabinet at once, since no other place could conceal a human figure. She would not have commenced her secret work if she suspected an intruder, and, unless Hiro moved or made a noise, she was unlikely to discover him at all.

Compared with the other places he had spent hidden nights, the cupboard was as large and as safe as his room at the church.

He heard nothing for some time. A writing brush made too little sound to carry as far as the cupboard, and Mayuri sat with the stillness and discipline of long study. Every few minutes a page rustled as she turned it, but otherwise the room remained so quiet that Hiro could hear the crickets in the yard.

After what seemed like at least an hour, Hiro heard small, light footsteps on the stairs. Someone else was awake, most likely on a late-night visit to the latrine.

He heard the outside door slide open and close again. The sound barely carried through the closet wall, and Hiro doubted it was audible in the office.

A page rustled, followed by silence.

A few minutes later the outer door opened again, more softly this time. Hiro almost missed it and would have dismissed it as the house settling except for a tiny whisper in the hall.

"There. Under the door."

Geta thudded on the wooden floor and the office door burst open with a clatter and a sound of paper ripping.

"Stop, thief!" a male voice yelled.

Mayuri shrieked in surprise. Papers fluttered and a book, most likely the ledger, thumped to the floor.

"What in the fire-jar hell are you doing?" Mayuri demanded.

Hiro winced. Even a man who didn't believe in hell could appreciate the evocative reference. In the fire-jar hell, lascivious monks and other promiscuous men suffered a torment appropriate to their misdeeds.

No one spoke.

"Who gave you permission to enter this house at night?" Mayuri shrieked. "In geta, and ripping my doors! Get out! Get out!"

"I—I'm sorry," a male voice stammered. "She told me . . . I thought . . ."

After a pause his voice turned angry. "You said there was an intruder in the office!"

"I'm sorry," Yoko whimpered. "I went to the latrine and saw the light in the window. I thought it was Akechi-sama's ghost."

"Ghost?" Mayuri hissed. "Do I look like a ghost to you?"

"Not much," Yoko stammered. "Not anymore."

"Get out, all of you! And don't you come back in this house tonight—not even if it's on fire!"

The geta clicked out the door, across the hall, and onto the veranda as more footsteps rumbled down the stairs. Mayuri's yelling must have awakened the others. Hiro suspected they had been listening by the staircase until they knew it was safe to descend.

"What are you doing here?" Mayuri demanded. "It's the middle of the night. You should all be sleeping!"

"Not with all that yelling," Okiya said.

"An ignorant mistake by an ignorant fool," Mayuri sniffed. "Go back to bed."

The stairs creaked as the women returned to bed. Hiro thought they had all departed, but a moment later he heard Okiya say, "It's late for accounting."

"I have things to finish and couldn't sleep," Mayuri replied.

"Three years' worth of things?" Okiya's voice moved into the room, and the door to the hall slid shut behind her. "I didn't speak in front of the others because I respect your privacy, but I have a right to know what's going on."

Mayuri didn't answer.

After a moment Okiya continued. "I don't insist on my rights very often, but I do own a third of this teahouse, and I have a right to know what you're doing."

Chapter 40

A ll right," Mayuri said, "sit down."

Hiro heard soft footsteps on the tatami and the rustling of a kimono as Okiya knelt on the floor.

"Hideyoshi's daughter found out about his interest," Mayuri said.

"You told me he kept it a secret, even from his wife."

"Apparently not," Mayuri said, "and it gets worse. I burned the ledgers the morning he died, because I was certain the prohibition on samurai owning businesses had kept him from telling anyone that he owned a third of a teahouse."

"You burned the books?" Okiya asked. "What made you do that?"

"I didn't think anyone knew about his interest. Nobuhide didn't mention it, and you know he would have demanded his rights at once if he had known. I thought destroying the ledgers would protect us.

"When the priest and his ronin dog started poking around,

I worried that they might see the books and think we were involved in the murder somehow—especially given that mess with Hidetaro and Sayuri's contract."

"I told you not to let Hideyoshi claim her," Okiya said. "We agreed the girls would never be sold or treated as slaves."

"It was a mistake," Mayuri admitted. "You're right, I shouldn't have done it, but he threatened to force himself on every girl in the teahouse if I didn't give him Sayuri. Including you."

Okiya laughed. "I'd like to see him try it."

"That's not a problem anymore, but we have a bigger one. Yoshiko is her father's heir and she knows about the teahouse. She was here last night demanding an accounting and wanting to know how much income she should expect.

"She demanded to see the books."

"Does she know the percentage?" Okiya asked.

"I don't know. I didn't ask. I was too surprised to learn that she knew anything. He always said he never told anyone, not even his wife."

"Not even his wife," Okiya repeated. "How long have you worked in the floating world, and you don't remember that men always lie?"

Silence stretched out between them. A page turned, and then another. After a minute or so Okiya said, "Worse things could have happened. We have another partner. At least this one won't be spoiling virgin girls like her father did."

"That's one expense I'll be glad to do without," Mayuri agreed, "and I suppose he did get his interest rightfully. I should have known that girl was an assassin. Her contract came far too cheaply."

"That was years ago," Okiya said. "You can forgive yourself now."

"It cost part of your interest as well as mine," Mayuri said. "That's what I regret."

"All this talk isn't getting your ledgers finished," Okiya replied. "I'm going to have some tea before I sleep. Would you like some?"

"Yes, thank you."

A kimono rustled and footsteps approached the cupboard.

"I'll use the big pot."

Okiya stood on the opposite side of the cupboard door. Hiro heard her hand touch the panel. The door rattled on its tracks.

"On second thought, I think I'll just finish these ledgers and get to sleep," Mayuri said. "If I stay up for tea, I won't be sharp tomorrow."

"Are you sure?" Okiya asked.

"Yes, thank you. No tea for me tonight."

"All right." Okiya's voice moved away from the door. She yawned. "I'll use the little pot in the kitchen instead.

"I wish Sayuri didn't have to take the blame for Hideyoshi's murder," Okiya added from the doorway. "I'm sure she didn't do it."

"Better her than us," Mayuri said.

"Better still to see real justice."

The room fell silent except for the rustle of ledger pages and, once, the grinding of an ink stick against the well.

Hiro sat on the blankets and thought through the facts again. He reconstructed the night Hideyoshi died, placing each of the relevant suspects in their places. Slowly, the bits and pieces became a whole, though the answer was not the one he expected, or even the one that seemed so accurate earlier in the evening.

By the time Mayuri put away her ledgers, Hiro knew who killed the samurai.

Chapter 41

Hiro remained in the cupboard for almost half an hour after Mayuri left the office and went to bed. The house grew still. Hiro didn't know the time, but judging by the tired ache behind his eyes, dawn was only an hour or two away.

Still he waited.

When he judged it safe to move, he slid open the door and stepped into the office. Working by feel alone, he rearranged the blankets to erase the depression left by his body. He didn't stop until the cabinet showed no sign of his presence.

He left the room without looking at the ledgers. The women's conversation had confirmed the suspicion that led him there in the first place. Hideyoshi's income would not support a teahouse lifestyle, and though it had taken Hiro a while to deduce that the samurai had owned an interest in the teahouse, the facts eventually lined up in his mind. Ironically, it had been the servant's broken sandals and Hidetaro's shabby robes that provided the final clue.

If Hideyoshi had income or hidden savings he could allow anyone to discover, he would have bought them better clothes, if only to ensure that no one knew of his poverty. But his only extravagance was the teahouse. When Hiro added together Yoshiko's visit, Sayuri's contract, and the destruction of the ledgers, it had grown clear that the teahouse finances were not what they had seemed.

The moon was low in the sky. The night seemed darker, as always just before dawn. Hiro crept along the veranda and checked the yard for the *dōshin* and his friends. He saw no one. He slipped the metal claws on his wrists and sprinted across the yard. He leaped into the cherry tree without a pause and without concern for the scars his claws would leave on the bark. By the time anyone might notice them, Sayuri and Father Mateo would be free or Nobuhide would be dead and Hiro preparing for seppuku.

He reversed his path across the rooftops as far as the river, where he paused to remove his cowl and claws, untie his cuffs and retrieve his sword. He jumped softly to the ground. Seeing no one, he stepped onto the road and headed for home. He swaggered with a slightly exaggerated roll, like a drunken samurai heading home from indulgences in Pontocho.

He reached Marutamachi Road without incident. As he passed the Okazaki shrine, the tall white torii gate shone brightly in the moonlight and the guardian lion just beyond seemed to grin even wider than usual, as though he knew about Hiro's successful mission. Hiro grinned back.

"If you do exist," he murmured, "thanks."

The statue did not reply.

A robed figure emerged from the shadows on the eastern side of the torii and floated into the road. In the slanting light of the setting moon, the figure looked like a ghost.

"Who are you?" it asked. "Where are you going?"

Hiro swayed slightly but didn't break character. He stopped and blinked at the figure in the road. "S'night time," he slurred. He raised a wobbling finger toward the setting moon. "Moon's up."

The figure stepped forward again, and the moonlight revealed her as the priestess who sold amulets by the gate.

She laid one hand on her hip and wagged the other accusingly. "You should not be out so late. What will your wife and parents think when you come home drunk at dawn? A samurai should set a better example."

"Maybe I'm out early." Hiro spoke with the slightly surprised tone of a drunk who knows he has said something very clever. "D'you think of that?"

"Maybe I can tell you're drunk, and drunks are only out late, never early." She sniffed and pointed up the road. "Go home."

"Trying to," Hiro mumbled as he wandered past.

He reached the church just before dawn and walked up the side of the house to avoid waking Ana or the others.

Father Mateo knelt before the cross at the far end of the yard.

Hiro stopped and waited beside the koi pond. When the priest finished his prayers, he rose, crossed himself, and turned toward the house. He startled at the sight of Hiro.

"I'm glad you're back," he said with relief. "I'd started to wonder if something had gone wrong."

"No," Hiro said. "In fact, it went exactly right."

"Is everyone alive?"

"I can't speak for all Kyoto," Hiro said, "but I didn't kill anyone tonight."

"Then come inside and tell me where you've been. We have some time before we leave for the teahouse."

"Not enough for talking," Hiro said. "I need to sleep, and I have a letter to send."

"At least tell me that you identified the murderer?"

"Don't worry about that," Hiro said. "Nobuhide won't be killing anyone today."

Four hours later Hiro and Father Mateo returned to the tea-house. The sun stood high in the sky but it was not quite midday.

Mayuri answered Hiro's knock. She seemed startled and oddly pleased to see them. She even bowed. "Good morning."

"Good morning," Hiro said. "We have come to see Sayuri."

"And Nobuhide," she said, with a hint of sorrow in her voice. "Please come in."

She escorted them to Sayuri's room.

"I apologize for my lack of hospitality," she said, "but I need to leave you alone. I have an important appointment in a few minutes."

"Of course." They bowed and Mayuri closed the door.

Father Mateo crossed to Sayuri and asked if she wanted to pray. They bowed their heads together and a moment later Father Mateo's deep, gentle voice filled the room. Hiro didn't necessarily believe in any god. He doubted the world had made itself, but he also put little faith in the competing stories people told. This one was an angry god. That one lived in trees.

Hiro was too busy staying alive to sort through them in search of a real one.

Still, Father Mateo's prayer was soothing on the ear, so Hiro listened as the Jesuit asked his Jesus god to spare Sayuri's life, and also his own, and if not to grant them entry into His Heaven for all eternity.

About halfway through the prayer Hiro heard the muffled sound of a knock on the teahouse door and female voices talking in the entry. As the women passed through the common room Hiro thought he recognized Yoshiko's voice. He waited until he heard a door slide closed and then slipped out of Sayuri's room and down the hall.

He stood outside Mayuri's office and listened to the conversation within.

"—you for coming," Mayuri was saying. "Again, I am very sorry for your loss."

"Thank you," Yoshiko said.

"I am a little confused about the reason for your visit."

"I am my father's heir."

"Are you seeking restitution for his death? A teahouse owner is not liable for the actions of an assassin."

"As I told you two nights ago," Yoshiko said, "one owner is responsible to provide the other owners with reports of profits and expenses."

When Mayuri did not reply Yoshiko continued. "Don't put me off any longer. I insist on seeing the ledgers."

Mayuri tried one more time. "Samurai don't engage in business."

"Five years ago my father was assaulted in this teahouse." Yoshiko's voice would have melted steel. "He did not drag you before the magistrate or cut off your miserable head because you offered him a percentage in lieu of restitution or revenge. You can either accept me as your partner now, this minute, or we will see how the magistrate feels about your unfortunate lack of memory."

Before Mayuri could answer, a loud bang echoed through the house.

Chapter 42

The front door of the teahouse banged again as Nobuhide's voice yelled, "Mayuri!"

Hiro barely had time to race across the common room and duck through the door of Sayuri's room before footsteps scurried through the house and Mayuri's voice called, "Just a moment."

Hiro was impressed. It took a lot to make an entertainer forget her training. Entertainers never yelled and Mayuri's feet never made a sound before.

Yoshiko's heavier footsteps followed Mayuri's across the common room. Hiro pushed the door open just a crack to listen. Behind him, Father Mateo's prayers stopped. Hiro suspected the priest and Sayuri were listening too.

"What do you want?" Mayuri's voice revealed her irritation. "Why are you yelling?"

"I have found my father's murderer!" Nobuhide said.

"Nobuhide?" Hidetaro's voice echoed through the house. "Yoshiko? Why are you here?"

"Hidetaro!" Yoshiko exclaimed, "I could ask the same of you."

Hiro smiled. The messenger must have delivered his letter precisely as requested, and Hidetaro had shown up right on time.

"I . . ." Hidetaro paused. "I came to see Sayuri."

"How convenient," Nobuhide said. "Shall we go together?"

Footsteps approached the door to Sayuri's room. Hiro backed up several steps and placed himself between Father Mateo and the door. Behind him, he heard someone stand up. The rattle of a scabbard told him it was the Jesuit and not Sayuri.

The door slid open. Nobuhide stalked into the room, followed by his sister, Mayuri, and a very confused Hidetaro. Nobuhide remained by the door, but the other three walked farther into the room.

Nobuhide startled at the sight of the priest. Apparently, he expected the Jesuit to run.

He pointed at Hiro. "You stand by the outer door. I don't want the murderer escaping."

"Father Mateo and Sayuri go with me," Hiro said. "I will not stand on the opposite side of the room."

Nobuhide pointed to the tokonoma. "Let them stand there, between us."

Hiro considered the distance from Nobuhide to the alcove. The *yoriki* would have to circumvent the hearth to reach the priest, but Hiro had no obstacle in his path. From the perspective of defense, it represented a better position than the one Hiro currently held.

The shinobi nodded.

Father Mateo and Sayuri walked to the tokonoma as Hiro took up a position before the veranda door.

"I didn't need your help to find the murderer." Nobuhide sneered. "I solved the crime myself, though you were correct that Sayuri was not to blame. I should have known a whore didn't have the intelligence or the strength to kill my father."

"Don't. Call her. A whore." Hidetaro's words came out as separate sentences. His hand rested on the hilt of his katana.

"Did you come to plead for her life?" Nobuhide asked.

"My business is none of yours," Hidetaro said.

Father Mateo changed the subject. "How did you identify the murderer?"

A superior look came over Nobuhide's face. "It was simple for me, because I am samurai and you are not."

"Would you mind sharing your discovery with us?" Hiro asked.

Nobuhide removed a small leather bag from his kimono. He held it high.

"This is the weapon that murdered my father. A shinobi weapon, though he was not killed by an assassin. He was murdered by someone who knew him well. Someone who had everything to gain by his death, and who used my father's own weapon to take his life!"

Nobuhide opened the bag and pulled out three of the *neko-te* finger sheaths. One had no blade in it.

"The murderer stole the weapon from our home the night my father died, used it to kill him, and sneaked it back to the house the following day. No one noticed because the pieces had fallen on the floor, thanks to my Uncle Hidetaro's shocking lack of gratitude and discipline." Nobuhide paused. "He threw away a dagger my father gave him as a gift. A fine way to repay our generosity."

Hidetaro clenched his fists at his sides. He took a deep breath and relaxed them. Hiro noted both movements with relief. He suspected a fight was about to happen, but he didn't want Hidetaro to begin it.

"I noticed the missing *neko-te* when I returned home with the body," Nobuhide continued. "They returned to their places later that morning, but one of the blades was broken and out of place. When I saw it, I remembered that there was a broken blade in my father's chest when I brought him home. I checked beneath his armor but the blade was gone. The killer had replaced it, and also the other *neko-te,* hoping no one would notice."

"You realize this means Sayuri is innocent," Father Mateo said.

Nobuhide nodded. "Indeed. I absolve her of all responsibility for the crime, and you as well, as soon as the real murderer pays the penalty for this crime."

"Who is the real murderer?" Hiro asked.

"A member of my own family." Nobuhide reveled in the moment.

Hiro wished he would get on with it.

"My father was killed by someone he knew and trusted!"

"That is why he did not fight," Yoshiko confirmed.

"We agree on that," Hiro said. "The question is—"

"I ask the questions," Nobuhide snapped, "and there is no need to ask. I already know."

"Then tell us."

Chapter 43

Nobuhide pointed at his sister. "Yoshiko killed our father."
Yoshiko's hand flew to the hilt of her sword. "That is
a lie!"

"It is the truth!" Nobuhide crowed. "You killed him and
you deserve to die."

Hidetaro took half a step backward. Mayuri paled and covered her mouth with her hands. Father Mateo took half a step
to his right to shield Sayuri with his body.

"Who stands to gain from our father's death?" Nobuhide
demanded. "You! You are his heir, and you knew it. You knew
about the will and what it said, and you killed him to get control of the family fortune."

"There is no fortune," Yoshiko said, "and I was at home
with Mother the night Father died."

"You were not at home," Nobuhide said. "Your shoes were
covered in mud the following morning. You were out that
night, after midnight, in the rain."

Yoshiko looked at the floor. "You're right, I was not at
home." She looked up. "But I did not kill him. After you and

Father argued with Hidetaro, I worried that Uncle might do something rash. When two men want the same woman, you cannot depend on either to act wisely."

Hiro agreed with that wholeheartedly.

"Hidetaro followed Father here, to the teahouse," Yoshiko continued. "He spied on the room from outside the veranda door, and when the night grew late he hid behind the latrine. I stood by the garden gate and watched, but Father never left the room.

"When Hidetaro left, I followed. I tried to practice stealth but he caught me by surprise. He said he intended no harm and I believed him so I headed home. Shortly after that it rained. My clothes and shoes got wet.

"I was not home in the early morning because I took my kimono to be cleaned, but I did not touch the *neko-te* and I did not kill my father."

"A convenient lie," Nobuhide said, "and all the worse because you expect our uncle to support your feeble claim. Here is what actually happened.

"You had been waiting to get your hands on Father's fortune because he would not allow you to pledge an oath or become a retainer to a real samurai. No man wanted to marry you, and without a fortune you would be no better than a beggar all your life.

"When you heard the argument between Father and Hidetaro, you knew your opportunity had come. People would suspect Hidetaro instead of you. So you waited until we left and took the *neko-te* off the floor. You chose them because you knew a shinobi's weapon would make you look even less suspicious."

"It is a woman's weapon," Yoshiko said with disdain,

though Hiro noticed her breathing speed up and heard a hint of fear at the back of her voice.

"Shut up!" Nobuhide barked. "You followed Father to the teahouse, waited until he was alone, and murdered him. He didn't struggle because he never thought his beloved daughter could kill him.

"In the morning you conveniently 'found' the will, with Mother's help, and revealed yourself as the heir.

"You would have gotten away with it, too, except for one mistake. You removed the broken *neko-te* from the wound instead of leaving it in the body, where it would not have attracted attention."

"Very clever," Hiro said. "You appear to have thought of everything."

"Your beloved priest and the little whore will get to live after all." Nobuhide drew his katana and brandished it before him. "I demand vengeance . . . against Akechi Yoshiko."

"Just a moment," Hiro said.

Nobuhide paused.

"There is something you haven't explained."

Nobuhide frowned. "What's that?"

"Your father's will was a forgery," Hiro said, "though it doesn't matter because under the law Yoshiko is still your father's heir.

"And one other thing. Yoshiko didn't kill your father. You did."

Sayuri gasped and raised her hands to her mouth. Hidetaro scowled, and Mayuri's eyes widened in surprise.

Nobuhide took a step backward. "Me? That's an outrage! I would never kill my father."

"I thought so too, at first," Hiro said, "and later I almost blamed Yoshiko too—for the very same reasons you just stated. Her actions make her look much guiltier than Sayuri, or even Hidetaro, though both of them had motives for murder too."

"Yoshiko did kill him," Nobuhide protested. "She benefited from his death."

"Possibly," Hiro said, "but not before he died. She had no reason to kill your father. You had several."

"I don't know what you're talking about."

"Your father refused to let you join Mitsuhide in Nobunaga's army. Despite your pleas, he forced you to remain a lowly *yoriki* in the service of a shogun who would never appreciate your skills. You could not disobey while your father lived, and your father's profligate spending at the Sakura made you worry that he would spend his entire fortune before you could inherit it, depriving you of the wherewithal to buy yourself a greater position than that of Kyoto policeman.

"But because you are a policeman, you knew that you couldn't just kill your father and walk away. You needed an opportunity to blame it on someone else.

"You heard your father argue with Hidetaro. You were present when Hidetaro threw the knife. You saw the *neko-te* scatter on the floor, and you scooped them up as you left the room, knowing no one else would enter your father's study while he was gone."

"*Neko-te* is a woman's weapon." Disgust dripped like venom from Nobuhide's words. "No man would ever use it."

"Which is exactly why you chose to," Hiro said. "You knew it would throw suspicion on Sayuri. I think you intended to claim a conspiracy between her and Hidetaro, to ensure that one or the other took the blame."

"But I couldn't have killed him," Nobuhide said. "I was at the House of the Floating Plums all night. Ask Umeha, she will tell you."

"That threw me too, at first," Hiro said. "It was clever of you to give her so much sake. You've known her several years, so I'm sure you know what happens when she drinks."

"She doesn't remember anything," Mayuri said. "I never let her drink sake when she was here, for that very reason."

"She fell asleep," Nobuhide said, "and so did I. There's no mud on my kimono or my shoes."

"He's right," Yoshiko said. "He came home in the same clothes he wore the night before, and they were clean."

"Because he wasn't wearing his clothes when he killed your father," Hiro said. "He was dressed as a prostitute."

Chapter 44

Nobuhide whirled toward Hiro with a snarl, but a clash of steel brought him up short. Hidetaro had drawn his sword with almost unbelievable speed. His blade held Nobuhide's at bay, and although he did not move, his eyes held a lethal warning.

"He is a liar," Nobuhide hissed.

"Let him finish." Hidetaro's voice was calm. "Step back and lower your sword."

For a moment no one moved. Hiro's hand fingered the five-pointed *shuriken* in his sleeve. He had seen Nobuhide's movement before Hidetaro, but stayed his hand when he realized Hidetaro would block the strike. Had Nobuhide moved two inches farther, or tried to fight, Hiro would have planted the metal star between his eyes.

"This is ridiculous," Nobuhide sniffed. "I would not wear women's clothes."

"Any man would wear women's clothes to get away with murder," Hiro replied, "and it almost worked. Mayuri saw you through the door and thought you were Sayuri. Someone else saw you in the road and took you for a prostitute.

"If Umeha hadn't mentioned her ruined robe I might never have put it together."

"But how did you know it was Nobuhide," Yoshiko asked, "and not me or Sayuri after all?"

"Sayuri was in the latrine when the murder happened, and you are much too tall to be the woman Mayuri saw." Hiro didn't mention Mitsuhide's comment about the woman's height. "In addition, I doubt you have ever dressed like a prostitute."

Yoshiko tilted her head. "True enough."

"Sayuri could have murdered him when she returned from the latrine," Nobuhide accused.

"I'm afraid not," Hiro said, "because Sayuri is not left-handed.

"The murder was committed with left-handed strokes that nearly ripped out your father's throat. Only someone trained in left-handed combat could have struck the initial blow so quickly that the victim had no time to scream or fight.

"I have seen Sayuri play the shamisen, and I have seen her draw a dagger. She is definitely right-handed."

Hiro looked at Nobuhide, who stood holding his sword with the left hand near the guard and the right below it, just at the base of the hilt. "This is the second time you've held your sword with a left-handed stance."

"But the will made Yoshiko the heir," Nobuhide said. "Why would I kill my father if I didn't stand to gain?"

"You were the heir until you killed him," Hiro said. "The will was created after your father's death, not years before as

Sato claimed. No one had seen it because it didn't exist until yesterday."

He looked at Yoshiko. "If I had to guess, I would say that your mother made up the story—and the will—because she worried that Nobuhide would spend your father's money on himself instead of caring for the family as your father would have wished."

"She did worry about that," Yoshiko said. "How did you know the will was forged?"

"Twelve years ago your brother was still a child. His name was Taromaru, not Nobuhide."

Yoshiko nodded. "I noticed that, too, when she mentioned his childhood name yesterday. When I confronted her after you left, she refused to admit the forgery, but I had already decided to investigate further once the other issues had been resolved."

"No need for that now," Hiro said. "The forgery is irrelevant. You have become your father's heir by force of law.

"A murderer forfeits all legal rights to inheritance, which disqualifies Nobuhide, and even if you were involved in the forgery—which I doubt—forging a will is not a sufficient legal ground to disinherit an otherwise valid heir."

"So Yoshiko inherits everything Hideyoshi owned?" Mayuri asked.

"Everything," Hiro repeated. "Without a will, Hideyoshi's estate will pass to the eldest surviving child who is qualified to inherit under the law. Murder disqualifies Nobuhide.

"Yoshiko is the heir . . . and in possession of the legal right to execute vengeance for her father's death."

Nobuhide narrowed his eyes at his sister. "You wouldn't kill me. You haven't got the fortitude."

"Do not test me," Yoshiko said. She took a deep breath. "I will not let you live, but I grant you the honor of seppuku. I will even act as your second."

Nobuhide raised his sword. "I would rather die in battle than by suicide."

"Even now, you lack the honor to behave as a samurai?" Yoshiko drew her katana with one hand. "You will die today. The only question is how."

Nobuhide whirled around and slashed at the sliding door that led to the common room. The door cleaved open with a crash, and Nobuhide jumped through the opening.

Yoshiko followed as Hiro jumped backward through the veranda door. Wood splintered and paper tore as Mayuri's outraged howl split the air.

Hiro raced down the veranda and around the front corner of the teahouse. He heard feet behind him and recognized Father Mateo's gait. Somewhere inside the teahouse, a woman screamed.

Hiro paused before the swinging doors, uncertain whether to wait or go inside. When no one came out, he went in.

Nobuhide lay sprawled facedown on the floor of the common room. His foot was stuck in the sliding door. His katana rested near the hearth, and Hidetaro was just bending down to pick it up as Hiro and Father Mateo entered the common room from the foyer.

Yoshiko stood over her brother with her katana in one hand and her *wakizashi* in the other.

Nobuhide started to rise but Yoshiko's voice cut through the silence. "If you move, you die with a sword in your back."

Nobuhide froze.

Yoshiko sheathed the *wakizashi* and shifted her katana to a two-handed grip. Hiro noted with satisfaction that she held it right-hand dominant, with the right hand above the left.

"Now, get up very slowly."

Nobuhide stood up and straightened his kimono. He raised his hands and smoothed his hair.

"Don't make me kill you, Nobu." Yoshiko sounded on the verge of tears, though her face retained a perfect samurai calm. "It's bad enough to have a patricide in the family. Don't add fratricide, even in revenge."

Nobuhide's face twisted with sudden and unexpected emotion. "It was his own fault! He never understood my talent. He let them force me into the police instead of insisting the shogun give me a command.

"He wouldn't even let me join Lord Oda's forces with Mitsuhide. That's all I wanted. He didn't even care!"

"Is that why you did it?" Yoshiko asked. "Because of Mitsuhide?"

"He wouldn't let me go." Nobuhide sounded like a child refused a favored toy.

Yoshiko looked at the others. "Leave us."

"I know what you have to tell him," Hidetaro said. He looked at Hiro and Father Mateo. "It is a family matter, and private."

Mayuri led the others into her office. They had barely closed the door when Hiro said, "I'm sorry . . . may I borrow your vase?"

He reached for the alcove.

"What are you doing?" Mayuri demanded.

"They need privacy, but I need . . ." He paused.

Mayuri looked horrified. "The latrine is outside." She pointed. "Go. No one will mind. Don't you dare touch that vase."

Hiro slipped out of the house, around the veranda and back into the room where the initial confrontation had occurred. He crept across the floor and listened beside the hole in the door.

"How could you believe our family was split between two daimyo?" Yoshiko was saying. "That one side supports the shogun and one does not?"

"What do you mean?" Nobuhide asked.

"Akechi Mitsuhide joined Lord Oda at the emperor's command, with the shogun's knowledge. It was Ashikaga gold—the shogun's gold—that bought the firearms Mitsuhide took to convince Lord Oda of his fealty."

"Mitsuhide said he stole that gold from the shogun."

Yoshiko laughed. "You still don't understand. Mitsuhide is a spy. If Lord Oda gets within striking distance of Kyoto, Mitsuhide has orders to kill him—or die trying. Our father refused to let you go because he didn't want his only son on a suicide mission."

Chapter 45

H e never told me." Nobuhide sounded miserable.

"He knew you couldn't keep a secret," Yoshiko said.

"Why did he tell you and not me?"

"He didn't tell me." Yoshiko's voice softened. "You know my lifelong habit of listening at doors. I overheard him talking with Mitsuhide when our cousin passed through Kyoto—the day he invited you to go along."

Hiro heard a thump as Nobuhide fell to his knees. A moment later Nobuhide asked, "Akechi Yoshiko, will you act as my *kaishakunin*?"

It was the formal term for the person who assisted with seppuku.

"I will," Yoshiko said. "Would you like me to bring the others back?"

Hiro never heard Nobuhide's answer. He was already racing around the outside of the house toward Mayuri's office.

A few minutes later, Hiro and the others gathered in front of the teahouse.

Nobuhide knelt in the middle of the street, facing the river, on a tatami they had brought out from the teahouse. Yoshiko stood behind him with her katana drawn. The street was deserted. A couple of neighbors poked their heads from their houses in curiosity, but when they saw the spectacle they withdrew and shut their doors without a word.

This was a samurai matter and no one dared to interfere.

Nobuhide drew his *wakizashi* and laid it on the tatami in front of his knees. He removed his obi and wrapped it tightly around the middle of the short sword's blade.

"What is he doing?" Father Mateo whispered in Portuguese.

Hiro leaned toward him and whispered, "To keep the blade from cutting his hand when he—"

"Understood," the priest whispered, too disturbed to let Hiro finish the sentence.

Yoshiko stepped to her brother's side and raised her katana behind his head. "When shall I strike?"

Nobuhide took a deep breath and exhaled slowly. "Allow me the honor of completing the cut."

Hiro was impressed. A samurai who committed seppuku didn't usually complete the disemboweling slice across the abdomen. The *kaishakunin* usually cut off his head the moment he plunged the dagger into his belly, sparing the pain of completing the ritual cut.

Nobuhide chose greater honor, but also much greater pain.

"Why does he have to do this?" the Jesuit whispered. "Surely there is another option."

"Not only did he kill his father," Hiro whispered, grateful

for the Portuguese that disguised his words, "he found out that he did it without a reason. This is the only way for him to recover his honor, and also spare his family the humiliation of a public execution. It is our way."

Father Mateo gave Hiro a sidelong look. "I don't like your way."

"You'll like it even less in about a minute."

Nobuhide opened his kimono to expose his chest and stomach. He bowed his head.

Hiro hoped the priest would not try to intervene. The seppuku ritual had existed for thousands of years. It prevented Yoshiko, or anyone else, from bearing the stain of Nobuhide's death and atoned for their father's murder in the best way a samurai could.

Nobuhide looked up at Yoshiko. She nodded. Her eyes were red but her jaw was set. She would do what she had to do.

Hiro couldn't help but admire her strength.

Nobuhide raised his *wakizashi*. He gripped the hilt in his right hand and the cloth-wrapped blade in his left. Rising up on his knees, he plunged the sword into his left side. With a grunt of pain, he pushed the sword across his belly and opened a fatal gash.

His breath came out with a rush but no one heard it. Yoshiko's sword flew through the air with an audible swish and sliced through the base of her brother's neck. She stopped the blade just before it severed his head completely.

Nobuhide's head fell forward against his chest, connected to his body by only a tiny flap of skin.

Blood spurted from the gaping hole in Nobuhide's neck as his body slumped forward. Dark blood sprayed the dusty street and pooled around the nearly headless corpse.

Yoshiko stood beside her brother, head bowed and sword hanging almost to the ground. Her shoulders heaved and she had her eyes shut tight. Her face screwed up with grief, but she did not cry. She did not make a sound.

After almost a minute she opened her eyes and looked at Mayuri. "Please move my brother's body from the street. I must arrange proper transport."

She looked at Hiro. "Thank you for your assistance. It is . . . unfortunate . . . that we did not meet under different circumstances."

Hiro bowed, and Yoshiko walked away toward the river.

Mayuri didn't seem to know what to do. She looked horrified at the thought of handling a dead man.

Hiro did not hesitate. He stepped forward to carry the corpse. When he bent over Nobuhide's body, he saw that Father Mateo had followed him.

"Some people think it's unlucky to touch the dead," Hiro warned as he grasped Nobuhide's arms. "They think it's catching—especially when there's blood involved."

"Bad choices are not contagious," the priest said, "only regrettable, and blood can be washed away."

He bent down to help Hiro carry the body away from the road.

After a cart arrived to remove Nobuhide's corpse, Father Mateo asked Mayuri what would happen to Sayuri.

"I'm taking her with me," Hidetaro said. He turned to Mayuri. "She's not your property. If you want money, I'll get it somehow, but she's not staying here another minute."

He gave Sayuri a hopeful look. "Unless, of course, she does not want to go with me."

Sayuri's face broke into a lovely smile. "I do want to go with Hidetaro. Please? I promise we will pay."

Mayuri looked at them for a moment. "That murder probably broke her spirit anyway. No teahouse needs a defiled entertainer. She's no use to me, and she has no value. I consider her contract paid in full."

Sayuri beamed like the sun breaking through storm clouds. Hiro finally understood what Hidetaro saw in her. When she smiled, she glowed, and even a man who didn't trust women could see her genuine joy.

Father Mateo and Hiro set out for the church on foot. The sun was high, the sky a cloudless blue that promised a hot afternoon.

As they saw the peaked roof of the church rising up before them, Father Mateo said, "I know you explained everything, but I can't quite believe you managed to put it together. I never would have guessed it was Nobuhide."

"Actually," Hiro said, "you were the one who solved it. The last piece of the puzzle came from you. Well, you and the kitten."

"The kitten?" Father Mateo asked.

Hiro nodded. "When she tried to escape with the paper and you said she didn't count on someone else being there to snatch the prize.

"Until then I suspected Yoshiko, but I hadn't been able to figure out her motive for killing her father. She had no reason for wanting him to die. Becoming his heir didn't change her life in any noticeable way.

"Your comment made me realize she wasn't the murderer at all. She snatched the prize from someone else. Last night, when I put everything together, I realized it was Nobuhide all along."

The front door opened as they approached. Ana stood in the doorway with the kitten. She held it in her arms like a baby and Hiro could hear it purring from the walk.

"Hm," she said. "Is this cat going to stay or isn't it?"

Hiro glanced at Father Mateo, but the priest didn't answer.

"It is," Hiro said. "It's my cat now."

"Then it needs a name," the housekeeper said. She stroked the kitten's head. "I can't keep calling it 'that cat' all the time."

"What's your word for 'paper'?" Hiro whispered in Portuguese.

"Don't you dare," the priest replied.

"Well?" Ana demanded. "I haven't got all day."

"Gato," Hiro said. "Her name is Gato."

Ana looked down at the kitten in her arms.

"Hm. I like it. You finally did something right."

Glossary of
Japanese Terms

B

bokken: A wooden practice sword, used for sparring or solo weapons practice.

Bushido: Literally, "the way of the warrior." The samurai moral code, which emphasized loyalty, frugality, and personal honor.

C

chonmage: The traditional hairstyle of adult samurai males. After shaving the pate, the remaining hair was oiled and tied in a tail, which was then folded back and forth on top of the head.

D

daimyo: A samurai lord, usually the ruler of a province or the head of a samurai clan.

dōshin: The medieval Japanese equivalent of a beat cop or policeman.

F

futon: A thin padded mattress, small and pliable enough to be folded and stored out of sight during the day.

G

genpuku: A traditional samurai coming-of-age ceremony, after which a boy was allowed to wear swords and take on the responsibilities of an adult.

geta: Traditional Japanese sandals (resembling flip-flops), with a raised wooden base and fabric thongs that wrapped around the wearer's big toe.

H

hakama: Loose, pleated pants worn over kimono or beneath a tunic or surcoat.

I

inkan: A personal seal, used in place of a signature on official documents.

J

jitte: A long wooden or metal nightstick with a forward-pointing hook at the top of the hand grip; carried by *dōshin* as both a weapon and a symbol of office.

K

kaginawa: A medieval Japanese grappling hook consisting of a metal hook (or hooks) attached to a length of rope.

kaishakunin: The samurai who acts as the second for another samurai during the seppuku ceremony.

kami: The Japanese word for "god" or "divine spirit"; used to describe gods, the spirits inhabiting natural objects, and certain natural forces of divine origin.

kata: Literally, "form(s)." A detailed pattern or set of movements used to practice martial skills and combat techniques, performed either with or without a weapon.

katana: The longer of the two swords worn by a samurai. (The shorter one is the *wakizashi*.)

kimono: Literally, "a thing to wear." A full-length wraparound robe traditionally worn by Japanese people of all ages and genders.

koban: A gold coin that came into widespread use in Japan during the later medieval period.

koku: A Japanese unit of measurement, equal to the amount of rice required to feed one person for one year.

kunoichi: A female shinobi.

kuri: The kitchen in a Zen Buddhist monastery.

M

mempo: An armored mask that covered the wearer's face, with holes for the eyes and mouth.

menhari-gata: A type of *tessen* (bladed war fan) containing sharpened metal ribs that allowed the fan to be used as a weapon.

miso: A traditional Japanese food paste made from fermented soybeans (or, sometimes, rice or barley).

mon: An emblem or crest used to identify a Japanese family or clan.

N

naginata: A weapon featuring a long wooden shaft with a curved blade on one end, similar to a European glaive.

neko-te: Literally, "cat's claws." A weapon consisting of metal or leather finger sheaths equipped with sharpened metal blades. The sheaths slipped over the end the wearer's finger, allowing the blades to protrude like the claws of a cat.

noren: A traditional Japanese doorway hanging, with a slit cut up the center to permit passage.

nuki-ashi: A specialized method of walking with sweeping, careful steps to minimize noise; one of many stealthy movements utilized by shinobi.

O

obi: A wide sash wrapped around the waist to hold a kimono closed, worn by people of all ages and genders.

odoshi: A lacing technique used to connect the plates of lamellar armor.

oe: The large central living space in a Japanese home, which featured a sunken hearth and often served as a combination of kitchen, reception room, and living space.

P

Pontocho: One of Kyoto's *hanamachi* (geisha and courtesan) districts, containing geisha houses, teahouses, brothels, restaurants, and similar businesses.

R

ronin: A masterless samurai.

Ryogin-an: One of the subtemples located on the grounds of Tofuku-ji.

ryu: Literally, "school." Shinobi clans used this term as a combination identifier and association name. (Hiro Hattori is a member of the Iga *ryu*.)

S

sake (also *saké*)**:** An alcoholic beverage made from fermented rice.

sakura: An ornamental cherry blossom tree (*Prunus serrulata*) or cherry blossoms.

-sama: A suffix used to show even higher respect than *-san*.

samurai: A member of the medieval Japanese nobility, the warrior caste that formed the highest-ranking social class.

-san: A suffix used to show respect.

seppuku: A form of Japanese ritual suicide by disembowelment, originally used only by samurai.

shamisen: A traditional Japanese instrument with a long neck and resonating strings strung across a drum-like wooden base. The instrument is played by plucking the strings with a plectrum.

shinobi: Literally, "shadowed person." Shinobi is the Japanese pronunciation of the characters that many Westerners pronounce "ninja." ("Ninja" is based on a Chinese pronunciation.)

Shinto: The indigenous spirituality or religion of Japan, sometimes also called *kami-no-michi*.

shogun: The military dictator and commander who acted as de facto ruler of medieval Japan.

shuko (also *tegaki-shuko*)**:** Spiked metal bands worn on the hands to aid in climbing walls, trees, and other vertical surfaces.

shuriken: An easily concealed, palm-sized weapon made of metal and often shaped like a cross or star, which shinobi used for throwing or as a handheld weapon in close combat.

T

tabi: An ankle-length Japanese sock with a separation between the big toe and other toes to facilitate the wearing of sandals and other traditional Japanese footwear.

tanto: A fixed-blade dagger with a single- or double-edged blade measuring 6–12 inches (15–30 cm) in length.

tatami: A traditional Japanese mat-style floor covering made in standard sizes, with the length measuring exactly twice its width. Tatami usually contained a straw core covered with grass or rushes.

tengu: A supernatural demon ("monster-spirit") from Japanese folklore, often depicted as a human-avian hybrid or with a long, hooked nose reminiscent of a beak.

tessen: A bladed war fan with ribs made of sharpened metal. The bladed ribs were disguised so that, when closed, the *tessen* looked like a harmless wood and paper fan.

tetsubishi: Metal caltrops, often used by shinobi to distract or slow pursuers.

Tofuku-ji: A Zen Buddhist temple located in Kyoto.

tokonoma: A decorative alcove or recessed space set into the wall of a Japanese room. The tokonoma typically held a piece of art, a flower arrangement, or a hanging scroll.

torii: A traditional, stylized Japanese gate most commonly found at the entrance to Shinto shrines.

Tsuten-kyo: A covered wooden bridge located on the grounds of Tofuku-ji (a Buddhist temple in Kyoto).

W

wakizashi: The shorter of the two words worn by a samurai. (The longer one is the katana.)

Y

yoriki: An assistant magistrate, tasked with supervising *dōshin* and other practical and administrative law enforcement duties.

For additional cultural information, expanded definitions, and author's notes, visit http://www.susanspann.com.

ML   7-13